MISSING OR DEAD

MISSING OR DEAD

A NOVEL

POLINA QUINN

Self-published by Polina Quinn

polinaquinn.com

ISBN-13: 979-8-9925398-0-6

To my family,
I love you all endlessly.
Thank you for always believing in me.

Prologue

Sound. Movement.

No vision.

I hear voices. I feel as though I'm in a moving vehicle.

Blindfolded? I cannot see anything, and I cannot open my eyes.

Drugged? Blurry memories and distorted headspace.

The vehicle goes over a bump, and I knock my head against something solid. The space I'm in feels cramped. I'm in a lying-down position. The trunk of a car?

Memories escape me.

Where am I? How did I end up here?

I search my brain for any logical explanation—coming up empty.

Another bump in the road. I hit my elbow, and pain reverberates through my body.

I squeeze my eyes shut tighter, willing my brain to remember.

Deep, calming breaths.

Nothing.

The voices sound distant, and I strain to hear them. Do I recognize them? I can't tell.

I'm tied up—arms behind my back, legs tied together. There is no duct tape on my mouth, which probably means I can scream as loud as I want to, and no help will come.

I try anyway and no sound comes out.

My legs are cramping, and I try to adjust my position.

My head is so fuzzy; this doesn't seem real. It's a dream. A nightmare.

It's so dark in here.

While I try to roll over onto my side the car hits another bump.

My head hits something solid.

Everything disappears and goes black.

Chapter 1.0

ALTAITOWN ACADEMY—THE SCHOOL I'VE been going to since pre-kindergarten. I remember my first day, coming through the front doors with my older brother and older sister. Truthfully, they had to alternate between pushing and pulling me in. I wasn't budging in the slightest as soon as we walked up to the seemingly never-ending stone path, which led to the entrance of this chaotic, mysterious place.

I was wearing a purple raincoat, and I hated it. It was a hand-me-down from my sister Beth, and I thought it made me look like Barney. Regardless, Beth and Trevor, my brother, always gave me confidence. Though my confidence sometimes faltered, they unconditionally and unwaveringly had my back. I miss and need them now more than ever as I approach this achingly familiar, yet strangely foreign, building after being absent for seven months. Seemingly, nothing has changed, yet so much has. I can't bring myself to look up as I trudge forward, dragging my feet along the stone path.

When I arrived and parked, exiting my car and walking toward the entrance, I stood still for a few minutes before forcing myself to plow forward. The ghostly feeling of Trevor pulling me by the arms while Beth pushes me from behind is the only reason I take one daring step after another. I only think about them as the reflective glass door entrance gets closer.

I enter the school alone, feeling exposed and vulnerable. It's so strange and unfamiliar. Nothing has changed around here. Maybe the reason I feel like I don't know where to go from here is because I'm the one who's changed. I stand by the entrance, one step inside, the glass door smoothly swinging closed behind me.

Trevor never forgave my mother for something no longer spoken about in our household. He moved out three years ago. I haven't talked to him or seen him since. My father and Beth disappeared seven months ago and were proclaimed a cold case by the people in my town not very long after. Are they missing, or are they dead? Nobody seems to care anymore. So much for hope and support, right? My father and Beth went out to buy some groceries, for god's sake, and there has been no trace of them since then. The police couldn't even find Dad's car. Nothing. Nothing. Nothing.

To this day, that is how I feel: nothing.

"Talia, dear, come along now." Grace, my over-caring best friend, comes up behind me. She has resigned to being my older sister. However, it's not helping.

I wasn't ready to return to school after seven months, but my mother told me I was. We don't have the best relationship, to put it lightly. Honestly, she has no relationship with any of her three children. Nevertheless, she insisted I rejoin school for at least the second semester of junior year. I don't understand the point of it. I have nothing left. I've spent the past months numbly staggering around town while eyes stared and mouths whispered all around me (*about* me, specifically).

Nothing can bring them back now. The police have slowed their investigation, and people have given up. From now on, it's essentially charity work for whoever volunteers. All my mom and I have left is a never-ending parade of bills. And nothingness. Emptiness. We have that.

Grace is somewhat of an angel. She cares for everyone and everything, which is why people constantly surround her, or maybe she surrounds them. Either way, she does no wrong.

"I'm not a dog," I reply semi-jokingly and untangle my arm from her grip.

She scrunches her eyebrows, perplexed, but then quickly smiles. "I'm happy you're back. We all are."

"I'm sure there were some people who were happy that I left for a while," I respond.

"Well, *some*, maybe. But those people don't matter, do they? Natalie is a royal pain in the ass. Did you know she reminded me six times that she donated to your dads' and sisters' search fund? I guess she got through to me because here I am telling you..." Grace trails off as my face falls at the thought of the "search fund". People have given up, and the money is going toward nothing. In the past three months, practically no more donations have come in. I'm not surprised. Who wants to spend their money on a lost cause?

"They aren't dead, T," Grace whispers, almost as if she's afraid to spook me. I'm unsure if she's trying to convince me or herself. Probably both. Maybe nobody in particular.

I nod. All I do is nod now. I can't bring myself to talk about it, about anything. I'm not being helpful, I know. But it's too much to handle for a girl who was a high school sophomore only a few months ago, with no worries other than overdue homework and a test she didn't study for.

"We can get the fund going again," Grace offers.

"Can we just—can we just go to class? I think the principal put me in the same classes as you because that would be easier for me since we take the same classes anyway." I smile slightly to show her I'm not rejecting her; I'm fine.

· · · · · ● ● · ● ● · ·

"Oh my god! I was so worried about you." My friend Kate rushes over as I take a seat in class. Her face is a mixture of relief and something close to fear as she pulls me into a hug.

"How are you feeling?" I ask, attempting to keep it light, but I can't help frowning. Kate looks thinner than the last time I saw her. She is always trying out these fad diets and working out until her legs buckle. I always tried to keep up her confidence when I was around so that she wouldn't dwindle. I guess with me gone, nobody took on the role.

"Stressed," Kate responds, releasing me from the hug and slightly looking away. When my frown deepens, she adds, "Because of you—I mean, *for* you." She catches herself, then looks at me with an anxious smile. "You don't seem stressed, though. How's the fund? Are the police making any progress? Do you think there's a chance of... you know?" She trails off, watching me cautiously. Kate's rarely this hesitant—she's never been one to hold back.

I shrivel down into my seat, eyes on my hands, as I wring them. I don't want the whole class to hear this. And they are, they are all hearing this.

"Sorry, T, I'm just very—I'm very..." Kate sighs. "I'll go sit down." She slumps down next to me, looking away again.

"Probably the best idea, *K*," Natalie chimes in mockingly.

Natalie. Well, that's someone to talk about. Natalie is one of those people who instinctively attracts you. Her silky blonde hair, her bright shining smile, her perfectly symmetrical face, and her laugh that echoes across the lands. Unfortunately, once the initial haze of her exuberant personality and enchanting looks softens, her true colors appear. They aren't as enticing as the exterior, to put it mildly. In reality, Natalie is full of venom, which seeps out of her pores continuously. She is like molten lava, destroying everything in her path and never looking back to assess or notice the damage. I wouldn't go as far as to say that she's the spawn of Satan... but if Satan is real and he has a spawn, I would assume she was it.

"Hey, Natalie," Grace says brightly. Her personality and undeniable naivety never falter, even with the worst of humankind.

"Did your friend tell you I donated to your search fund?" Natalie barrels on.

"I did," Grace answers, still smiling.

Natalie keeps ignoring her while glaring a hole straight through my head. I can see her in my periphery, seething with fakeness. I keep my eyes down, playing with the holes in my sweater.

"I heard they think your dad and sister ran away together. You know, as in some *incest* thing. I doubt it. They weren't *like that*, right?" Natalie continues her one-sided conversation.

"You have no shame, you psycho bitch," Kate snaps, spinning around in her chair.

I sit there, silent, unsure of what to do or say. My face burns, my pulse races, but I feel hollow.

"I'll take the rude silence as a 'they weren't like that' and 'thanks for donating'," Natalie says, rolling her eyes and disregarding all my friends' commentary. "Nice talk, you mute train-wreck." She turns back around, smirking at her friends.

I take a deep breath, keeping my gaze down, and murmur, "Shut up, Natalie. You don't know anything."

My whisper somehow cuts through the classroom noise. The chatter dies, and for a moment, the attention flickers between me and Natalie. Then the teacher walks in, and the class begins.

•••••••••••

The day passes in a blur of pitying looks, whispers, and hollow condolences. I stay silent—not out of rudeness, but because I don't know what to say. Grace and Kate try to cheer me up, but every well-meaning look or comment just makes it harder to keep believing Dad and Beth are still alive. I can't stand the thought that they might be gone.

They aren't.

"So, Tal, are you ready to talk about Michael?" Kate asks casually but with an edge of apprehension as we walk toward her car after school.

"Kate," Grace hisses in warning while her eyes start searching my face. I haven't looked up yet, ever since my first class. I keep examining the ground before me as if it will give me answers or guidance.

"Hey, don't worry about it," I say quietly and steadily to Grace. "Kate, I don't think I'm ready to talk about that yet," I say, somehow quieter. I don't want to upset her, but I can't handle another strenuous conversation today.

"Not ready to talk about your infidelities?" Kate's laugh is strained, her attempt at humor comes out rather condescending and a little too harsh.

Grace glances at me, her face a mix of pity and regret—an expression I've become all too familiar with lately. She stays silent this time, offering neither defense nor judgment.

"Yeah," I respond, a bit louder than before. "I'm trying to leave that for later." I try to smile; it feels like a grimace. It's the thought that counts. Clearing my throat, I look up slightly to make eye contact with Kate's chin, not having the courage to look into her eyes yet.

"It's been six months. You know he never gave up trying to help you through the hard times. You're the one who pushed him away," Kate continues, seeming to be more worked up now, and that's justifiable.

I take a deep breath, knowing I have to respond. But where do I start? This isn't even a conversation I should be having with Kate. Carefully, I say, "Kate, I'm sorry for what I put your brother through. I know I hurt him, but you can't put all the blame on me. Please try to understand—I was in a terrible place. I take full responsibility, and I'm truly sorry. But this is a conversation I need to have with him, not you." I pause, forcing a shaky laugh. "Can we go home? I need a nap after today."

I got my license taken away a couple of months ago due to... "an incident". Kate's been driving me ever since, which was a relief—I'd rather spend forty minutes with her than with my mom.

Ahead of me, I can hear Grace giving Kate a piece of her mind. Somehow, even when Grace is stern, she keeps it amiable. She's fiercely protective of her friends, and though she's patient, Kate's bluntness and temper often push her to her limit.

There are many decisions I regret from the past seven months. If I had to choose one, though, it would be pushing Michael away. He didn't deserve it; he was only trying to help. But I was sinking, weighed down by grief, with no way to pull myself up. Looking back, maybe I did him a favor. Who wants to hold on to dead weight?

Ultimately, I resorted to alcohol and sex. "Five stages of grief", they say. I sure fulfilled the anger stage. As for the others... what's the stage where you want to drink away your problem and have sex with strangers? Some would call it the stage of denial or depression. I call it a constant stage of loneliness and nothingness.

Denial. Anger. Bargaining. Depression. Acceptance.

I never made it to acceptance because, as my therapist unhelpfully stated, I never got closure. I have no proof that Dad and Beth are dead. I never saw the bodies. I never buried them. I don't even know if they're dead or alive. They're just... missing. It's been nearly a year, and I have nothing to hold on to, no proof that they'll ever come back. I'll never reach acceptance because I have nothing to accept.

Chapter 1.1

"HOW WAS YOUR DAY?" Mom asks the second I open the door. She's standing by the stairs, directly facing me, like she didn't want to miss my return.

I pause, giving her a questioning look as the door thuds shut behind me. A small eye-roll slips out. Sure, it's nice she's asking, but I can't help wondering about the intent behind her inquiry. Cautiously, I offer, "You know, the usual: people staring, saying they're sorry for my loss, me breaking down in the bathroom with Grace and Kate, Kate bringing up Michael, Grace being overprotective." I can't help the condescending tone. Honestly, how else would my day have gone?

"Please watch your tone," Mom warns. "You just got out of that phase where every one of your words was dripping with sarcasm," she adds, sounding annoyed.

"Yeah, yeah." I sigh, rolling my eyes again.

"Kate brought up Michael, you say? Do you think that's ever going to blow over?" Mom asks, her disappointment barely hidden.

I throw my head back, groaning a little before finally meeting her gaze. "Mom, nothing I've done in these seven months is going to 'blow over.' People might pretend to forget, blame it on my 'bad mental state,' but they'll always see me as the depressed, trashy girl

I've been. That's my legacy here." I drop eye contact and head to the kitchen, grabbing an apple. Dramatic, sure—but not wrong.

"I made soup," Mom says, ignoring my heartfelt speech.

"Not hungry."

"Do you have any homework?"

I sigh. "No, because school is being nice and trying to 'ease me in' without it being *too stressful* for me. They wouldn't want me to have another breakdown, would they?"

"Well, what will you do for the rest of the day?" Mom questions, without hesitation, once again ignoring my words.

I roll the apple around in my hand. "I was thinking about going to the local bar and leaving with some random dude. You know, the usual Monday afternoon." I start walking out of the kitchen and toward the staircase, evading eye contact again.

"Talia," she warns. "Don't push it. I swear if you start this again, I will not—"

"Fine," I interrupt her quickly. "I'll go upstairs and read a book," I snap. I start walking up the stairs slowly as I wait for her to say her parting words, which will most likely be full of disappointment and disdain.

I feel her eyes tracking me as I walk up the stairs. Finally, out of the corner of my eyes, I see her shake her head. "I wish you'd talk to me instead of acting like a brat. We could have gone through this together, but instead... instead you just ruined what was left of this family's reputation."

At the top of the stairs, I turn back to face her, looking at her closely this time, with harshly direct eye contact. Her stare stays unflinching, piercing through me like a drill through ice. "Mom, stop kidding yourself. We have no family left. Face it, we're the only ones now, and we're not known for being particularly respectable community members."

Mom blinks for a few seconds before finally turning away from me. She doesn't move but merely stands still, facing away from me. I don't expect any fight from her anymore. I don't expect anything. And she doesn't expect anything from me either. We're both tired of fighting with and for each other. We've had enough. Our relationship is now labeled as "acquaintances", or maybe even "roommates" at this point; nothing familial remains.

Upstairs, I continue rearranging my room. During my "anger stage" (also known as my reckless phase), I threw most of my stuff out the window. Now, in my so-called recovery, I'm restoring what I can. Most of it's broken or can't be replaced, not that I want everything back the way it was. I'm not the same person I was seven months ago, so my room shouldn't reflect the innocence and hope I no longer feel. I'll keep a few things, but the rest? I'm swapping it all out to fit this new "persona." Even though I don't fully know who that is yet. I'm not sure if this is really me, or if it's who I'll stay, but it's who I am right now, and I no longer have the energy to fight it.

I hear a knock on the front door and run downstairs before my mom can reach it.

"Talia, baby," Derek greets as I open the door.

Derek is an interesting story. I'm unsure if going into detail is the best idea when it comes to describing our relationship. In short, Derek was a mistake I made during one of my wild adventures over the past seven months, and I haven't been able to get rid of him since. I also don't want to. It's not as though I'm in love with him. Most of the time, he even annoys me. Nevertheless, ultimately, I need to figure out if he should stay in my life for the future, but since I haven't figured that out yet, here he is.

"Oh, hey," I reply cheerily. Derek does bring back some good memories, even though I was at my lowest when I met him. My best memories from the past seven months solely revolve around him.

"That's all I get? Come here, babe." Derek pulls me into a quick hug and plants a kiss on my forehead. "How was school today, my youngling?"

"Um, fine, I guess," I respond, scrunching my nose and awkwardly patting him on the back. I'm not the physically affectionate type. "My mom's home. Want to go somewhere else to talk?"

"To talk or..." He releases me from the hug and raises a suggestive eyebrow.

"Yeah, we can 'or' as well." I let out a laugh, my first real laugh of the day.

"Who is it?" Mom yells from the living room, where she is watching *Lost* on a loop. It's been months and months of *Lost*. No offense, but I will never understand how she can stomach watching it more than once. It's possibly one of the most frustrating TV shows of all time.

"Derek!" I yell back.

"Oh! You are not going anywhere with him." I hear the TV sounds pause and angry steps stalking toward us.

"Hi, Mrs. Turner. Always a delight to see you," Derek says in a friendly and blatantly sarcastic tone.

"Derek, you get your ass off my front porch and never come back," Mom snaps. Don't be fooled, this is not lighthearted banter. Mom has never tried to hide her dislike of Derek.

"Oh, Mrs. Turner, not a chance. But I promise I'll have Talia back safe and sound in a few hours." He grabs me, closes the door, and hustles me to his car before she can say another word. "Think she'll kill you when you get home?" he asks, steering me to the passenger side.

"That's the hope." I grin at him. I glance back at the house, knowing perfectly well that Mom won't try to run out after me.

Once in the car, I can finally breathe. Derek's presence and my mom's absence make me feel lighter. I can't exactly explain why, but something about Derek makes me forget everything else. Not that he makes me happy, but he makes my newfound world bearable. As he drives, I close my eyes, enjoying the quiet for a moment.

"So, seriously, Tal. How was your day?" Derek asks after a couple of minutes.

Unfortunately for me, Derek decides to be chatty today.

"Well, nobody asked me about who I'm dating right now, so that spared me the awkwardness of explaining my frowned-upon sexual relationship with a twenty-year-old," I respond, letting out a feeble laugh.

"I act more childish than you, and I'm hot. It's more like I'm eighteen, anyway," Derek muses.

"Still slightly frowned-upon, babe," I say.

"Sorry, I forgot you're twelve." Derek snorts.

"Fuck off." I laugh. It's not too concerning. I'm seventeen. Which, I guess, is still upsetting for some people (my mom). But who gives a fuck, right? I surely do not.

"But, like, how'd you hold up today?" He asks. Why is he still prying? Ugh.

"Fine. Except for when Kate brought up Michael, that was a downer." I keep my eyes closed so I don't give away any excessive emotion.

"Michael's the one that—"

"Yeah," I interrupt.

"Oh. And Kate is his—"

"Sister, yeah. Can we not talk, please? You're here to give me some fun, right?" I finally open my eyes and look over at him. Even though Derek knows most of the stuff I have been through, I am not in the mood to have a conversation right now.

"Well, we can talk as well," Derek offers slowly and softly. Is that hurt that I hear in his voice? Or is it pity?

"I'd rather not. I've had enough of talking today. I need something to get my mind off of it. And you're going to be that something," I state decidedly, closing my eyes again.

"Right," he replies tightly. "Sex and alcohol are the only answers to Tal's problems."

"That's why I keep you around," I say evenly, with a slightly joking hint. I honestly don't know if I'm joking, but Derek seems more emotional today, and I don't want to hurt his feelings too much.

"Tal—"

I open my eyes again. "If you're going to talk this much today, we need to stop at the liquor store first," I say, not hiding my annoyance.

"I just want you to be okay," he says softly.

I sigh heavily with irritation and roll my eyes before answering, "I told you. I'm fine. I had a great day. Now move on. Please get me drunk and fuck me. It's what I want. Look, I'm seventeen, almost eighteen, and can make my own decisions."

"That's barely an excuse. You're still young." He sighs this time, keeping his eyes on the road.

"Let. It. Go."

He sighs again, and I can feel his frustration now. "You're right. We will both need something to drink if this is how the night will continue."

"I'm always right," I state in a calm voice, closing my eyes again and leaning back in my seat.

I can feel him eyeing me, but I honestly don't care. Sometimes, he irks me.

Yeah, maybe what I'm doing is morally wrong—or even illegal—but I honestly don't care. The last few months have been the worst of my life, and even though I plan to get through it, I'm not there yet. Right now, I'm on a five-thousand-mile, uphill dirt path, and it'll be a long time before I reach the end.

My phone rings as we pull into Derek's driveway, startling me. I was starting to drift off a bit because today has been exhausting.

"Mom?" Derek asks me as he parks.

"How would I know?" I snap. I know he doesn't deserve my attitude. I can't help it.

I look at my phone and the number is unknown. It could be because a few months ago, I threw my phone across a bar, and it went to shit, so now I have to use my flip phone from seventh grade. On the other hand, I recovered most of the phone numbers of the people I talk to, so I have no idea who this might be. Who would even be calling me?

"It's my dealer. Give me a sec," I say to Derek.

"Tal, you get your weed from me. You don't have a dealer." Derek looks over at me with confusion and concern.

"This one's for coke. You told me you don't have that," I reply while opening the door to get out of the car.

Derek gasps almost inaudibly. "Cocaine? Tal, seriously?" he asks, definitely more concerned than confused now.

"I'm sorry. Who do you think you are, *my dad*? Give me a minute." I get out of the car, my phone still ringing. "Yeah, hi," I answer apprehensively.

"Mom called me. I'm coming tomorrow," a voice says, then hangs up. But I know exactly who it is—no introduction needed.

My brother is coming back home for the first time in three years.

· · • • • • • • · · ·

"So, your mom called? And for some reason, you're listening to her and coming back home?" Derek asks as he drives, his voice strained with worry that only annoys me further. He goes quiet, waiting for a response I don't bother to give. Finally, he asks slowly, eyes on the road, "Are you... breaking up with me?"

I let out a deep breath, not looking at him and keeping my eyes straight ahead. "Derek, don't be stupid. We're not dating. We're friends with benefits, minus the friends and extra plus the benefits." I try to sound as light as possible, to hide my annoyance with him and the uneasiness I feel after that phone call.

"Wouldn't that be called fuck-buddies?" Derek asks, with the same light-hearted tone I used, although he also includes a side of hurt, concern, and frustration.

"Yeah, sure, that," I respond, leaning back in my seat.

He mutters, barely audibly, "Nice." His face tightens, eyes fixed on the road, his jaw set in a way that tells me he's pissed. I'm not sure why, and right now, I don't care enough to ask. I squint, scratching my neck, wondering if I should say something.

After a long silence, I bite my lip and glance over at him. "Look, Derek. I met you when things were... rough for me, and you stuck around. Now's the easy part. So don't start getting serious on me. Be the guy I met at that bar in New York—the guy who just happened to be from my town and was up for something spontaneous. I don't know what you're trying to do right now, but... but I think you know me well enough to know..." I pause, unable to complete the sentence without sounding like a complete bitch. *"To know I don't want anything else from you."* I can't bring myself to say the words out loud, especially when he's clearly more emotional today.

Derek stays quiet for ages. After a while, he sighs deeply and murmurs, "That's all you want?"

"That's all I want," I say without hesitation.

"Fine," he agrees. He still doesn't make eye contact with me, and the car's aura is unpleasant. We stay silent for the remainder of the ride, looking at the road ahead without acknowledging the others' presence. There's no denying the heaviness of the air around us.

"Thanks for the ride," I say gently as we pull into my driveway, and I quickly jump out of the car before it even comes to a complete stop.

At the front door, I brace myself, knowing I won't get past Mom without a scene. She called my brother to reel me back home, deliberately exploiting one of the only people I'd drop everything for. I cannot begin to fathom what possessed her to pull this stunt. Just when I was beginning to find some semblance of stability, she decides to stir up a 7.2-magnitude earthquake in my life. But that's typical for her; Mom wouldn't know how to be nice if someone wrote her a guide on it. Instead of actually being helpful, she decided to pull my brother back into the fray. He's the only person I've truly looked up to, even though he's been out of my life for three years now. Dealing with her—or him, for that matter—is the last thing I want right now.

"You're home early," Mom's voice is smug as I slip through the front door. She's been waiting for this.

I refuse to walk over to where she's sitting at the kitchen table, obnoxiously leafing through a magazine. Instead, I opt to stand by the stairs in order to make a swift escape in case the conversation escalates. "Well, you did call your long-lost son and tell him how much of a mess I've been so that he would feel bad for you and come back to babysit me. So, yeah, when I found out about that, I wasn't really in the mood for sex anymore," I retort.

"I simply told him you have been a bit troubled," Mom replies calmly, not looking up from her magazine.

"That's an understatement," I say dryly. *Wow, way to burn yourself. Good one, Talia!*

Mom sighs deeply and finally looks up at me, scowling. "Talia, for once, can you try to be a smidge more tolerable to deal with?"

"Why would I try, Mom? What's the point? Is anything going to change between us?" My voice rises in pitch with each question.

"Talia, please don't start this again. You know I hate fighting and yelling, just—please don't start again. You can go to your room if you aren't interested in a civil conversation. I am not in the mood for your attitude," she responds in a monotone voice, lowering her gaze back to her magazine.

I give her a snarky laugh. "Typical. When are you ever in *the mood*? And you wonder why I don't talk to you. Have a nice night, Mom. Oh, and thanks for ratting me out to the only person who didn't yet know that I'm a complete wreck." I'm not going to cry. I'm angry.

These are purely angry tears, but I won't give her the satisfaction of seeing them.

"If you gave me a break once in a while, I wouldn't have to take extreme measures," she counters, still using an unaffected tone and not looking up.

Oh, that is rich, seriously.

"'*Extreme measures*'? When did you become an actual mom who cares enough to take '*extreme measures*'? Did you take extreme measures with Trevor? Or Beth? Or maybe with dad? Hmm, I don't recall! But hey, maybe that's why one-third of them haven't talked to you in three years, and the other two-thirds are missing or most likely dead. But sure, let's try it out on me. Maybe I'll stick around," I'm yelling at this point, tears pooling in my eyes.

Mom's eyes are still plastered on the magazine, although I can tell she isn't focusing on it. I take a deep, centering breath. I don't want her to look at me as the first tear rolls down. "Alright. Good night," I say tightly once I realize she won't respond.

I know how harsh my words were. They hurt me probably more than they hurt her. But that woman put me through immense amounts of torment and pain. She separated our family and made all of us miserable.

No wonder everybody but me is gone.

Chapter 1.2

FOUR A.M. I KNOW I won't be falling back asleep. Too many thoughts are swirling in my head, and there isn't enough time to think them all. I had mild insomnia before, and the stress of the past months hasn't made sleeping any easier. Honestly, I don't feel like going back to sleep anyway because anxiety overpowers me, and restfulness seems like a faraway phenomenon. I'm well-rested enough to function, at least at a fifty percent capacity, and that's what matters. Nobody expects more than that from me, anyway.

There is a soft but insistent knock on my bedroom door. "I know you're awake," Trevor's voice comes through the door. Won't you look at that? This is the second time—in twenty-four hours, no less—that I've talked to him. He hasn't spoken a word to me in over three years. What a treat. Although, I haven't gotten a "hello" or "how are you" yet. That's the relationship we have now, I guess. He used to be better before Mom broke him. Not surprising.

"Yeah," I say slowly. "Come in."

He waits for a few seconds, hesitating, before eventually opening the door. "Good morning?" he attempts, the greeting coming out as more of a question than a statement.

I give him an evaluating look. He looks different. Unfamiliar. Naturally, of course, since I haven't seen him in a while. He's twenty-one now, all grown up. He has a beard, too, which suits him, I guess.

"So, when did you get in?" I ask, getting up to open the window and let in some fresh air. The crisp morning breeze stings my face, but I welcome it.

"Two," he states, not making eye contact with me.

"Does mom know you're here?" I ask, still examining him and cataloging the differences I see. He looks *so* different, not at all like I remember him. He looks like a stranger.

"She does."

"Shame. You could have snuck in, talked to the person you came here to talk to, and snuck out without the devil noticing." I smirk, only half-joking. Actually, no, I'm not joking at all; I'm serious.

"You don't mean that," he says, still looking at the floor. He's completely stoic, only his mouth moving to form words, and such ridiculous words at that.

"Don't act like you don't think that."

"I don't."

"Well then, I don't know who you are."

That is true. I don't know who he is, either.

My brother takes a deep breath, finally looking up and staring straight at me. "Talia," he starts. "Mom called me for a reason. I'm, well, I'm not here to play games. I will be here for as long as it takes to see you get back on track. I was finally able to take a break from work, and I'm—"

"That wasn't necessary," I interrupt.

"—moving in." He keeps going, ignoring my comment. "I'll stay as long as it takes to see you doing better. I'm not doing this for Mom. I might be helping her out, but I'm doing it for you. And... for Dad and Beth."

"You're an asshole," I say, turning around to look out the window. Tears in my eyes, not this again. Why do they come at the most inopportune moments?

Trevor pauses but then continues in the same manner, "Call me whatever you want, but I'm staying for good. I'm moving in for a month or two, or three, or a year. Whatever it takes. So you better start getting used to me being around."

"Nothing is going to change." I shake my head, turning back to look at him, tears threatening to spill at any moment. "Now, seriously, leave my room."

Trevor meets my eyes briefly before looking away. I know he won't say anything else—three years might have passed, but I still know him. He's a good guy, studying finance at Berkeley, with some impressive job lined up. Living in a sunny state, with sunny people, and a sunny outlook. That's not how we operate here in Washington, D.C. We don't have time for small talk or thinking about others' feelings. *I* don't have the time or patience for this bullshit.

He finally turns around and silently walks out the door. Before closing it, he says, "I like what you've done with the place."

I'm not sure if he's mocking me or being sincere. Probably a mix of both. Either way, I don't care, and I'm done with the conversation.

"Get out," I choke out as the door shuts.

I flop back onto my bed, staring up at the ceiling. Not long ago, I installed a mirror up there—so I could face my miserable reflection each morning, maybe motivate myself to start the day. Sometimes I wish it would just fall and crush me, shards of glass piercing through my skin. It's too early for these dark thoughts. I suppose it's just wishful thinking. Currently, the mirror is a reminder of all my senseless, irreversible decisions. I might as well face it in all its cold, brutal clarity.

"Tal?" I hear a quiet and low voice call out outside my window. I jolt up and run to it because I know exactly who it is.

"Michael," I say breathlessly, leaning over the windowsill and feeling the frigid air on my face.

Michael is standing on the icy lawn, the frosty winter morning breeze blowing through his way-too-light-for-this-weather jacket. The look on his face is glum and despondent... it's hard to explain. Despair might be the best word. Definitely not anger, as I was expecting.

"Can we—can you come down?" he mutters questioningly, looking down at his feed and kicking the frozen ground.

Wow, I am getting a lot of undesired visitors at this hour, aren't I? What a lovely start to the day.

Selfishly, I want to slam the window shut, lock myself away and disappear. But since he came all the way here, I have to accommodate. "Want some tea?" I ask uneasily, still standing at the window. Why did he come, and what in the hell would he want to discuss with me?

"Sure," he says softly, offering me a sorrowful, yet somehow encouraging, smile.

One thing that I cannot do is deal with him smiling at me right now. I duck back into my room and decide against changing into something more presentable. I don't try to be quiet as I trudge down the stairs and open the front door. Mom and Trevor are probably awake, but I'm certain they won't leave their rooms until I leave the house (if then).

"Hi," I greet, opening the front door and moving aside so he can come in. Being quiet and shy is out of character for my "new self." But it's *Michael*.

"Talia," he greets in return, giving me an awkward nod of acknowledgment and shuffling his feet inside.

I stand at the open door for a while, holding on to the doorknob. After taking a deep breath and gathering myself, I walk over to the kitchen counter and fill the kettle with water before turning it on.

I turn around to look at him. If we're going to do this, I assume face-to-face is the most proper way. "Um, so, how did you know

I was awake?" I ask after what feels like an eternity of agonizing silence.

He sighs, rubbing his eyes tiredly. "Took a wild guess. I stood under your window until I saw you open it. I hoped you would hear me and wake up. It could be any of those options, honestly. Or, you know, all of the above."

I giggle quietly, inappropriately, and quickly suppress it. "Do you want some cookies with that tea? I didn't go to sleep until late last night, so I baked."

I'm working on three hours of sleep here.

"They don't have weed in them, right?" he asks, using a rather jokey tone, but I presume it's a genuine question.

"I don't do that anymore..." I respond, frowning and slightly defensive, although I have no right to be. I can be internally offended, but his preconception is justified.

"Sorry." He gives me another solemn smile. "Nothing has changed much around the house." He glances around, trying to small talk.

I'm *really* not in the mood, but I humor him anyway. It's the least I can do. "You should see my room." I laugh. But then immediately stop, deciding that's a bad idea. Clearly, he's here to talk about our relationship. Michael was my first love, my first boyfriend, the guy I thought I would end up marrying, honestly—as corny and cliché as that sounds. But that was all before I stopped caring about how my life would end up. That was before everything got fucked up. That was before.

"Kate told me you had a decent first day back at school and—you weren't too bad," Michael swiftly changes topics. His voice sounds unsteady. Uneasy. Forced, even.

"She said I wasn't *too bad*? Wow, Kate, thanks, I guess," I say sarcastically but with a smile.

He smiles back. I love that smile. I used to love him. He was my sun, my air, my everything. I was consumed by him. I remember thinking I couldn't survive if we ever broke up, like the world would go dark. And in a way, it did... yet here I am. Alive. Not well, but alive. Although sometimes it feels like I'm withering away, I suppose that happens when the sun disappears forever.

I place two mugs of tea on the kitchen table and sit across from Michael, anxiously waiting for him to start the dialogue. It's been months since I've seen him, and last time, I shattered his heart. Mine got crushed too, but that's beside the point.

"I saw you at school yesterday, but I decided not to come up to you," Michael starts carefully.

"Probably for the best," I say quickly, lowering my eyes to my cup of tea. I didn't mean for it to come out as rude as it did, so I correct myself, "I mean, um—it would have been difficult, probably, and I don't want to have to work things out in public." Does that sound any better?

He's silent for a second, scanning my face. "So, what exactly are you planning on working out?" he asks slowly and cautiously.

I knew he would pick up on that wording; I regretted the words the moment I said them. I sigh and twist my hair into a bun, stalling for time while I come up with something to say—no such luck. "I—I don't know," I answer weakly. I don't think he can even hear me.

He probably doesn't because it's silent for the longest time. Finally, he takes a deep breath. "Well, that's honest for a change," he says in a rather harsh tone.

"I've been nothing but honest with you," I object. I know I'm in the wrong. I know. But my first instinct is to be defensive. It's not the best trait.

"Please don't say things like that. It makes things worse, and you know it," he says, the harshness leaving his tone as the hurt sets into his voice. I still can't tell if he's mad, sad, or trying to start a fight. Maybe he's trying to get back at me.

"Why did you come?" I ask after another dreadfully long pause.

"Honestly, I—I have no idea. But I couldn't leave things the way we did. You're better now, and I hope we can work things out... because I can't live properly without you in my life." His voice cracks at the end. I can't look up to see his face; it's too painful.

I shake my head and squeeze my eyes shut. "'*Better now*'? You're speaking to me as if I've been a mental case for the past months, and now I'm finally out of my psychotic breakdown—"

"Isn't that what happened to you?" he asks.

My eyes open to glower at him. At this point, he is either being exceedingly annoying or enormously condescending. Either way, he's being plain disrespectful. Maybe he is honestly trying to figure out what happened to me, but his tone is not making me feel any better about myself, which in turn is making me bitchy. I will stay quiet to avoid making the situation worse by saying the wrong words.

Michael sighs again, rubbing the back of his neck and closing his eyes. After a moment he opens his eyes and makes hesitant eye contact. "You hurt me a lot, Tal," he says slowly and softly. Lowering his eyes, he gently reaches for his mug and takes a small sip.

It almost seems as if he doesn't want to admit I hurt him, but he doesn't even have to because I know I did. I know I did. I know I did. And I'm so sorry and wish I could take it back. I wish I let him go in an easier way rather than the horrendous way in which it happened.

My inner thoughts and feelings stay on the tip of my tongue, never making it out. Instead, I take a small sip of my tea, stare at the table, and keep quiet.

• • • • • • • • • •

During the first month of my going through my self-imposed stages of grief—while I was still on the cusp of staying a good person but already becoming the person I am now—Michael was by my side. He would go everywhere with me and try to stop me from making bad decisions.

It obviously didn't benefit him since most of the time, I would go out without him, do some dumb shit, and at the end of the night, he would end up holding my hair back while I puked.

Toward the end of the first month, everybody around town knew all of my business. Most people avoided me at all costs, but Michael stayed. I pushed him away with everything I had because I felt suffocated by everything around me, including him. And why would he even want me? Nevertheless, Michael was not keen on getting pushed away.

On one of my foolish nights out, I went to my new favorite place: the local bar. The bartender there knew exactly who I was and how old I was and still poured me a drink every time. It was probably because he wanted to fuck me. I guess I knew that subconsciously and took advantage of it. All I wanted was to drink.

Here's a joke: A drunk girl walks into the bar in a short-fitted dress from Forever 21 that she has been wearing for the past couple of days... sorry, I can't remember the rest because the bartender got me too drunk.

Moving on...

"Hey, Talia," Jack—the bartender—says while pouring me a shot of tequila.

"Hey, bartender Jack," I say and shoot him a flirty smile after taking the shot.

"You know, you don't have to call me by my profession every time. You come in here often enough for us to be on a strictly first-name basis," he answers, sending me a flirtatious look of his own.

I grin. "Keep pouring the shitty stuff because I'm running out of money, Jack." I'm not going to lie, I came into that bar already halfway wasted.

"How about something nicer this time? My treat?" Jack asks, walking over and reaching toward the upper shelves.

"If I didn't know any better, I'd think you're trying to pick me up at your own bar," I say, smirking.

"How do you feel about that?" Jack asks, with a more serious edge this time.

Honestly, I didn't feel like anything about it. But I can't say that because then the conversation would be over, and that is not how you get free expensive drinks. I honestly didn't care if I would end up having sex with him or not. I felt nothingness—the usual.

"Let's see how much good stuff you can carve out for me first," I respond, perching myself on top of the bar counter.

"However much you want, Talia." He grins, grabbing a bottle of Clase Azul Reposado tequila and pouring me another shot. Tequila is my poison of choice, and Jack knows that better than anyone. Circling back to the sex talk, Jack is twenty-three, so not illegal, but undeniably questionable.

I put my hair in a bun and drink for the next half hour. As does he. He knows once I've reached my complete limit because I have reached it so many times at this bar.

"You know I live right above the bar?" Jack asks casually, feigning innocence, as he stands between my legs.

"Oh, how convenient for you," I tease. No more thinking. I lean over and kiss him. Long story short, I'm sitting on the bar top, and a whole lot of first and second base is happening.

Unexpectedly, I hear the bar door slam, and I twist around slowly, lips still not fully unlocked from Jack's. Jack tries to pull away, but I grab his shirt tightly to keep him where he is.

Michael is standing at the front door, stuck in mid-motion. "Talia," he says, his voice cracking. Without another word, he lowers his eyes and slowly starts walking out of the bar. As if he's my disappointed father, and that infuriates me.

"What are you going to do about it? Oh, right. Nothing! Because you never do!" I yell. Honestly, I don't know if that came out comprehendible or as a complete jumble of random sounds. "I'm not even sorry!" I add as the door to the bar bangs shut.

Jack finally pulls away from my grip. "Tal, I can't do this to him," *he says, shaking his head.*

"Don't act like you care about my relationship with him, now," I say in a snarky tone.

"Talia, I don't think you have a relationship with him anymore. *You fucked that up. Michael is a good guy, and I'm an asshole. You chose. Good guys don't deserve this shit."*

"You're not making any sense. Are we going to have sex or not?" I ask. I am getting frustrated by his sudden change in attitude. And Michael left me furious and flustered.

"No," he says firmly, looking me directly in the eyes. Or at least I think he is looking me in the eyes. It's hard to keep track since I am considerably dizzy, and everything is spinning.

"Fine. Can I at least crash at your apartment tonight?" I ask, pointing upstairs.

"Talia, I think you should go home. When was the last time you saw your mother?" Jack's voice sounds almost concerned and caring, making me want to hurl. Whether it be a bottle at his head or my insides onto his precious bar floor—that's up to fate.

"My mother? My mother?*" I question loudly, not quite yelling but getting worked up. "Fuck. You." I adjust my dress clumsily and get off the counter. "You are not who I thought you were. What a disappointment," I say, turning around and walking to the door.*

"Talia, look at yourself. You are seventeen years old. Get yourself together, go to school, drink at high school parties, fuck with guys your own age. Stop acting like a hooker and get some new clothes." He looks genuine, but the words he's saying are utter bullshit and frankly misogynistic, especially considering his actions just a few moments ago.

"You done?" I snap. "Get a life, Jack. About five minutes ago, you were serving drinks and about to fuck a minor. So don't try to act all holier-than-thou because you are just as horrid as the rest of them. It's just that you got caught, and now you feel bad, turned off, or whatever. Fuck you, honestly," with those parting words, I laugh (hysterically)

and slam the door behind me. I have no idea what time it is, and I have about fifty bucks stuffed into my bra. So, naturally, I go to the nearest train station and catch a train to New York City.

There, I meet Derek. But that is a whole different story, and truthfully, not a very interesting one. We know how it ends.

· · · • • • • • · ·

The memory is etched into my mind, no matter how desperately I wish it would fade. Painful memories have a way of sticking around, of replaying themselves just when you'd give anything to forget.

"Yes, I hurt you," I say steadily. "But—and don't take this as me making any kind of excuse for my actions, I was hurt too. I try to forget, but I can't. I remember it all. I remember trying to make myself numb, and it never worked; I felt everything. I still feel everything, somewhere deep down." Even though I feel empty inside. Nothingness surrounds me. I can still remember feeling at one point—feeling too much and feeling helpless.

I know I'm seventeen, but sometimes it feels like I'm a lot older. With everything I've been through—and put myself through—it feels like I've got one foot in the grave. You'd think age would tell you how much people have been through, but that's not true. I used to be a normal girl with a normal—well, mostly normal—family. I wasn't well-known, I didn't cause trouble. I lived life like anyone else, with its ups and downs.

Now I'm the girl with the worst reputation in town, the one everyone would rather see gone. I wrecked relationships. I hurt people. I hurt myself. From the outside, you wouldn't pin me as someone tragic or destructive, and I don't like to think of myself that way either. But I know who I've become, and it's hard to change that. There's a saying I heard once. I don't remember it exactly, but the gist is: be good your whole life, and no one notices; make one mistake, and it defines you forever. I made seven months' worth of mistakes. How do I get people to forget that?

"Talia, what I'm trying to say here is, I don't want us to end up hating each other or—"

"I don't hate you," I interrupt, frowning and finally looking up at him. "Not at all."

"I don't hate you either," he replies, sighing as he holds my gaze. "All I'm saying is I want us to be on good terms. Because I don't enjoy fighting, whether it be physical or verbal or any other kind, you know that."

I nod, my gaze not dropping from his face. I want to say something, anything, and all that comes out is, "So... it's mid-January, and it's not even snowing. What's up with that?" Thanks, brain-to-mouth filter. As if this wasn't already painful, I had to make it worse by asking about *the weather*.

Michael gives me a strange look but goes along with it. "It did snow on Christmas, so that was nice," he offers.

I nod overenthusiastically and smile.

He smiles back.

This is more awkward than I thought it would be.

Michael finally stands up. "I think it's time for me to head back home. Everybody at home will be awake soon, and if they see me coming in from outside, that's a lot of difficult explaining that I do not want to be doing," he says. His voice sounds a little lighter now, making me feel warm. I savor it.

I nod. "Some cookies for the road?" I ask, offering him the container.

He hesitates. "Um—sure, why not?" He shrugs and takes a couple, wrapping them in a napkin he grabs from the table.

"Well, I'll talk to you later..." I trail off, unsure whether I should make it a question or a statement. It comes out as a mumble, my voice uncertain and shaky.

31

He takes it as a question and nods. "Yeah, I think we will. We have more to discuss, but not at your house and not at five in the morning."

I laugh softly, walking past him and toward the front door. "Okay, good. Bye," I say as I hold the door open for him.

He smiles again and walks out the door. I'm about to say something else—anything else—just as the door closes. Honestly, I have nothing to say, but I wanted to keep talking to him, to keep hearing his soft voice and seeing his shining smile. I'm about to stupidly run out after him, when my phone rings. Saved by the bell, I suppose.

Who is calling me at this hour? Still staring at the closed door, I answer, "Hello."

"Talia, honey, sweetie, hello my dear," Natasha's—my sweet, sweet psychic—voice sounds through the speaker.

"Oh, hey Natasha. What's up?" I light up and finally peel my eyes away from the door, instead leaning against it.

Natasha is a psychic, my friend, and my rock. I met her one night in downtown D.C., when I was completely wasted and lost. She took me in, nursed me back to health, and we bonded. She's helped me make better choices since then—or at least tried. She's never asked for anything in return, just took me under her wing. She's the mother figure I never had, and though I still sometimes mess up, I don't know where I'd be without her. I also genuinely think she has psychic abilities, I wholeheartedly believe and trust her.

"I have some news for you," she starts. I hear her take a deep breath and proceed, "Okay, so I still have not seen your father or sister yet, which is part of the good news. Remember what we talked about?"

"Natasha, of course I remember. I haven't had a drink in nine days. I know that if you haven't seen them yet, it means they are still alive." I smile at that thought. A sad, hopeful smile.

"Yes, yes. Anyway, I heard from my PI about the request you sent to the FBI regarding your sister and father a few months back. You know the one we did together? Well, it is finally under review and might be up for investigation."

I almost shriek with joy, "Are you serious? That is AMAZING! Oh my god, that is such thrilling news! Natasha, thank you so much. You are an extraordinary person, and I could never have done this without you." This woman has genuinely become the rock I can lean on over the past months, and I am eternally grateful to her. She dealt with me when I was at my worst. However cliché all this sounds, this woman really did help me. I'll go as far as saying that she saved my life.

"Yes, honey, I know this is great news. But remember what we talked about? Please continue down the road you have been going for the past couple of days. You are finally on the right path, and if you continue with this and mend all the bridges you burned—well, you know the rest. I know this is a lot of chitter-chatter for five in the morning, but you should listen."

"I always listen to you, Natasha," I say, rolling my eyes slightly.

"Good," Natasha affirms. Her voice always sounds stern, yet somehow soft.

I hesitate for a moment but decide to bring it up anyway, "I talked to Michael this morning. He was at my window until I let him in. By the way, my brother is back home, and I had a conversation with him this morning. Michael seems to want to work things out." My thoughts are all over the place, spilling out in a jumbled mess.

Natasha is quick to respond, "Your brother is back home? Honey, let's put a pause on Michael for a few minutes. Your brother is back home?" She seems to have a worried edge to her voice, although she always knows how to work through a situation step by step.

"Yeah, he came back last night. Mom called him and snitched on me, so now I have to deal with that too," I complain.

"What did we say about your mother?" Her voice sounds odd. I choose to ignore it for now, focusing on her words.

"We don't say bad things about her. She wants the best for me," I recite and roll my eyes.

"Don't roll your eyes, sweetie, or else they'll get stuck that way." Natasha's voice is calm but firm. "Now, let's use better language. She didn't 'snitch' on you, but rather, she called your brother because she's genuinely worried about you and doesn't know how to handle it herself. She needs support. Remember, you told me once that your older brother was a role model for you before he left three years ago. So, I have to agree with your mom here. Honey, she's trying to do the right thing. Give her a chance. She is your mother." Natasha's voice trembles a bit with emotion. Her sensitivity isn't her best trait, but I appreciate her sincerity.

"Okay, Natasha. Thanks for calling and letting me know. Are you still in Vegas, or will I get to see you soon?" I try to change subjects to avoid talking about my mother any longer.

"I'm sorry, Talia, but I will still be away from D.C. for a few more weeks. You know I have other clients that require my guidance and support." I can feel her smiling, although I know she's being serious. I definitely believe that this woman works with more serious people than a measly seventeen-year-old girl.

"Yeah, yeah. I'm still your favorite," I reply jokingly.

"I have a client now. Talk to you later, dear." She hangs up.

I yawn and walk over to sit down at the kitchen table.

I think about what my life has become. I used to have a normal life, as normal as any life can be. Our family had problems, of course, and we fought a lot... but we were a family. Now, I'd be lucky to gather enough people to even make a family, let alone a normal one.

"Hi, sis, you ready to go to school?" Trevor walks into the kitchen, grinning and looking cheery overall.

"It's five-thirty in the morning. What are you talking about?" I snort.

"I was just trying to casually slide in the fact that I'm taking you to school today," he responds nonchalantly.

"Yeah, good one. My friend is taking me," I say while grabbing a banana for breakfast.

He sighs and throws his head back dramatically. "I don't think you understand this arrangement, Tal. *You* won't be making the decisions from now on. You are going to be a normal child and—"

"Yeah, a normal child with a dead father and a dead sister," I add in a snarky tone.

"Yup, just like that," he says without missing a beat, although I hear a shakiness in his voice.

I eye him carefully. If he's going to play hard-ass, I can play his game and make it fun.

"Alright. Well, I'm going back to sleep now. Wake me up at six-thirty." I stand up from the table and walk upstairs.

Back in my room, I lock the door behind me. I look around, remembering when this room felt full of life. I've tried to bring it back to life but now it's cluttered with memories I'd rather erase. All I want is an empty space—a bed, a desk, and a chair. Nothing more.

Every object in here reminds me of the past. There's the chair where Beth used to sit and read to me every night when I was little. The lamp that Trevor broke years ago, only for him and Dad to fix it together. The pink fluffy pig I stole from Beth's room when I was seven. The souvenirs Dad brought home from his business trips. The photo frames that Grace and Kate helped me fill with pictures of family and friends. I used to have a life. A happy, memorable life. I used to connect with people and share pieces of myself.

I used to.

Chapter 1.3

TREVOR IS SILENT AS he drives me to school. Grace sits in the back, a casualty of my family drama since Kate would normally pick us both up. But since Trevor is driving me today, Kate went straight to school, leaving Grace to endure the tension in the car.

It's majorly, uncomfortably silent in this car.

After about ten minutes, Grace can't seem to hold it in anymore, "So, Trevor, the last time I saw you I was thirteen years old. You got anything new going on?" I know she is trying to be friendly and help the awkwardness, but I can also hear the criticism in her voice.

Trevor eyes her through the rearview mirror, otherwise not making a move to respond for a minute.

"Mom asked me to tell you and Kate to come over for dinner tonight. We can discuss things then," he responds eventually.

"That's so nice, I can't wait! Save me a seat next to Anne. I need to catch up with her," Grace says excitedly. Anne is my mom's name, and I used to despise how close Grace and her were. However, now I take it for the blessing that it is (it gets Mom off my back). This is what I love about Grace: she always knows how to make a situation light. She is the most positive person to ever exist. The rainbow at the end of my rainstorm.

· · · · **·** · **·** · · ·

School drags by, as dull as yesterday. The only difference is Kate's enthusiasm over my "hot brother being back in town," which makes me gag. She insisted she's going to "wear something nice for him" at dinner, and I had to resist the urge to punch her. Just because I dated her brother doesn't mean she can go around saying shit like that about mine.

"It's not a problem. I'm sure Mrs. T wouldn't mind; she's super chill," Kate says, shrugging and grinning delightfully.

"Kate, if you say one more thing about my brother, I have the siblings' right to punch you," I say for the eleventh time today.

"Trevor and I have always had a connection," Kate continues. When I actually swing at her, she ducks away and giggles. "Speaking of…" she trails off, pointing toward where Trevor just pulled into the parking lot.

I am being treated as a prisoner. Home—school—home. This is my life now.

"Ah, anyway, you know I'm kidding, babe. I already have a boy lined up, and all I need is help for him to fall in love with me. So, dinner at seven?" Kate asks.

"You need *help* for a boy to fall in love with you? What has happened in these past seven months?" I ask. Kate is gorgeous, with a great sense of humor. And yes, she has a bit of a temper, but she is one hell of a catch.

"Oh, you remember how Jason L. tried to start up a thing with me last year? Well, we've been talking recently, even though he has a girlfriend. By the way, we've only hooked up three times—and only one of those was while he was with her, and I was drunk and didn't know. Anyway, now I'm starting to like him. He's dating a freshman, so I'm working on breaking them up. Sounds bad, I know, but he wants me too. All the freshman girls hate me now, but you gotta do what you gotta do, right?" She gives me a wicked smile. "You do what you want, babe. Just tell me beforehand so I know who to protect you from and who to hate." I laugh shakily. That's quite a story. But nothing compared to mine. So, who am I to judge?

Kate rolls her eyes at me but laughs. "Alright, let's go home." She drags Grace toward her car.

"Hey, sis." Trevor drives up to my side.

"Stop talking to me," I say as I climb into the car and slam the door. "This is prison, so we might as well act our part. You're the guard, so take me back to my cell, and no pleasantries are required."

He gives me a look and rolls his eyes. "We used to have such a good relationship. What happened to that? Or will I be afraid to hear the answer?" He genuinely sounds cautious as he says this.

I don't honor him with a response.

"I guess I'll be afraid to hear the answer," Trevor says with a sigh as he starts driving out of the parking lot. "Talia, I'm not keeping you as a prisoner. You can leave whenever you want and do whatever. I'm here to keep you safe, and if you want to rejoin as a family, it's all up to you."

I let out a slight grunt of derision. "Trevor, what family?" I ask. "We have no family."

"We have the three of us, Tal. So we might as well make the best of it. Don't you want to?" His voice is almost pleading.

Frankly, I don't know if I do. How would we make a family work? Does that mean Trevor is staying here, or will he return to Cali? I have too many questions, and I don't want to ask them. But I don't think we can make it work.

I decide to sit quietly, watching the haze of trees and curves of the road as we drive home.

• • • • • • • • • •

Dinner is sufficiently dreadful.

I didn't realize that my mother invited Michael and Derek as well. That was... a painful revelation. Which I wish I had been more prepared for. When I took Mom to the side to discuss this strange arrangement of people, her justification was that she wanted everyone who cared about me to be around the dinner table tonight.

Currently, Grace is in a deep conversation with my mother about something that apparently requires lowered voices.

Michael is slightly glaring at Derek while Derek is gobbling down plate after plate of food.

Kate is chatting with Trevor, asking him about what he's been up to in the past three years.

I have no clue what to do. So I sit. Not touching my food and not making direct eye contact with anyone. I sit there—staring at my hands on my lap.

"How about a toast?" My mother finally says, standing up from her chair. I can tell that she's already pretty tipsy. Shocker.

"Yeah, go, Anne!" Grace cheers her on.

Mom smiles back. "I'll keep this short and simple," she begins, looking around the table. "You're all close enough to our family to know what happened seven months ago. It hit us hard. Obviously. I just want to say thank you. I'm thankful all of you stuck around. And while some of you only came into our lives during this time, you still offered support." She pauses, glancing at Derek—not exactly warmly, but it's a start. Her gaze shifts to each of us, voice softer. "I hope you'll all stay in our lives and keep supporting Talia. Maybe that's asking a lot, but my job as her mom is to ask. You all mean a lot to her, and because of that, you mean a lot to me." She raises her glass with a heartfelt smile. "I hope we can have dinners like this more often—"

"And cheers to them being less awkward than this one!" Kate interrupts, raising her glass.

"Cheers," my mom smiles, taking another gulp of wine. "And kids, I'm sorry I didn't introduce you before... this is Derek, everybody. Derek, this is Kate, Michael, Grace, and Talia's brother, Trevor," she says, pointing at each person respectively.

Grace cheerfully says, "Nice to meet you!"

Everybody else smiles politely at the introduction.

"Dinner was amazing, Anne. But I'm afraid Michael and I have to be back home by ten p.m. on school nights, and it's nine forty-five," Kate says, rising from the table.

How the hell have we been sitting here for almost three hours? It feels like five minutes and, at the same time, feels like five hours.

"Aw damn, I have to catch a ride with you guys. I guess I have to go. Love you, Tal. Nice to meet you, Derek. Bye, Trevor and Anne," Grace smiles at everybody as she gets up from the table. She also helps my mom clear the table before leaving. Mom insists she doesn't have to do that, but Grace will always leave a house cleaner than the way she found it.

"It wasn't half as bad as I expected," Mom comments as she closes the door behind Derek, who stayed behind to chat with me for a bit after everyone else left.

"If that wasn't half as bad, I have no idea what is going on in your head," I say as I walk up the stairs.

"We did this for you, Talia," Mom says, her voice wavering.

I turn my head to look down and see Trevor standing next to her at the foot of the staircase. They have these agonizing, expectant looks on their faces. I turn back around and continue walking up the stairs. At the top of the staircase, I turn around again to look at them, and they are still standing there and staring at me.

"It wasn't the worst experience I've ever had," I say, and give a tight smile. I'm glad the dinner went well enough that I didn't want to end my life.

· · · · ● · ● · · · ·

The next morning, I realize the mistake of my nice comment last night. My mom has now taken on the responsibilities of a "real mother". The new rules are as follows:

-Family breakfast and dinner every day

-Family movie night on Friday or Saturday (or both!)

-"Family outings" once a week—whatever that means

-Each family member has to have at least one friend over every week

-Trevor has to transfer to Georgetown for the rest of the semester and, if need be, for the rest of next year (which is his last year of college)

I guess my mom made some calls since her friend is the Dean at Georgetown.

"So, now we're going to have to follow rules on how to be a functional family? Not sure that's how it works," I say snarkily, as my mom serves pancakes with whipped cream and maple syrup, bacon, scrambled eggs, fresh fruit, and orange juice.

I make a mental note to ask Kate to stop for iced coffee before school. Mom insists coffee isn't a "sufficient meal" to start the day, even though I can't function without it. At least I convinced her that Trevor driving me every day is impractical, so Kate's back to chauffeuring me. Thank. God.

"Honey, we have to get into the flow of it again first, which is why we will follow some *guidelines*. Just some helpful tips on how to get back to standard family functionality," Mom replies in her motherliest tone.

I purse my lips. "Right," I say and take a bite of my banana.

"Eat a pancake, would you?" Trevor says. "It's only polite. And honestly, they are delicious," Trevor says in a monotone voice, and he doesn't make eye contact with Mom. One has to appreciate his effort, though.

"We're all going to try to step up our game, Trevor." Mom smiles at him.

He doesn't respond to her or say anything else. Fortunately for me, the past is not easily forgotten, and Trevor and Mom aren't going to become besties overnight.

"Well, nice talk. I'll see you guys after school." I start to get up from the table.

"Talia Marie Turner, you come back here this instant and finish a sufficient meal with your family. I will not repeat myself twice, and if you leave through that door right now, you will never hear the end of it," Mom says in a stern yet unsure voice. I almost want to laugh at her trying.

"The end of it," I mutter, slipping out the door. Am I being immature? Hell yes. But I refuse to let them mold us into this bizarre new version of a family.

• • • • • • • • • •

I decide to call Natasha today, even though I spoke to her yesterday, and she insists that I not call her out of the blue. She assures me that she will call me whenever she has essential information.

I dial anyway.

"Yes," Natasha answers the phone. She always answers the same way because she does not save any numbers on her phone and has no time for pleasantries.

"It's Talia, hey," I say softly. I'm skipping English class for this, and if I get caught, I'm screwed. I'm currently sitting in a bathroom stall. You'd think that would be the low of my day, but it will most likely be the high.

"Hi, Talia," Natasha responds. Her voice sounds a little off, but I choose to ignore it for now since I have an important conversation to uphold.

"So, have you found anything out yet?" I inquire. "I might be coming to visit you soon. I know you said you wouldn't be back—"

"Having issues at home?" Natasha asks distractedly.

"My mom's trying out something new. She wants to be a family again, and she's making us follow these—"

"Look, honey, I'm so sorry. I don't have time to talk right now. I am very busy. Can I call you back later? Thanks, darling." She hangs up abruptly without waiting for my response.

I'm a little startled because she's never been so curt with me, but I guess she has some critical high-level dealings to get to. Of course, she can't blow that off for some petty troubles of a teenage girl.

I wonder if I should skip school altogether today. But then I think about the past seven months, and I think about Dad and Beth—their disappointment... my disappointment.

"Sorry I'm late," I say as I enter English class and sit next to Kate.

"You came to class. I thought you were skipping," Kate whispers, grinning at me.

"I decided I need to get back into the flow of school. The anxiety of school work will help me focus less on home stuff, you know?" I smile back at her. Could this be me maturing?

"Nice." Kate nods. "English is horrible, by the way." She turns back around to look at the board. I have no idea what we're reading or discussing, but I try to focus and take notes anyway.

Classes go by very slowly and longer than I remember, although it could seem that way because I have no clue what is happening in any of them. I try to take notes and keep up, but everything is moving too quickly, and everything seems to be in a foreign language. If I knew that missing half a year of school would fuck me up this bad—well, I'd probably still miss it, but at least I'd know.

"A bunch of us are going to hang out at the pink coffee place after school if you want to join. After that, we're going to the movies, because Jason wants to see this new *hilarious* movie and well, I need to go if he's going. His little girlfriend isn't coming this time, so the seat next to him is mine," Kate says during lunch. It's raining outside (nothing new for early-January weather), and all that makes me want to do is drink. Because this weather makes me sad, and sad equals drinking. Have I become an alcoholic? Perhaps. Perhaps I need help. Maybe I'll ask my mom. Ha-ha.

"I think that's a great idea. It'll get you back in the flow of things, and it can count as extra points with your mom because you're hanging out with friends, right?" Grace encourages.

I shrug and keep staring out the window. I haven't had a drink in a week and two days, and I want one badly. Alcohol makes everything feel warmer, fuzzier. It lets me be happy, even if I'm not. And lately, I'm rarely happy. I didn't drink like this before, just here and there at a party or a concert. But now... it's different.

"I'm going to need some verbal confirmation from you, and I'll text Mel," Kate says while getting her phone out of her pocket.

"Mel?" I ask, finally tearing my eyes away from the window and looking at the girls.

"Oh, yeah, we're friends with Mel now. She kind of joined our group when she started dating Tom. She can be annoying sometimes, but she throws awesome parties, so I don't mind her that much." Kate shrugs nonchalantly.

Melanie used to be the girl we all hated. One of those girls who "matured" early, and she wasn't exactly friendly. Early freshman year, she ditched her friend group and started hanging out with older guys. Now, I guess she's with Tom, which means she's with us. Tom, Brad, Grace, Kate, and I have been inseparable since kindergarten. It feels strange having someone new in the group. Or maybe I'm not part of the group anymore?

"That's going to be such an odd group of people," I say, frowning slightly.

"It's just the usual, plus a couple of dates. Nothing weird about it," Kate responds defensively.

"I didn't mean you and Jason, I—never mind." I shake my head. I've been out of the loop lately, and I think my social skills are currently lacking.

"If you don't want to come, you don't have to," Kate states. She seems kind of pissed off now, but I haven't forgotten Kate's temper, so I don't take it personally. "Anyway, I have class. See you later. Or not." Kate doesn't finish her salad, throwing it in the trash as she walks away.

"What's up with her?" I ask Grace.

"She's very upset about the whole Jason thing. She went through a very depressing stage a couple of months back, and she's recovering," Grace says with a dejected sigh.

"How about you and I go somewhere after school, and you can catch me up on stuff?" I ask.

Grace makes an unusual facial expression I have never seen her make before. "Oh—um—sorry, I'm going to the coffee place with everybody. I'm kind of going with someone," she explains, stammering through it. "We can totally chat there, though," she recovers.

"Who are you going with?" I ask, confused once again.

"I kind of have a thing with—um—Kyle." She smiles.

"Didn't you swear off guys or something?" I ask. I distinctly remember her saying something along those lines. Although that was over seven months ago, now that I think about it.

"Okay, not the reaction I was expecting when I tell you I'm dating the football player that everybody is in love with. Anyway, don't tell anybody for now. I'll see you later." She gets up and walks away as the first bell rings.

I stand up and throw away my trash. Then, I head over to my next class. I'm still confused and a little offended and upset.

What happened to everybody in the past seven months?

•••••••••

The pink coffee place is a local hangout. It doesn't have a name, so everyone calls it the "pink coffee place" due to the pink walls, furniture, and dishes. Basically, everything is pink. They also have good coffee and pastries.

As I walk in, I see Kate and Jason across from Tom. Tom and Jason are in a deep—and loud—conversation about basketball. Kate is trying to cuddle up to Jason while Melanie sits beside Tom, her head resting on his shoulder as she seemingly texts. Grace and Kyle are flirting at a separate table. Brad, who's sitting next to Tom, is eyeing Grace and Kyle while also trying to join the basketball conversation.

And me? Well, I just walked in. I don't fit into any of these little scenes. I've known these people almost my whole life, but now I feel like the jagged extra piece in a completed puzzle. I'm not one of them anymore. I feel a rush of nerves and start backing out, hoping no one notices.

"Hey, Sparkles! Join us." Tom waves and grins at me.

Too late.

Tom has called me "Sparkles" since elementary school because when I was younger, I was obsessed with glitter and would always spill it everywhere, including myself and those around me. Funny how that stuck. (Pun intended?)

Everybody stops their talking and stares at me as I walk over. It's not necessarily hostile expressions that I see on their faces, more like... hesitant, but not entirely unfriendly. Brad and Tom both stand up to give me a hug.

"Nice to have you back, bud," Brad says, sitting back down.

"Here, take my seat," Tom offers. Melanie doesn't look pleased with that arrangement.

"It's cool. I'll just pull up a chair," I say, and pull one up next to Brad.

"Haven't seen you in forever. I'm not going to ask how you've been. But I will ask, how has it been coming back?" Tom asks.

I shrug. "I mean, it's only been three days. So much has changed since I've been... away. I don't even know what to say or how to feel."

"Yeah, '*away*,'" Melanie mutters, rolling her eyes, but still doesn't look up from her phone.

"Excuse me, do you have something to say? Say it to my fucking face," I say, looking directly at her.

Everybody's eyes widen as they stare at me, and then they slowly turn to see Melanie's reaction.

Melanie is wide-eyed as well, but she recovers quickly. "Okay, I will say it to your face, princess. Your perfect little life is over. Get ready to be a big girl now, Talia. You need to learn to make decisions since you have no family left to make them for you. Stop trying to act like the past seven months didn't happen. They did. You know it, I know it, we all know it. It happened. It will always be there. Learn to live with the repercussions." She pauses for a second, contemplating if she should pour more salt on the wound. "Tom, we're leaving," she says after a second, standing up and walking right out the door without hesitation.

Tom is quiet for a second, then says, "Um—she's my ride. I'm really sorry, Tal." With that, he walks out. One of my best friends since kindergarten just chose his new girlfriend over me.

"That was hard to watch," Jason states while sipping his drink.

Kate nods slowly, still looking at me with wide eyes.

"This was fun. I'm going to leave," I say, standing up.

Brad jumps up. "I'll give you a ride. You got your license taken away, right?"

Grace's head turns from the table next to us, eyeing Brad's enthusiasm to drive me home suspiciously. I can't read her face. She's gotten some new facial expressions over the past seven months. I used to know all of them.

I nod at Brad. "Bye Jason, Kate. Grace, Kyle, see you later," I nod again and head out the door.

What a train wreck that was. Maybe it's me who's the train wreck, and everybody should simply stay away.

············

I thank Brad for the ride home and get out of the car. But as soon as I shut the door and turn to head up the driveway, he's suddenly right in front of me, his eyes unsettlingly intense.

"Oh my god!" I jump a little, clutching my chest. "You scared me." I didn't realize he got out of the car when I did. I assumed he would drive away as soon as I got out.

He stands there for a second, and within a split second, his face is moving toward mine. I barely avoid his lips touching mine as I lean further back against the car door.

"Brad, what the fuck are you doing??" I demand, my eyes wide—full of shock and confusion.

He looks startled for a second but recovers quickly and smirks. "My parents went to the Bahamas for the week. Do you want to come over to my house?" he asks.

I try to back away because Brad is still tremendously close to my face. I end up practically lying back against the car door. "Brad, what is this?" I ask, still incredibly confused.

"What do you mean?" he asks, as if he didn't try to fucking kiss me a few seconds ago.

I think about what to say for a moment. "Like—um—are you trying to do this right now because you're not over Grace and you're jealous of Kyle?" I ask finally. I might as well make it clear.

He pauses, then asks, "Are you saying no?"

I keep level eye contact with him as I respond, "If you want to go to your house and talk, or watch a movie or something, I'm up for it. But Brad—"

"What?" he snaps, eyes narrowing.

I try to lean back even farther away from him. The look in his eyes is dangerously intense, alarming me. "Nothing is going to happen between us," I confirm.

He doesn't seem to notice my discomfort and continues standing a few inches away from me.

All he does is chuckle. "Talia is saying no, that's a first! Alright then, you can go home now. I'm not keeping you." He finally steps away from me.

"You're serious?" I glare at him in astonishment and slight outrage. I've been friends with this kid since childhood, and that's all he has to say after he tried to kiss me out of the blue?

"Oh, come on, be real." He rolls his eyes. "You've always known that I want you, and you've led me on for years. Even when I was dating Grace. But I guess I'm the only guy in this town you won't sleep with. So, the conversation here is over," he snaps.

"You're being a dick," I say, glued to my spot.

He doesn't budge or speak. He just stands there, unblinking.

"Fine, have it your way." I lean away from the car and push past him. "I thought you were my friend," I say as I walk toward the front door.

I'm about to open the front door to my house when I hear the car door slam and the tires screech as he pulls out of the driveway.

Could this day seriously get any worse?

· · · · · · · · · ·

Two a.m.

A text from Brad: ian sorjroy

Me: what

Brad: sory

Me: are you drunk? where are you?

Brad: bar whith freids

Me: do you need my help?

Brad: I',ma ok

I get out of bed and dress in a hurry. I put on a hoodie and leggings before heading to the local bar. Fortunately, it's only a ten-minute walk. Unfortunately, it's the bar that bartender Jack owns. I assume Brad is there because there aren't other bars in our town, and I don't think he's in D.C.

I walk in and see Brad is there with some suspicious people I have never seen before.

"Talia, it's been a while," Jack announces as he sees me come in. "New outfit?"

I refuse to humor him with a response.

"Brad, we're going home," I say as I come up to the counter and grab him lightly by the shoulder.

"Oh, look, Brad, your mom came," one of the guys says.

"Funny," I say, looking over at him. I turn back to Brad, "Brad, let's go." I take his arm and try to pull him into a standing position.

"I don't need your help," Brad snaps.

"You need it, trust me," I say, still tugging on his arm. I need to get out of here, or else some backsliding will occur.

"Hey, you're Talia Turner, aren't you?" The "funny" guy asks me.

I keep my eyes on Brad, ignoring everyone else. "Brad, please. Please come with me. You need to go home," I continue.

"Talia, give the guy a break. You rejected him earlier today, and now you come in here, all worried, trying to get him home. Stop playing games with him," Jack says.

"Yeah. Now you're trying to act like my girlfriend," Brad adds smugly.

"I'm not acting like your girlfriend; I'm acting like your friend," I state. "Now get up and let's go. Seriously, stop with this bullshit." I try to pull him up again.

"Look, Talia, I don't need this, and neither do you. Go home," he says, gesturing for another round.

"Jack, don't you dare," I say. "Brad, you are cut off, no more. What is happening? Why are you acting like this?" I try to make eye contact with him, but he keeps avoiding it.

He jerks away from me, his movements sharp and almost violent, and then meets my gaze with a cold, piercing stare. "I'm sorry, princess, that you didn't realize while your life was falling apart, that some of your friends needed support, too." His voice drips with bitterness. "Kate was having a breakdown for three months and wouldn't come to school. She almost... she almost killed herself, Talia. Grace lost it, too. She went off the rails and hooked up with the whole football team. And Tom? He started dating Melanie, for god's sake! *Melanie!*"

He shakes his head, looking at me with pure disbelief. "And where were you? Drinking? Sleeping around? Having fun? Actually... apparently, you weren't even having fun. So why couldn't you have been there for your friends? We would have been there for you a thousand times over. We could've helped each other." His voice cracks slightly, but he continues. "But you cut us off. So what are you expecting now? It's been *seven fucking months*, Talia. You don't just get to waltz back in like nothing happened."

My mouth goes dry as he leans in, his face set and angry. "We kept going, kept living, while you were stuck in the hell you created for yourself. So don't pretend you're somehow better than me now. I don't need you to look out for me, or take care of me. I can take care of myself just fine."

His words hit me like an avalanche of guilt. My friends have gone through so much, and I've only been worrying about myself. All I've talked about is myself. All they asked about was my well-being, but I never asked them about theirs.

I take a deep breath. My priority is getting Brad out of here. "Brad, I'm genuinely sorry. I understand you're going through a rough time as well. You love Grace, I know that, and I know all of this is hard for you. Please let me take you home, please," I beg, but I don't dare to touch him anymore.

"Fine." He stands up and starts stumbling toward the door.

Thank god the walk is only ten minutes because I have to half-carry and half-drag Brad along the way and into his house.

Once we're inside, I guide him to the living room couch and lay him down. I sink into the nearby recliner, suddenly exhausted. My phone's still at home. How am I going to wake up? I can't leave him here alone—he'll start puking soon and I can't risk him choking in his sleep. I guess I'll wake up when I wake up. Or I'll stay awake all night.

With that thought, I drift off.

Chapter 1.4

"WHERE HAVE YOU BEEN?" Mom demands as soon as I walk through the front door in the morning.

My new life reminds me of a terribly-cast, low-budget, nonsensical movie.

"Friend's house," I respond as I walk upstairs. It's eight-thirty a.m. already, and I'm trying to make it in time for at least my second class.

"Come down here and communicate with us," Trevor chimes in. "I'm serious. Come down here."

"You can't just continue disappearing now that you are on the path back to being a normal teenager. You have to act your age, which means letting me know when, where, and with whom you're going out. As well as if you plan on sleeping over at someone's house," Mom says.

I purse my lips and take a couple of steps down. "Okay, um—not going to lie, I'm feeling attacked by the both of you right now. I told you I was at a friend's place, and now I'm home. I'm sorry I didn't call, but he really needed my help, and it was late at night, and I forgot my phone," I say.

"He?" Mom exclaims as if we're in a soap opera. "You were at a *boy's* house? How many times are we going to go through this,

Talia? You're seventeen, for god's sake! You cannot sleep over at boys' houses anymore."

"Calm down. It's not a big deal, it was Brad." I roll my eyes.

"Go to your room, Talia. We will discuss this later," Mom says sternly. It makes me want to laugh.

"Good try, but I'm actually going to school. See ya." I walk back down the stairs and out the door. I'd rather walk three miles to school in last night's clothes than deal with my family any longer.

I haven't even walked a mile before I'm totally done with walking. I call Derek to pick me up.

"Ah, the bad girl is finally back! Skipping school, are we?" Derek says, pulling up to the corner to pick me up.

"You're literally driving me to school, so I don't know what you're talking about," I say, getting into the car.

"Wait, we're not going back to my place?" Derek turns sharply to me, making a confused face.

"Did you really—" I start.

"I'm *kidding*," he interrupts. "I know you're a studious, good girl now, and I accept it. I'll drive you anywhere you want, honey." He grins.

I grin back. "You're so full of shit."

I come into chemistry very late, but the teacher doesn't comment on it. I'm not surprised because nobody says anything to me anymore. Nobody wants to confront a girl who completely went off the rails not so long ago and whose father and sister are still missing (most likely dead).

"Why were you late to chem?" Grace asks as we walk out of class. Her voice is full of concern, which, for some reason, causes irritation to spark through me.

"I was—I slept through my alarm. I just—getting back on track wasn't as easy as I thought. I'm used to sleeping in." I offer her a half-hearted smile, following my flimsy excuse.

Grace laughs. "Yeah, I guess months of waking up hungover after noon takes a toll."

I keep the smile plastered on my face. I don't want to lie to Grace, but I also can't tell her I slept over at Brad's. I'm unsure if she'll freak out or just keep it all inside and be internally mad (which is worse), but I don't want to risk either. I hope Brad doesn't open his mouth. I doubt he will since he's nursing a horrendous hangover today and most likely regrets a lot of what occurred yesterday.

Kate stomps up to us, already in a mood. "Earth to Talia! Why weren't you answering your phone yesterday? I was having a crisis, and I thought that after months of being MIA, you would be constantly on your phone, ready to help me." Typical Kate. No "hello", no "how are you". Straight to the point. Classic, confrontational Kate. I missed her.

"Hi, yes, what crisis were you having?" I ask with a slight chuckle.

"This isn't *funny*, Talia. I thought something happened to you again. And I needed your help because I've been getting advice from Grace for the past several months, and you know how that is." She rolls her eyes.

"Excuse me," Grace interjects. "As far as I'm concerned, my advice got you closer to Jason. So, I don't want to hear it."

"Right. That was all thanks to you." Kate rolls her eyes again. "So, yesterday Jason texted me, and he—"

"Are you ladies planning on going to class?" Principal Hughes comes up to us.

We all smile at him. We all hate him. He's the worst.

"Yeah, sorry, I was just in the middle of a very important story, and I really need Talia's help. And since, you know, she's been gone for the past seven months, I kind of need her advice ASAP," Kate says, with a sarcastic tone and tooth-achingly sweet fake smile on her face.

My eyes grow big. I raise my eyebrows, looking at Kate and then at the principal. He is going to kill us. Grace is already backing away. The final bell rings.

"Get to class," Principal Hughes says. "You can discuss this *very important* um—thing during break after next period. Bye, girls." He stands there, waiting until we all scatter, fumbling to get to our respective classes.

I don't feel like going to math, but I also don't know any trig, so I probably should attend if I want to pass this year.

"You're late," says the teacher as I walk into class.

Everybody goes silent.

I look up at him and realize that he's definitely new and has no idea what happened to me. Now that I think of it, Grace told me that we got a new math teacher a couple of months back because Ms. Masters (our previous math teacher) had to quit under some unfortunate circumstances.

I decide that nothing bad will happen to me, so I respond without a filter, "I'm late to every class."

He looks at me with shock and surprise. He was definitely waiting for some kind of excuse or apology. "Take a seat," he says quickly, turning back to the board.

He's actually kind of cute. He probably just got his degree and is definitely in his twenties. My type. (Kind of).

I sit down next to Grace, surprised to see she got to class before me. Oh, right, I stopped by the cafeteria for a bagel and coffee.

"Are you okay?" Grace asks. There's that concern in her voice again.

"Yeah," I answer, not looking up at her as I take a notebook out of my backpack.

"You don't seem okay. You just snapped at a teacher for no reason. What's wrong?" Grace asks. She isn't trying to be condescending. Nevertheless, I take it that way. The concern in her voice is really starting to get to me.

"Nothing is wrong with me," I whisper harshly, looking up at her. "Can you ever mind your—"

"Miss Turner, would you like to share with the class?" the teacher asks. I have no idea what his name is. But he seems like a Richard (get it? Haha.)

"Are we in middle school?" I ask, amused.

His face slightly flushes. "We can talk after class. Now stop disrupting everybody else."

"Actually—" I start to argue.

"I said after class," he says, in a voice that sounds like he's about to burst from anger. Maybe I did take it a little too far. He has to show his authority, and, well, I don't mind that.

The class ends, and I'm about as lost and confused as Katniss was when she woke up in District 13. Honestly, I have no idea how I will ever catch up—it seems unmanageable. I stay after class, having no idea what to expect from this teacher. There appears to be a pattern forming: I have no idea about anything.

"Talia," the teacher says once the room has emptied. He gestures for me to sit across from him at his desk. Reluctantly, I take the seat, squirming and avoiding eye contact. He studies me for a moment, like he's trying to figure me out. Finally, he speaks. "I know you've been out of school for a while," he starts, his tone uncertain but kind. "And I know why. But now that you're back, I expect you to behave like a student. I'll be lenient with your work, but I can't let your behavior slide." He pauses, clearly hesitant. "I'm here if you need help with schoolwork. For anything else, there are school counselors, or you can talk to your family..." he trails off awkwardly.

My face twists into a painful scowl, and I look up at him momentarily before looking back down and playing with the holes in my jeans. Honestly, if he left that last part out of his little speech, he would have been doing well.

"I want to help you get back on track," he continues after a moment, his voice softer now. "I believe that you are a smart girl and that you will catch up. It will inevitably take time, maybe even months since you did miss a lot, but I believe you can do it. And as

I said, I am here for help. Whenever I don't have class, or whenever there is a break—you can come here, and we can go over material..." he trails off again, as if unsure what else to say.

I assume he expects me to respond in some way. "Okay," I say slowly, finally making eye contact. "Thanks."

He nods, giving me a quick smile. "I hope we've come to an understanding."

I nod in response, stand up hurriedly, and start walking toward the door.

"Talia," he calls out as I near the door.

I turn around. What more could he want?

"We could start now," he says with hesitation, yet a hint of determination, in his voice. "We have fifteen minutes of break, but I can at least explain some of what we did today if you felt lost."

I think about Kate. "Tomorrow," I say. "We'll start tomorrow." I walk out the door quickly before he can say another word.

I meet Kate and Grace in the cafeteria.

"I heard you got in trouble with Mr. Hottie today," Kate says teasingly.

I smirk softly.

"He is not hot," Grace says while pouring herself coffee.

"Oh, come on, be serious, Grace. Yeah, he's older but extremely attractive," Kate says.

"I'm not into older men," Grace responds. She then glances at me, not at all subtly.

I choose to ignore Grace's look. "Anyway, what were you going to tell me, Kate?" I ask, trying to change the subject.

"Oh, yes! So, anyway, yesterday, Jason texted me and told me he isn't going to break up with his girlfriend. There was a lot of heated back and forth. Ultimately, he called me a psycho bitch, and I obviously left him on read after that," she says. She stops and looks at both Grace and I, awaiting our reactions.

"What the hell? You didn't tell me this. I'm going to beat that dickhead up," Grace says in an infuriated tone. "I'll make Kyle beat him up, too," she adds.

Kate shrugs. "I think I'm over it at this point. It's been all too much, and I don't want to get all depressed again... so I think I need to end it. At least take a break from him and all the drama that comes with him."

"I doubt you can stop yourself from being around him," Natalie joins our conversation out of nowhere. Where does she always appear from, and how does she always know what we're discussing?

"Eavesdropping much?" Grace asks, at the same time as Kate asks, "How is this any of your business?"

"Oh, Kate, sweetie. Everything is my business. I see, hear, and know everything." Natalie gives us a fake smile before walking away.

"She creeps me out so much," Kate says, shuddering dramatically.

I nod in agreement.

Here's a short story: Natalie and I were inseparable during freshman year—best friends, really. Then she started dating this guy, Ben, around November. They broke up in February after she accused him of constantly flirting with me. Her words, not mine. I never saw this flirting, or maybe I just didn't notice. I definitely didn't encourage it. But after that, things changed. I guess some friendships just don't survive the bumps. We couldn't get past that silly argument over a guy, and eventually, we went our separate ways. Natalie has hated me ever since. Sometimes I wonder if we could've worked things out, especially since it was over something so stupid. But some friendships inevitably end, or you outgrow them. It happens. Now, I simply wish we could be more amicable, but that's up to her.

"Earth to Talia." Kate waves her hands in front of my face.

I look at her with a confused look on my face. What did I miss?

"We're going to the movies today after school. Care to join us?" she asks. Her annoyed tone signifies that this isn't the first time she's asked.

"Who's going?" I ask, keeping my fingers crossed that it wouldn't be the same people from the coffee place fiasco.

Kate pauses, sensing my reluctance. "Um—well—pretty much everybody who was at the pink coffee place the other day. Besides Jason, of course, because he is no longer invited to go places with me. You have to go because you're my date, or else I will be all alone, surrounded by couples, and very, very sad." Kate pouts at me. She's good at it.

"I don't think it's the best—" I start to say.

"You're going," Kate interrupts me. Her voice is calm and firm.

I don't want to. I don't want to spend time with Melanie and Tom. I don't want to see Brad. If we're being completely candid, I don't want to go to the movies at all. "Listen, Kate—" I start again.

"No, no, no. Come on. We used to go to the movies all the time." Kate still sounds firm but also slightly pleading. "We can sit a couple of rows away from *the couples*." She looks over at Grace pointedly before looking back at me. "You're going."

I throw my head back in frustration and take a long, deep breath. "Fiiiiiine, whatever, I'm over this conversation."

"Perfect. I'll pick you up at seven. The movie is at seven forty-five." Kate smiles in satisfaction and spins around on her boot heel, swiftly walking out of the cafeteria.

I smile softly and shake my head before looking over at Grace.

She's already laughing. "Haven't you missed Kate?" she asks, with a fondness in her voice.

I roll my eyes, still smiling. "I've missed you both. Promise me, we'll go out just the three of us sometime soon?"

Grace nods while smiling before linking our arms and strutting with me down the hallway, chatting about nothing. It feels so nice, so normal. I have really missed this. A couple of weeks ago, at this time of day, I would have most likely been asleep, coming back home hungover, or already drunk and hooking up with someone. That thought makes right now feel so much more blissful. It feels good to walk down the hallway with my best friend and talk about nothing—as peculiar as that might sound. It feels like I'm floating on a cloud.

However, like with everything else in my life, the moment is fleeting and a storm hits not long after. I end up plunging toward the ground.

"Hi," Michael says, walking up to Grace and me while we're at our lockers.

Michael and I haven't talked since that early morning in my kitchen, where we left off on "good terms"—I think that's how he put it.

"Hey, Michael," Grace interrupts the unbearable silence while I stand still and stare at him.

"So... how have you guys been?" Michael asks, looking increasingly uncomfortable at my reaction (or lack thereof).

"Not bad. You?" Grace continues the conversation cheerfully, seemingly oblivious to the atmosphere surrounding this situation.

At long last, I come out of my stupor. "Yes, yes, I've been super good. We're actually going to the movies today. I don't know what movie we're seeing, but it should be good. You should join," I blurt out all in one sentence, without taking a single breath or thinking about what is coming out of my mouth.

Grace stares at me in bewilderment.

Michael seems very taken aback and stays silent for what seems like an eternity while never breaking eye contact with me. It feels like he's staring straight into my soul and burning it alive.

"You want—you want me to come to the movies with you?" he asks finally, slowly and uncertainly.

I shake my head vigorously. "I mean, like—not a date. Obviously. Just like—friends, good terms," I continue blabbering. I could probably disintegrate right here, right now.

I look over at Grace with a horrified expression, and she still seems shocked but is also biting her lip, definitely holding in a laugh.

Michael eyes me carefully, suspiciously even.

I can't stand this any longer. "Kate is picking me up at seven. Figure it out with her before then," I say before running to my next class without waiting for a response.

Slumping into my chair in history, I put my face in my hands and don't know if I should laugh hysterically or burst into tears. I scream internally and throw my head back. It could have gone worse, right?

I don't pay attention to the rest of my classes at all. Instead, I focus on overthinking.

"I heard your brain stopped working while talking to my brother today," Kate says while we walk to her car after school.

"Kate," Grace says warningly while simultaneously stifling a laugh.

"I heard you invited him to the movies with us today. Should be interesting since I invited you as my date, and now my brother is apparently coming as your date," Kate ponders, both sarcasm and amusement evident in her voice.

"I'm sorry," is all I can say.

"So, is he like... coming?" Grace asks, looking slightly confused.

"Yeah, I told him to," Kate says nonchalantly, shrugging her shoulders.

"Why would you do that?" I ask, suddenly distressed.

"Well—" Kate starts.

My phone rings.

I look up apologetically, but I have to answer because it's Natasha.

"Hey, Natasha," I whisper so Kate and Grace don't hear me. They don't know about Natasha. They don't know about a lot.

"Hi, honey. Listen, I'm returning to D.C. tomorrow, and I really need to meet up with you. It's important, but I can't talk much right now. When will you be available to come?"

"Um—I'm kind of leading a normal life now, so I don't know if my mom will let me randomly go to D.C.," I whisper.

"Figure something out. Go with friends, make a day of it. I just need thirty minutes of your time. Okay, bye, sweetie." She hangs up.

Typical.

Chapter 1.5

THE LEVEL OF UNEASE surrounding me right now is reaching some kind of record. Seated between Kate and Michael, I feel like I might lose it. Why did I have to open my big mouth? In an alternate universe, my other self is probably enduring torturous punishment for my stupidity.

To make matters worse, Kate insisted on getting a mega-sized popcorn bucket for the three of us. "It's cheaper," she argued, "and I'd rather share than feel like a pig eating a personal one by myself." I'm not particularly thrilled about the prospect of my hand accidentally brushing Michael's when he reaches over to grab a handful of popcorn from the bucket on my lap. There's an excruciating ache deep inside my chest, as I feel the heat of his elbow next to mine, immensely close to brushing mine, yet also unbearably out of reach. He's manspreading (in a typical guy manner), and his knee almost knocks into mine as his leg bounces anxiously, waiting for the movie to start. Why do I do this to myself?

I can barely concentrate on the previews that are currently playing.

"What movie are we seeing?" I ask Kate, realizing I don't know what I'm waiting for. I didn't even pay for my ticket because Michael insisted on paying for Kate and me.

"Some new horror movie, no clue what it's called," Kate whispers, not taking her eyes off the screen.

"Horror movie?" I repeat cautiously.

Kate looks at me, rolling her eyes. "Yeah," she responds. "Why, you scared?"

I scrunch my nose. No, I'm not scared. I love horror and thriller movies. I enjoy watching them alone, in a dark room, right before bed. The real problem here is that I used to drag Michael to every horror movie that came out when we were dating. It was our thing. Even if the movie was terrible, we'd sit in the back, mostly flirting or making out. Or laughing at how ridiculous the movie was. It was *our thing*.

"No," I respond simply. Mostly because I've been silent for so long after reminiscing, and Kate is still staring at me with a now-confused smirk.

Suddenly, I remember I have to ask Kate something, but she seems too entranced by the previews. I look at my watch and we still have about ten minutes until the movie starts. I don't want to sit here silently, thinking about Michael's warm body sitting close to mine. I need a distraction, so I twist around to face Kate again.

"I have a question for you," I say.

I can see Kate's annoyed face before she even turns around to look at me. "You have more questions? What do you want to know now—who the cast and crew are? Where was the movie shot? What the soundtrack is like?" she asks in a sarcastic tone.

I pause for a second. "Um—no. It's actually not about the movie at all, so don't get heated," I reply, trying to lighten her annoyance. "I was wondering if you and Grace might want to go to D.C. this weekend?"

Kate's face instantly turns confused. "Why?"

I pause again. I haven't gotten as far as to think of a motive for going to D.C. I must look like a whole mess of suspiciousness right now as I scramble to come up with a reason. "Well—you know—um—just I've been cooped up for so long... and like—fun. We could have fun—walking around—like museums maybe? Or like—shopping? Walk around." It would have been better if I said nothing than that whole spectacle.

Kate still looks confused but laughs. "Did you just have a stroke or something?" She looks at me quizzically while still giggling. "I'm not sure why you want to go, but I'm down. I just have to ask my mom."

I let out a quiet breath, glad she didn't try to press me for an actual answer. "Okay, great, I—"

"If you girls want to chat, why don't you go outside and do it?" a middle-aged woman sitting behind us asks as she leans forward in her seat to breathe right on my neck.

I swallow down my instant anger and turn around with as much of an apologetic smile as I can muster. "Our apologies," is all I can say.

The woman seems to accept that, leaning back in her seat, satisfied.

Kate shrugs while rolling her eyes and goes back to watching the previews.

On autopilot, I glance at Michael, and find him already looking at me. My face goes hot, instantly flushing. I drop my gaze quickly, pretending to focus on something in my lap. I can still feel his eyes on me, setting me on fire. Every part of my body seems to be burning; blood boiling, cells bursting—like the universe is finally punishing me for my senseless decisions.

The movie inevitably starts, and I can't help but slightly lean away from Michael in order to breathe properly. The first fifteen minutes are already jam-packed, and the next fifteen are even more intense. I find myself leaning more and more toward Kate. Until finally, somewhere halfway through the movie, she turns around to look at me. Our faces almost touch since I have practically smushed myself against her side.

She shoots me a questioning look. "Are you okay?" she whispers.

"Yeah, I—um—am a little scared," I manage to find the words.

Kate giggles quietly. "I thought Talia never gets scared of horror movies." She moves her hand to pat my cheek in a playful and slightly condescending way. "It's okay, babe. You hide your face in my shoulder if you need to." With a wink, she turns back to the screen while I uncertainly lie my head down on her shoulder. I guess I'm going to have to proceed with this narrative.

The movie eventually ends, and the lights in the theatre turn back on. I've begun to get sleepy toward the end of the movie, but I quickly take my head off Kate's shoulder and rub my eyes before stretching out my limbs.

"That wasn't bad," Michael remarks.

I almost jump at the sound of his voice, but thankfully, I compose myself in time. I end up flinching a little, but it goes (hopefully) unnoticed.

"Yeah, I liked it. Cool concept," Kate agrees.

I nod along, wanting to leave this place as soon as possible.

"Shall we go?" Kate asks as she picks up the trash around us.

Now, that's a concept I can get behind: leaving.

I stand up slowly and slightly shakily. I can feel Michael's warm presence close behind me as we walk to the theatre exit.

Kate decides to leave me alone with Michael after Jason randomly calls her, and they start yelling at each other.

Michael and I stand outside the movie theatre. It's dark, the air is chilly, but I like it. It feels nice. Kind of like the emptiness inside me—a cold, quiet sort of peace. I look up at the sky, spotting a few stars. They make me smile. If something as dark as the night sky can hold such beautiful sparks of light, then surely I'm not a lost cause after all. Maybe there's still hope. A small spark of light in the overwhelming darkness.

"Penny for your thoughts?"

I almost jump at the words. For a moment, I forgot Michael was standing right next to me.

The heat returns to my cheeks, even as the cold wind blows against them. Windburn, that's what it is. That's all it is—cold wind.

I laugh lightly. "Who says stuff like that anymore?"

"I do, I guess." He shrugs.

I pause for a second. "I was just admiring the stars and thinking," I say, looking back at the dark sky.

"Thinking about what?"

I stay silent for a while. "I don't know. Just... thinking," I admit. I can't say what I actually want to say. Michael and I have just returned to "good terms", and I can't ruin that.

Somehow, he accepts that answer, and in my periphery, I can see him looking up at the sky as well.

"I missed hanging out with you," he admits out of nowhere, after three hundred forty-seven seconds of silence. I counted.

I lower my eyes from the sky and look at him. He's still looking up but meets my gaze after a moment.

He sighs. "I mean, you did spend the entire movie trying to get as far away from me as possible. But..." he trails off, shrugging. He looks upset.

I grimace slightly. "You caught that, didn't you?" I murmur slowly.

He raises his eyebrows. "I didn't know you were doing it purposefully... but—why were you?" he asks.

I sigh and shake my head. "I don't know. I, well, um... I just—I remembered how we used to go see scary movies together. It was our thing, and I guess the memories just hit me harder than I expected. It's kind of weird being around you now," I admit. I grimace again. "Sorry, that came out wrong. I don't know how to act around you anymore." I look down and shuffle my feet, wishing I hadn't said anything.

He doesn't say anything for a while. He clears his throat finally and then admits, "I get that. I kind of feel the same way."

I breathe out. Good. I mean, it's not the best thing to hear from someone, but at least I know I'm not alone in this. I'm not completely losing my mind.

I look up at him again and smile. "This is going to take some getting used to if we really want to be friends," I say.

He nods slowly and quietly says, "Friends."

Kate returns, looking tremendously pissed.

"You okay?" I ask, finally breaking eye contact with Michael and looking over at Kate.

"I'm sooooo done with Jason. It's not even funny. Like, I am done forever and ever and ever. *So done*," Kate almost screams, venom dripping from every word, and she's using the angriest voice I have heard from her. That says a lot.

I walk over to her and put an arm around her. "You want to talk about it?" I ask.

"Yeah, not really. At least not now," she mutters. Nonetheless, she puts her arm around me and we start walking toward the car, with Michael following us.

As I later walk through my front door, up the stairs, and into my bedroom, I realize maybe this night wasn't so awful after all. I seem to have made progress with Michael, and maybe somewhere in the future—no, I shouldn't start fantasizing yet. For now, we are friends, and that's all we should be (for now).

I fall asleep with a small smile and some form of faith for redemption blooming inside me.

· · · · ●· ● · · ·

It's Saturday. Somehow, Grace's mom, Kate's mom, and my mom have given us permission to go to D.C. I called Natasha earlier and let her know I can meet her today. I'm not sure what excuse I'll use to sneak away from Kate and Grace for half an hour, but I'm working on it as Kate drives to pick up Grace.

"This is so random," Grace states as Kate and I pick her up from her house. She sits in the back and leans over to the front to give Kate and me a quick, one-armed hug.

"I know. But Talia insisted we go to D.C. today." Kate shrugs.

"We used to go to D.C. all the time," I insist, trying to make myself sound less suspicious.

"Yeah. For, like, school field trips," Grace counters.

"You didn't have to come if you didn't want to," I respond.

Grace sighs. "Well, I'm here now. It could turn out to be fun. We might as well do some sightseeing. We live so close to the capital, and we haven't even explored it. There's also this restaurant that my mom and I used to go to all the time. It was super fancy, and the food was delicious. I'll call her and find out what it's called." Grace picks up her phone.

After Grace is done talking on the phone, Kate says, "Talia is in charge of AUX, so be prepared for a lot of One Direction."

I smile and roll my eyes. "Stop lying to yourself, we all know you would sell your soul for Zayn."

"I'm more of a Niall girl myself," Grace adds, giggling.

"And we all know Talia is a slut for Harry." Kate laughs.

"Don't be crude!" I faux gasp. "But you're not wrong."

We listen to everything from "Infinity" to "No Control" to "Act My Age". I couldn't be happier. Driving with my best friends, feeling so, so normal for the first time in months, and jamming out to some of the best music. No shame. Anyone who says they don't like 1D is lying to themselves or missing out. I said what I said.

I look at the time. It's ten-fifteen a.m. I promised to meet Natasha after lunch, around two p.m.

"Hey guys," I say as we park. "So, after some sightseeing and lunch, I kind of have to ditch you for half an hour." I try not to sound suspicious. I still do.

Kate gives me a weird look. "Okay, mysterious. Where are you going?"

I search my brain for one last time, thinking maybe an excuse is stored on a top shelf somewhere in there—unfortunately, no such luck. So, I decide to go with the truth. More or less...

"Um—I'm going to see a—um—therapist," I manage to say, faltering slightly. Not exactly the truth, but I can't say I'm going to see a psychic who might have found my sister and father—they would think I've gone off the deep end.

Kate and Grace glance at each other briefly.

"Oh. Well, that's good." Grace smiles at me, full of encouragement. "I think that will be really good for you."

Kate nods in agreement.

They seem to have bought my excuse. Thank you, brain! It's the first time in months that you haven't completely messed with my life.

"But for now, we're going to have fun and become a little more educated," I say excitedly.

Little did I know that this would be one of the best days I have ever spent with my best friends. We did some tours, visited monuments, ran around, took pictures, and ate lunch at the place Grace talked about (the food was undeniably mind-blowing).

By the time we finish lunch, it's one forty-five p.m., and I have to run to Natasha's. Fortunately, her local office is nearby. I tell the girls I'll meet them at the Washington Monument in roughly an hour.

• • • • • • • • • •

"Talia, dear, come on in," Natasha says as she opens the door to her office.

I smile at her and walk in. Suddenly, I stop in my tracks because two huge men are standing at either end of the room.

"Don't worry, sweetie, these are just by bodyguards." Natasha ushers me to the couch. "A woman in my position can never be too safe."

I'm unsure what that means, but I shrug and sit. "Sure," I say, feeling a bit cautious.

Natasha closes the door and locks it.

Something prickles in the back of my mind as the lock clicks into place. Even though I know Natasha is guarded and not trusting, something feels off. The locked door makes me uncomfortable. I know she has gone through a lot in her life, and she works with some powerful people, which I assume means she could have some powerful enemies as well. I push everything aside because, nonetheless, Natasha is one of the most trustworthy people in my life.

Natasha perches on her desk and looks over at me, not saying another word.

I clear my throat. "So... you said you needed to talk to me about something important? It's about my sister and father, I'm assuming, yes?" I ask anxiously. I can't wait any longer. I have been restless ever since Natasha called me two days ago. Even before that, when she told me that the FBI finally had my sister's and father's files under review.

Natasha sighs heavily and cracks her neck. "Look, Talia, I am very sorry..." she trails off as if she doesn't want to continue.

I immediately tense at her words. The shaking in my hands starts, and I feel the tears begin to well up. They're dead. I know it. This is what she called me here for. She knows they're dead.

Nervous energy floods through me, and I stand up from the couch. The two men respond immediately, moving closer in a way that feels... off. I frown at them, then glance back at Natasha. She doesn't seem fazed, but her expression is pained. I sit back down, forcing myself to remain calm. I need to hear her say it.

"Say it," I request.

Natasha looks at me, a bit of perplexity on her face. "Say what?" she asks.

"Tell me that they're dead," I say, with a strain in my voice. The tears inevitably start to form as I say those words, and my hands begin to shake as the distress and anxiety set in.

Natasha shakes her head and looks at the floor for a second before looking back at me. "They aren't dead," she says without a hint of hesitation in her voice.

I am overjoyed at her words. There is still a sting of uncertainty and confusion within a dark corner of my mind, but my body responds immediately, and I can't help but smile through the tears. They turn into happy tears immediately. Blissful tears. Hopeful tears. Tears of joy.

That's all there is for a moment until I register something that Natasha added after her statement. My smile immediately falters as I look back over at her.

"What did you just say?" I ask shakily.

Natasha doesn't hesitate to respond now, "I said they are alive. At least, for now."

For now.

For now.

FOR NOW.

For now?

I stare at her incomprehensibly, my eyes widening. "What does that mean?" I manage to choke out.

My head is spinning, and I feel like I might pass out.

For now.

Natasha sighs and stands from the desk. "It means exactly what it sounds like," she replies flatly. I catch the faintest smirk tugging at the corner of her lips as she walks over and sits beside me on the couch. "Talia, you're only seventeen. You're not an adult. And look at yourself—sneaking away from your loved ones, meeting a strange woman in the city. But I know you're not as dumb as you act. You should've known this wasn't going to end well. Or maybe you are that dumb. Who am I to say?" She shrugs, a smug look on her face now.

After a moment of consideration, all I manage to croak out is, "You're not a strange woman." I can't even begin to process her words. I am so confused, but I'm also becoming increasingly frightened.

All Natasha does is let out a high-pitched laugh and look over at the two men. She looks back at me, and I can almost see a hint of remorse in her eyes before a determined and alarming glimmer replaces it.

"You're going to have to come with me," she says eventually after looking me over for a couple more minutes.

I recoil from her. "Come with you... where?"

She rolls her eyes and sighs. "I'm tired of these questions and this whole situation. You will come with me, and everything will become clear."

I sit for a moment and contemplate. My head is spinning, and I still feel like I'm about to pass out. However, a certain clarity is starting to form in that deep, dark part of my brain. "No," I respond in a determined voice.

Natasha stands up and walks back to her desk, but she doesn't sit down. She looks back at me, and I notice the glimmer in her eyes amplifies. "I'm sorry, dear. I must not have made myself clear," she says, her voice eerily calm. She leans against the desk, folding her hands in front of her.

I feel the sweat on my skin, my hands shaking uncontrollably. This fear is unfamiliar. I've never been afraid of Natasha before. I'm *not* afraid of her. She's always been someone I trust, someone who helped me when I needed it. However, in this moment, fear is taking over all my other senses.

I shudder in my seat and can't even look back up as I play with the holes in my jeans, trying to force myself not to pass out and stop shaking. The anxiety is building up, and I can't take it any longer. Fortunately, I don't have to because the next words Natasha says make me stop cold.

"You're coming with me. That was not a question," she asserts, her voice chilling calm.

The next moments are a blur as one of the guards rushes over to me. I flinch away, but it's too late. I feel a prick. My adrenaline spikes. I try to stand, to run.

Too late.

As I fall to the floor, legs buckling and head spinning, all I hear are Natasha's previous unsettling words reverberating through my head.

Chapter 2.0

I BLINK MY EYES open and realize I'm lying on a bed. The ceiling looms above me, cold and blank.

No mirror.

A drop of water splashes onto my right eye. I sit up slowly, my head pounding violently. The room around me is frigid and dark, and I can't make sense of how I got here—or where *here* is. The air smells damp and musty, with a hint of rubbing alcohol and cleaning supplies. It almost makes me gag.

The room is tiny, nothing besides four concrete walls and the bed I'm sitting on, which is positioned squarely in the center. That's it. The floor, the walls, and the ceiling are bare and bleak. The entire space feels oppressive, suffocating. Miserable.

A wave of nausea hits me as I look around. Panic rises in my chest. No door. There's no exit.

I think back to the last thing I remember.

"Natasha?" I whisper inaudibly.

I clear my scratchy throat. "NATASHA!" I yell as loud as I can. Silence.

I scream her name again and again until my voice gives out, leaving me coughing uncontrollably. I look around the room once more, closing my eyes in the desperate hope that I'll wake up in my own bed, that this will all be some twisted dream. I have a fucked-up mind, so it wouldn't be the first time. What is it doing to me now?

But when I open my eyes again, there's no change. This is not a dream. It's reality. I'm stuck in a small, square room with no way out, and I have no idea how I ended up here.

What happened to me? Why am I here?

I close my eyes and rub my temples, trying to force some clarity, but my thoughts are a storm, each question and worry crashing into the next. Some of them beg for answers, others threaten to overwhelm me entirely. I can't focus. I press my hands against my head to keep the noise from consuming me. I can't take it anymore. I throw my head back and scream. The sound that escapes me is foreign—it's raw, animalistic, bouncing off the nasty walls and vibrating through the room.

"NATASHA!!!" I yell again, louder this time. She's the last thing I remember, so she's the only thing I can focus on.

There is nothing but silence in response.

I feel the tears coming and bury my head in the pillow. I try to fumble for my phone in my pocket but come up empty. My phone, money, and keys are all gone. I groan.

Who is doing this to me? And can they just kill me and get it over with?

It's my own fault. I was naïve, and reckless—leaving my friends, wandering into the city alone. Classic egomaniacal me. Honestly, I'm surprised this hasn't happened sooner. And of course this happens now, when I'm finally trying to make things right and get my life back on track. I laugh to myself. *Irony, thy name is cruel.*

I can't stop laughing hysterically as tears stream down my face.

After an indiscernible amount of time, I finally wipe away the snot and tears. I try to calm myself down, but the panic is still there, clawing at the back of my mind.

Okay, so what if I'm stuck here? There's not much I can do about it at this point. I sit cross-legged on the bed and explore the room with my eyes. Not much to see, but I focus on the minute details. Eventually, I get up and begin pacing around the room, dragging my fingers along the rough, bumpy surface of the walls. I keep walking, lost in thought, until finally sliding down to the floor. I sit with my back against one of the walls. It looks the most damaged, so I've decided it's my favorite.

Since I'm already down here, I start to examine the floor. It's just as bleak as the rest of the room. Unsurprisingly, considering I'm literally in a concrete box.

Suddenly, I notice something under the bed and swiftly stand up. I move the bed to the side and stare.

A latch.

With a trapdoor underneath it.

I freeze, staring at it. I can't bring myself to touch it. My logical side tells me it's pointless. It's definitely locked. There's no way it'll open. Absolutely *no way*. But that stubborn shred of survival instinct—which I presumed was long gone—pushes me forward. The "fight for your life" instinct we all have, the one that urges us to try and never give up.

I take a deep breath and yank the latch with all my strength.

To my surprise, the trapdoor swings open easily, causing me to fall back.

What?

I sit back, baffled. Why would someone put me in this room and leave the trapdoor open? This doesn't make sense. My instincts kick up a notch, and I shift uncomfortably on the floor, trying to figure out my next move. I have to go down, don't I? What do I have to lose?

I carefully lean over peer into the opening. Below me, I see a short ladder—no more than ten rungs. The floor is visible beneath it. Leaning further down, I catch a glimpse of a hallway stretching both to the right and left. A dim light casts eerie shadows along the hallway, but I can't see the source of the light. It doesn't look too horrifying. In a way, I feel like I'm in a horror movie. I like horror movies. Though, let's hope this one's American, since those usually end with a happily ever after.

I descend the ladder cautiously, keeping my back to it. My eyes are wide open, unblinking, scanning every corner, every crevice. I can't afford to miss anything. When I finally reach the last rung, my eyes catch the flickering light source above—some weak, intermittent recessed lights in the ceiling (though "ceiling" feels too generous a term in this scenario).

Cautiously, I step off the ladder and plant my feet on the ground, quickly scanning the hallway left to right. My senses are on high alert, searching and listening for anything that might seem out of place.

I decide to go right. Because why not? It's not like my instincts have let me down before. Hah. I walk slowly, glancing over my shoulder every now and then. I don't want to be the stereotypical horror movie victim, so it's best to be cautious. After a few steady steps, I decide to walk sideways, my back pressed against the wall. It feels safer that way, less exposed, and I'm able to see the full hallway without constantly looking back. Nobody is sneaking up on me—take that horror movie cliché.

Suddenly, something hard hits my spine. I jerk forward, clutching the spot where it struck, wincing in pain. I whip around, heart racing.

A door knob.

Connected to an actual door. *Duh, what a surprise.*

There's no harm in trying to open this door as well, right? I look around one last time and freeze, noticing another door not far from me, on the opposite wall. I take a deep breath, looking at both doors. Which one should I pick? I decide that since the first door I stumbled upon abused my spine, I'll pick the other door. Seems logical. I walk over to that door and grab the knob, twisting it. I push it, but it doesn't budge. I twist it again, pressing my whole weight against the door. I hear a sound, yet the door still won't budge. I keep pushing, but nothing happens. Disappointing. I thought I was on a roll.

As I walk away from the door, I hear another sound. I can't tell where it's coming from, but it seems like a voice... a whisper or a whimper? I try to listen for it again, but it's dead silent. I walk over to the first door I stumbled upon, trying to open this one.

No luck.

Shit. *So, what happens now?*

I sure as hell don't want to go back up to that concrete box. But staying in this creepy hallway isn't exactly my idea of a good time either. Maybe I should go left instead?

I slowly lean back, my hands brushing the rough wall as I inch along, cautiously making my way back to the ladder. Once there, I stop and take a deep breath. Left it is.

I move steadily to the other end of the hallway, but after a few steps, I reach a dead end. It's neither surprising nor disappointing. I don't know what I was expecting. I glance back toward the other end and sigh, frustration creeping in. My only option is to try one of those doors again. I head back to the other end until I reach the abusive door, ready to try again.

I twist the handle one more time. But it still won't budge.

I sigh again and throw my head back, glancing back to the other end of the hallway. Turning back toward the door, I decide to go completely insane.

"Is—" I start cautiously. "Is anyone in there?" I ask.

I don't expect a response. I just feel so alone right now that I might as well start talking, even if it's to myself.

I knock on the door. "Hello?" I say a little louder this time.

I hear that same sound again. It's definitely a whimper.

"Hello?" I say, even louder this time, while knocking on the door again.

There is silence.

I start knocking continuously because I am sure I heard something from behind that door. And whatever, or whoever, that was has to make a sound again inevitably.

"Please..." I hear.

I stop my knocking and shut up, pressing my ear to the door.

For a few minutes, nothing else happens.

Until I hear the whimper again. "Please... just stop... just come in," a soft, hurt voice pleads.

I freeze completely.

The voice sounds so familiar. "I—who is this?" I ask awkwardly and rather loudly.

Silence.

And then...

"Talia?" the voice asks in an uncertain, shaky, almost breathless voice.

If I was stagnant and cautious before, I am now trembling and on the verge of tears.

Because, *Beth.*

"Talia... Talia, is that you?" the voice asks, with more conviction now.

And now I'm sure that it's Beth. It's my sister. She is alive. She is behind this door. I can't wrap my head around the fact that it's her, but that is undeniably her voice. I can't be mistaken. However, I have to know for sure. I have to hear her again. I have to *see* her.

I step closer and put my hands against the door, leaning in closer, putting my ear against it. "Beth—my god, is that you, Beth?" I ask, almost indistinctly. I don't want to believe it. But more importantly, I so badly do want to believe it.

It's quiet for a while, but not as long as before. And when I hear her voice again, it feels so much closer to me. "Talia, what are you—"

Those words are enough to confirm it. I know this is Beth. I *know* it's her.

Without wasting another second, I start banging and kicking the door with everything I've got. I don't care if I can't break it down—I'll try anyway, as idiotic as that might be. Tears stream down my face as I slam my fists and feet into the door again and again, each bang a desperate plea.

Unfortunately, the movies lied. Kicking down doors isn't as simple as they make it look. It's not a swift kick—it doesn't work like that. *There is no use; just stop, or you will hurt yourself.* I can feel the bruises already forming, my legs weak, my arms limp. But I can't stop. I won't stop. I'd rather die right now than give up.

I scan the hallway, frantic, searching for something—anything—that might help. But this space is void of any objects. For a moment, I think about bringing the bed down from upstairs, maybe using it to ram the door open. But the rational part of my mind immediately reminds me of reality. How could I manage that? And how would it even work? Dragging a bed down, pushing it into the door—what would that accomplish?

But I can't think clearly right now. My thoughts are jumbled and my mind is clouded with panic. My sister's on the other side of this door. She's *so close*.

Exhausted, I collapse against the door, my arms and legs giving out. Despair washes over me as I feel the weight of hopelessness settle in. What if I never get to her?

"Beth," I breathe, placing my forehead against the door.

"Talia," she responds instantly. I can hear her. So close to me. She must be leaning against the other side of the door. She's so close, yet I can't see or hug her. I cannot get to her, and the panic keeps building inside me. I don't know what to do. My whole body seizes in hopelessness.

I can hear her breathing just inches away through the thick wooden door. How pitiful am I? I can't even break through a wooden door. It's not even metal. It's wood, for god's sake! I feel the adrenaline start pumping again as I pull myself together, stand up, and start banging and kicking again.

"Talia, please! Please, stop! You will hurt yourself," Beth shrieks from the other side of the door.

I fall against the door again, feeling wholly powerless.

A hush falls over us while I try to stabilize my breathing and shake away the anxiety, anger, and numerous other unidentifiable emotions currently brewing inside of me.

"How are you here?" Beth finally whispers.

I shake my head. "I don't know how I got here," I say truthfully. "But I'm here now, and I'm not leaving without you."

"If you have a chance to get out of here, you have to take it," Beth insists.

"No," I respond firmly. There is no way I'm leaving without my sister. The only way I'm leaving here without her is if someone is dragging my corpse. That sounds dramatic, and obviously, it's not my best-case scenario. But there is no way I am leaving. "There is no way I am leaving here without you," I say out loud.

There is silence on the other end, and I pause before speaking again. "Where is Dad?" I ask tentatively.

There is still silence, and I wonder if Beth is okay. I don't want to start thinking about what has happened to her here and what kind of condition she is in.

"I don't know," she answers quietly, her voice trembling. She's lying. I can hear it in her tone.

"Beth, what happened?" I press. I need to know.

I need to know.

I can hear her shift against the door as if she is sliding down to sit against it. I do the same. I have no more energy left in me to keep on standing anymore. I lean back, angling my head slightly so my left ear presses against the door.

"It's a long story, Talia," she says, sighing heavily.

"I've got time," I reply, the words coming out bitter. A part of me wants to laugh, but it's not funny. Nothing about this is funny. It's just fear and anxiety that are making me emotionally unstable.

She doesn't say anything for a long time. I sit in silence, listening to my pounding heart. What do I say? How do I even begin to ask the daunting questions? This is such a bizarre situation, I almost want to laugh again. I have no idea where I am, how I got here, or if this is even real. I found my sister. At least, I hope it's really her. She's been missing for months. I haven't even seen her face yet. What is happening?

I strain my ears to catch Beth's breathing. It's irregular, hitching with something unspoken. It worries me. But I can hear her. My sister. She's alive. *She's alive.*

"How have you been?" she asks out of the blue.

I can't help but laugh at that question. Seriously, *how have I been?* Oh, where do I even begin, sister? The truth is, I don't want to tell her how much of a mess I have become. The pain I've caused the people around me. The pain I've inflicted on myself. How much of a disappointment I've turned into.

What kind of question is that, anyway? I'm assuming she doesn't think I would just brush it off and keep living my life normally after she and Dad went missing. The question, in this current setting, seems rather inconsiderate.

"I really don't know how to answer that," I reply honestly. I wouldn't know where to begin, what to say, how to phrase it. Moreover, I don't want to disappoint her, as I have everybody else. She's my big sister. She is the closest person I have. I grew up looking to her as my role model and idol. How could I tell her what I have been doing for the past months without her completely losing faith in me and shaking her head in disgust and dismay?

"How's mom, then?" Beth asks, her voice tentative. My relationship with our mother has never been great, even before I went off the rails. Since Trevor left, it's been strained, and that's putting it lightly. Beth's relationship with her has been just as rocky. Why is she asking about her now? I wonder if she actually cares or is just trying to fill the silence. Maybe, after everything she's undoubtedly been through, she's forgotten what Mom is like.

"Just her usual self," I say tightly. "If not worse," I add, with a harsh edge to my tone.

"Still not getting along?" Beth asks.

I exhale sharply. "As if we ever could," I respond, with a bitter edge to my tone.

I can almost see her roll her eyes. "You're still such a baby." She giggles slightly before the silence settles in again.

My smile fades as we sit in silence, and the reality of our predicament slowly sets in.

I want to bond with Beth. I want to laugh, to joke, to talk about everything we've missed. But this isn't the time. This isn't the place. I could sit here forever with her, but reality is too brutal, too terrifying. It's impossible to ignore.

I can't keep pretending that everything's fine and dandy. I'm sitting against a dirty door in a dim, eerie hallway, while my sister is locked in—what I assume is—a concrete cell, not unlike the one upstairs. I don't know where we are. I don't know if we're still in Washington, D.C. or even in America. We could be anywhere. How long have I been out? Why can't I remember what happened after being in Natasha's office?

"I'm not a baby," I insist after a long silence, trying to lighten the mood slightly. I know this is no time for chatting or bantering, but nothing else comes to mind as I sit in this sordid hallway. I might as well make the most of my time with my sister.

"Of course. You're all grown up and everything now," Beth teases. But her attempt at lighthearted laughter sounds strained, and it breaks my heart. I try to picture her the way she was the last time I saw her. I can't bear to imagine what she looks like now, in these conditions, after who-knows-what she's been through.

"I am," I admit proudly. "I'm trying to be, at least. Although, I have to admit that it's been a struggle. It was hard after you—it was hard to do it by myself. But I'm really trying now. At least Trevor is back now." I gasp and clasp my hand over my mouth at the last sentence. I don't know why that came out. I don't know why saying it out loud to Beth sounds so bizarre. I didn't even mean to tell her that Trevor is back. She hasn't seen him in three years as well. It kind of slipped out.

I hear her gasp as well and then go completely silent for a while. Probably processing the information, I abruptly threw at her. "Trevor is back?" she eventually whispers, almost as if she doesn't believe me.

I feel like continuously hitting my head against the door for letting that information slip out of my mouth without any preliminary preparation.

"Yes, he's been back for a week. He's so different," I say. "He has a beard," I add with a laugh.

"I can't even imagine that." Beth lets out a laugh as well. "This is honestly shocking. What, how, why did he come back?" she stumbles over her words in disbelief.

"Because of me," I reply, shrugging. "Mom called him, and he came back to help out with me, I guess. I have no idea what happened, or how she convinced him... or why he even picked up the phone when she presumably called... but it happened, and he's back now. For the time being."

"Why does she need help with you?" Beth questions.

"It's... complicated." I shake my head, looking down. I still don't want to tell her what I have been doing over the past months. It would be too grueling for me to explain and for her to listen to. "I guess she can't handle all of this," I reply, laughing softly, gesturing toward myself.

"You realize I can't see you, right?"

I stop smiling and mentally slap myself for my stupidity. "Right, sorry. I just meant—eh, I don't know what I meant." I shrug and laugh again.

Beth chooses to ignore my awkwardness. "I still can't believe Trevor would come back. I just can't believe it," she continues. I don't know if she's saying this to me or just trying to process it herself.

"Yeah, it was a surprise to me. He called me out of the blue while I was with Derek and simply said he's coming back. Then he hung up. I was so stunned I didn't know how to react. And now he came back, and he's acting like nothing happened, acting semi-normal and being all brotherly and stuff," I say.

"Who's Derek?" Beth asks immediately after I finish speaking.

Shit. Another slip-up. What are you doing, brain? Do I even have a filter? Do I think before I speak? Come on! I mentally slap myself again.

I cringe before mumbling, "Um—well... he's like my... he's a new friend."

"Oh my god, like a *boyfriend*?" Beth asks teasingly.

I groan. "No, no. No. Not like a boyfriend," I say quickly.

"What about Michael?" Beth follows-up.

Kill me now.

I feel like I need to physically slap myself now because mentally slapping myself doesn't seem to be working. "We broke up," I manage to get out quickly and emotionlessly.

Beth gasps. "Why? I was already planning your wedding! You two were so in love! What happened?"

I close my eyes. No tears. Please. "Just—can we not talk about this right now?" I plead quietly.

She must have heard the hurt and desperation in my voice because she doesn't continue to press me for more information. "How are Grace and Kate? And everybody else?" she inquires instead.

I smile before it hits me, and my smile quickly turns to dread. *Grace and Kate*. I was supposed to meet them after going to meet with Natasha. They must be so worried. Oh my god. I wonder if they're still waiting by the Smithsonian, or if they are looking for me, or if they went back home. Fuck, I don't even know how much time has passed! It could be hours, or days, or longer. I could be in the same building that Natasha's office is in or across the country, for all I know.

"Well—" I start before I am startlingly interrupted.

"You know, if you wanted to open the door, you could have just asked for the keys," a deep, chilling, frighteningly-male voice booms from somewhere to my right.

Next comes a harsh chuckle and the sound of keys jingling.

I whip my head around urgently, with what I can assume is a look of shock and horror in my eyes.

Chapter 2.1

MY EYES WIDEN AS I spot a tall, muscular figure in the dimly lit hallway. They are too far for me to make out clearly. Startled, I leap to my feet, instinctively backing up against the door, unable to look away from the new, looming presence.

The figure doesn't move, but I hear them let out another honking laugh. "Nothing to be scared about, darling," the figure says calmly, the voice sending chills through my veins, making my blood turn to ice. It's a male voice. He pauses momentarily, then adds, "I'm Luke."

I stand rooted to the spot, unable to speak, move, or even breathe. Have I been breathing at all? I feel light-headed and nauseous. My eyelids feel heavy, yet I can't bring myself to blink. My gaze is fixed on him, ready for any sudden movement.

I hear him sigh heavily, and then he begins walking toward me at a maddeningly slow pace.

I can't move. I'm frozen, like prey waiting for the kill. There is no panic or anxiety coursing through my body, only an overwhelming, paralyzing fear. The rest of my body feels like it's ceased to exist.

Finally, he stops a foot away, and only then can I really see him. He can't be older than twenty-five, with dark hair, piercing blue eyes, and an extraordinarily chiseled facial structure. He's tall, maybe six-two, and his muscles are defined even under the loose gray joggers and white T-shirt he's wearing. I might find him attractive under different circumstances, but the fear and dread are too strong. I can't afford to think about how he looks when he's potentially responsible for my current predicament.

"You look a lot like your sister," he observes with a smile, tilting his head slightly.

I can't take my eyes off him, but I still can't speak a single syllable or move a single inch.

He takes a deep breath and rolls his eyes. "So, you're just not going to say anything?" he asks, in a faintly exasperated tone, his features hardening and smile faltering. His voice travels throughout the hallway, vibrating against the cement walls, bouncing off the floor, and echoing within my head.

Finally, I hear Beth speak from the other side of the door. "Luke, please—" she pleads in the same voice as when I first heard her, shaky and weak.

"Beth, come on, I'm just trying to be nice," he shushes her quickly, but his voice doesn't sound angry. It sounds almost... tender? Caring?

I'm losing my sanity.

Somehow, though, this new timbre of his voice brings me out of my horrified stupor.

"I-I'm T-Talia," I stutter out. Stupid. *Why are you telling him your name? You really are an idiot.*

"I know." He smiles, his face relaxing.

That's extremely disturbing.

But strangely, his voice begins to calm me, like a gentle wave in a storm. I look into his eyes again—*so* blue—and there is something there I can't quite place. They aren't warm, but they're not cold either. It unsettles me further, and I instinctively shrink back further against the door, trying to put more distance between us.

There is something indisputably unnerving about this situation, yet I can feel my body and mind relaxing, defrosting from the icy fear.

"Leave her alone," Beth speaks. Her voice sounds more determined now, yet still extremely soft and cautious as if she is afraid. Of course, she's afraid... right? There is something I can't place in her tone of voice as well, and it unsettles me.

"Beth, I'm just trying to have a friendly conversation here," he says calmly, almost pouting. Only his eyes give away how he truly feels; for a second, they slightly widen and flash indescribably. His smile doesn't falter this time.

While they talk, I try to build up the courage to open my mouth again and contain my shaky breath and trembling hands.

After a long stretch of silence, I blurt out, "Who are you?", forcing myself to make eye contact with him. Surprisingly, my voice comes out loud and sharp.

He looks momentarily startled by this sudden display of courage as well. However, his facial expression changes to amusement fairly quickly. "I'm Luke," he responds smugly.

Groaning with irritation at this *man*, I throw my head back against the door. When I look back at him, his expression of amusement has deepened.

"I mean, why are you here?" I push on without another moment of hesitation. A rush of fresh adrenaline and confidence fuel me as I continue, my voice now full of agitation and rage, "More importantly, why am *I* here? Why is Beth here?"

I should probably shut up, but I can't. I'm not in control of myself anymore, throwing the questions at him, practically spitting them in his face. "How long have I been here? And where is *here*, exactly?"

With every word I throw at him, his amusement visibly grows. He looks virtually delighted by the end of my outburst. His smile widens, and I feel my blood boil. It's infuriating. Who does he think he is? What is he trying to achieve?

"Well, Talia, answering all of those questions would be a rather long conversation. Wouldn't you rather I open the door, and you can spend time with your sister?" he asks.

"No. I want you to answer my questions," I press on unwavering. Where did this conviction come from? I'm honestly stunned at myself. I think I'm having an out-of-body experience because I am not forming these sentences or speaking these words, yet I hear my voice saying them out loud.

He tilts his head to the side, examining me slowly. I can't tell if the way he looks at me is more as if he's looking at prey or a complicated piece of art. It's like he's x-raying my insides and trying to figure out my soul.

I stand my ground. "Answer me," I demand. My voice has calmed down a bit, so the words don't come out as forcefully.

I also don't want to push him because even though he seems unshakably composed, I still fear him snapping. I have no idea who he is, but I can only assume that he is the one who has been keeping my sister (and father?) captive. Where even is my father, and is he okay?

"Maybe you want to speak with your father, then?" he asks as if reading my thoughts.

That makes my blood run cold. My façade falters as I stand completely still with a gaping mouth and wide-eyes, breathing coming in short, and muscles tense.

"Where is he?" I whisper, my voice weak but full of venom. I grit my teeth while awaiting his response.

Where did all my confidence run off to?

He studies me for a while, analyzing every inch and twitch, before he gives a subtle nod toward the door on the opposite wall—the second one I noticed earlier. The non-abusive one. I'm not surprised; I should have predicted this. It makes sense.

I nod and compose myself, trying to restore some of the vigor I had minutes ago. I shake away the irrational feeling of him reading my mind. "I still want you to answer my questions," I insist, my voice regaining some of its previous feistiness.

He doesn't seem to buy it. "I can't help but admire your confidence and persistence," he says, smirking and shaking his head with that maddening amusement. I can't help but think about how it sounds like he's mocking me.

"I don't understand why it would be so hard for you to answer my questions. They are not that complicated," I say, trying to copy his tone. It still comes out somewhat too shaky for my liking.

He raises his eyebrow, eyeing me carefully. "Quite sassy," he remarks, a smirk curling at the corner of his lips.

I narrow my eyes and glare at him, trying to express that I do not appreciate his attempt at banter. I stay quiet, waiting for him to address my questions.

He takes a deep breath while throwing his head back exasperatedly. "Look, I can't answer all your questions. That's not really how this is going to work. But I can tell you this..." he trails off and seems to think deeply about his next words. "You're here for a reason," he conclusively states.

"And what reason would that be?" I inquire. My confidence slowly starts to creep back in as I get increasingly irritated by this guy.

"Talia, as I said, I can't answer all your questions." He sighs, rolling his eyes in a bored way. His voice is calm, with slight annoyance starting to shine through in his tone again.

"But—" I start objecting.

He raises a hand, jingling the keys in his grip and silencing me. "I'm going to open Beth's door, and we're going to have dinner. That's why I came down here. I honestly assumed you were still up in your room. But you're a sneaky one, aren't you?" He eyes me with a slight tilt of his head, amusement still dancing in his voice.

I glare at him but take a few steps back, giving him room to unlock the door.

He nods, clearly satisfied with my silence, and moves toward the door.

My heart skips a beat for an instant, then starts working overtime as he slides the key into the lock. In just moments, I'll see Beth. My sister, who I haven't seen in over six months. It's surreal, almost impossible to process. So much has happened today, so much has changed. Has it only been a day? Time seems meaningless in this hellhole. But this hellhole is also giving me the chance to see my sister again. The thought of seeing her brings a rush of relief.

Until the door opens and I actually see her.

Beth steps hesitantly and unsteadily into the doorway. The sight of her nearly knocks the air out of my lungs. My hands fly to my mouth, holding back a gasp as tears pool in my eyes.

Beth has always been pale, with raven-black hair, so I used to call her Snow White when I was younger. I thought it was fitting and funny. But now, looking at her, she doesn't look like a princess—she looks like a ghost. Her skin is almost translucent, and her hair, once smooth and silky, is now ragged, matted, and uneven. It's as though it's been ripped out in places. I don't want to think about what would cause someone to do that or have it done *to them*.

Her eyes—those strikingly emerald eyes that once sparkled like spring grass—are now dull and cloudy, like the ominous sky before a storm. They're glassy, red-rimmed, as though she hasn't slept in days or has been crying incessantly. Maybe both. I hope neither, but I also know better. How much pain has she endured?

I scan her quickly, but the sight is too much. I lower my gaze to the floor, unable to linger any longer. It's a tragic scene. I want to remember her the way she was, before she left with Dad to go to the grocery store. I long to hug her tightly, to feel her warmth. But I'm terrified of hurting her even more. She looks so fragile, like a cracked window that could shatter at the slightest touch.

"Hi," Beth croaks out timidly. From the corner of my eye, I notice her trying to straighten out, holding her head up higher.

It pains me to an extraordinary extent. I feel an agonizing pit in my stomach and my chest.

"Beth..." I breathe out, glancing up at her for no longer than a second before looking back down at the floor. I can't bear it. My voice sounds like I am in pain, pitiful, but I can't find any source of energy inside me to hide it. I feel disgusting.

"Talia, look at me, please," she pleads, her voice now full of anguish and worry.

"Alright, enough sister bonding for now. You'll have more time during dinner. Let's go now," *he* says, while slightly pushing Beth toward the end of the hallway where he first appeared. His hand is gentle on her shoulder, almost caring.

That confuses me. If it's him who did this to her, why is he acting so tender now? If he's playing some kind of mind game, I won't fall for it. All of this so messed up, and I refuse to be manipulated.

I close my eyes and take a deep breath to steady myself before following them. Beth keeps glancing back at me and stumbling as he leads her forward with his hand resting lightly on the small of her back.

We reach the end of the hallway, where a door awaits. I curse softly under my breath for only checking the left side earlier and never considering going to this end of the hall. *You're so dumb.* However, it's not like I could have opened this door even if I had noticed it. It's a dark metal door that blends seamlessly into the wall. I couldn't even break through a simple wooden door. Stumbling upon this one wouldn't have helped me. But still, I mentally slap myself for not even trying.

He opens it, and I wince, shielding my eyes as a bright light hits my face. After being in that dimly-lit cave for however long, the light hits me hard, instantly giving me a headache. As I try to walk forward blindly, following him and Beth, I trip on a step and stumble, falling forward. Thankfully, a pair of hands catch me by the waist before I hit the floor face-first. I turn slightly and look up as my eyes adjust, and I see blue eyes looking at me worriedly, with a slight twinkle. Scratch that; I'm not thankful. I don't want this creep touching me in any way, even if he's helping. I would rather have fallen to the ground and busted my chin or broken something.

"You're welcome." He smiles down at me as I squirm out of his hold. He lets go of me easily but keeps watching me intently.

My eyes have finally adjusted, and I take a look around. It's a regular(ish) room. Linoleum floors and walls painted a dull beige. No windows. Across from me, in the right corner of the room, there is a kitchen. A dining table stands in the middle of the room. As I look to my right, there is a sofa and a coffee table across from a flatscreen TV. Other than that, there are a few potted plants around the room, a few odd paintings on the walls, and some other "homey" décor. It looks *too* ordinary, comfortable, and soft for the current situation.

But it's the door to the left of the kitchen that catches my eye—another steel door. This one's painted beige to match the walls and once again blends in almost perfectly.

"Are we underground?" I ask. I don't know where that question came from, but suddenly, I feel this strange feeling in my gut.

He chuckles as he walks over to the kitchen and opens the refrigerator. He doesn't say anything, the silence stretching out as he takes items out of the fridge.

"Am I supposed to guess whether that was a yes or no?" I question.

After a while, he turns around to look at me, closing the fridge. He crosses his arms as he tilts his head and examines me again. It's infuriating that he keeps doing that. I feel as if literal steam is coming out of my ears, as seen in cartoons—my whole body heating up with rage.

"You really are the talkative type, aren't you," he says, chuckling again. It sounds more like a statement rather than a question.

God, I wish I could snap his neck here and now.

I notice Beth sitting on the sofa with her legs propped up on the coffee table. Her arms are crossed across her chest as she blankly stares at the wall above the TV. I furrow my eyebrows at the sight. She seems so comfortable here, almost as if she's at home. It's disturbing and doesn't help with my growing anger. I turn and glare at him again, noticing that he's still looking at me, *examining* me.

"I don't appreciate banter, and I'm not looking to chat with you," I snap. "Why can't you just answer the questions I ask?"

He shrugs nonchalantly and turns around to start unpacking the items on the counter. "Like I told you, Talia, I can't answer all your questions. I've already answered one. That should be enough. You can go watch some TV while I make dinner."

"You haven't answered a single one of my questions," I argue, fuming. I try to calm myself down because he is not worth all of the tension inside of me that is causing a brain-splitting headache. The fact that I can still feel the ghost of his touch around my waist when he caught me doesn't make things better. If anything, it's making me more nauseous.

"Talia, just let it go," Beth says quietly and slowly as she snaps out of her trance and looks at me.

Confusion and disbelief flare in me as I meet her eyes. How can she be so calm? So accepting? I feel a pang of betrayal. Doesn't she want answers? Why does she look so... at peace? After everything, how can she be okay with this? How can she act like she belongs here? So comfortable, so normal.

"There's no use," Beth continues, reaching for the remote and turning on the TV. "Sit down and let's watch something. We can watch *Parks and Rec*. That's still one of your favorite shows, right?"

I am unable to move a muscle. How and why is she so calm?

There's no use.

"You sound like someone who's given up," I say, the words rushing out before I can stop them. "And I'm not about to stand here and pretend like that's okay. Like any of this is okay. I have no idea what you've been through, and—" I shake my head, my voice faltering. "I can't even imagine it. But that's not the point. How can you just give up? How can you act like this? This isn't you! Do you have no fight left in you? Is that it? Have you completely given up on everything?!" My voice cracks as I yell at her, my anger bubbling over.

Immediately, I feel a wave of guilt as I see her shrink back into the couch, her eyes wide and frightened.

Complete silence follows my outburst. I feel his eyes on me, but I continue looking at Beth as she darts her eyes between him and me, still looking alarmed. Nobody says anything for what feels like an excruciating amount of time.

"Do you like pasta carbonara?" he eventually asks, placing a pot of water on the stove.

Beth doesn't say anything, simply turns back to the TV. She puts on *Park and Recreation*, shifting a bit on the sofa, settling in comfortably.

I close my eyes and take a deep breath, but the tension in my chest refuses to ease. I know anything I say right now won't make a difference, yet the words still swirl in my head. Shaking my head in disappointment, I walk to my left where a tall potted plant sits. I sink to the floor beside it, leaning against the wall. I bang the back of my head lightly against the wall, then pull my knees up to my chest, resting my forehead against them. The pounding headache and the nausea haven't let up, and I'm left with nothing but the heaviness of both. So, I sit there, frozen in place.

The same nothingness I felt weeks ago creeps back in. I thought I was leaving it behind, that my life was returning to some semblance of normalcy. But now, here I am, drowning in that familiar numbness. I close my eyes tighter, wishing I could just will it all away. Oh, how I long for Dorothy's ruby slippers, so that they could take me anywhere but here. If only I could grab Beth and Dad on the way out and disappear.

"Dinner is ready!" he announces cheerfully.

The smell reached me unexpectedly, and as if on cue, my mouth waters, and my stomach growls. I realize how hungry I am, hating the thought of it. I don't want to give him the satisfaction of eating the food he made. But I don't know when the next time I am going to eat will be. Also, I have to figure out a plan to get out of here. Maybe eating will soothe my headache and nausea, leaving me with a clearer mind to come up with something.

I slowly lift my head and see Beth already sitting at the table, waiting patiently. He is standing in the kitchen with plates and utensils. He's not looking at me, so I stand up swiftly and walk to the table, sitting one seat away from Beth. I still can't believe the way she's behaving.

"Pasta carbonara, as promised," he says while setting down the plates.

I don't spare him a glance as I dig into the pasta.

"Someone's hungry!" he exclaims contentedly. "I hope you like it."

Once again, I don't look up from my plate as I shove the pasta in my mouth. But I do give Beth a quick glance and see her twirling her fork in the pasta without taking a single bite.

"If you're not hungry, Beth, you can go back to your room," he says in a monotone voice. Somehow, he still sounds calm and caring but with an edge to his tone.

"No, I am," she insists quietly as she picks up her fork and warily picks up one piece of pasta.

We eat in complete silence. The sound of him chewing and Beth dragging her fork around the plate is all I hear. I finish first and end up sitting there, staring at my now-empty plate.

"How was it?" he asks eventually.

I stay quiet and still, staring down at my empty plate.

"I asked: *how was it*?" he asks again, more forcefully and harshly this time.

I stand up abruptly, pushing my chair back with a scrape that rings through the room. I walk back to the corner where I was earlier, slipping into the same position as before. My headache and nausea haven't subsided, unfortunately. I guess hunger wasn't the cause after all.

I can't believe I'm in this situation. I don't even know what this situation is. It's safe to assume I've been kidnapped, but by who? Natasha? This guy? Someone else entirely? Why is no one else here? I have so many questions, and I know none of them will be answered anytime soon. Maybe not ever. I might die here. I have no idea what he even wants with me. What will happen to me? Judging by Beth, it can't be anything good. Is this my life now—locked up in that concrete box, only allowed out to eat? Is that all I can hope for?

I can hear him sigh and get up from the table. "Talia, you have to communicate, or else I don't know what you're thinking or what you want," he says. His voice is back to that annoyingly calm and kind manner. It makes me sick—sicker than I already feel. "You have to talk to me. Communication is key," he adds.

Communication is key?

What the fuck does that mean? Did he decide that we're in a fucking relationship or that we're some kind of screwed-up family? No, thanks. I have enough messed up family drama as it is, and I'm surely not going to be in a relationship with anyone anytime soon, *especially* with him. Very much, *especially with him*.

"Talia," he says again, a hint of warning in his voice.

"Just talk to him, for god's sake!" Beth screams.

I jerk my head up, the force of her words rattling through me. I look at her, my eyes narrowing in disbelief. How can she be taking his side? She's still at the table, picking at her pasta, but her expression is strange. A mix of perplexity and... fear? Something in her eyes sends a chill down my spine.

I look over to where he is standing in the kitchen. "I don't have anything to say. What do you want from me?" I ask, forcing my voice to sound monotone and bored.

His jaw clenches, and I catch a brief, unsettling flash of something menacing in his eyes. If I hadn't been watching him so intently, I wouldn't have noticed, because it's gone almost instantly, replaced by that same unruffled calm. "Fine. I will answer one of your questions," he concedes, with a dismissive roll of his eyes and a slight scowl. "You've been here for about two days," he states, turning away to place the dirty dishes in the sink.

I frown. "How come I don't remember anything?" I ask.

"You were knocked out, I guess." He shrugs while turning on the water in the sink.

Yeah, now I'm infuriated again. "You *guess*?" I hiss at him.

He doesn't respond, continuing to wash the dishes.

I jolt up from my seat, my body tense with anger, but remain standing in place. "Oh, now you're giving me the silent treatment?! After telling me I was knocked out, YOU *GUESS*?" My voice is at an alarmingly high decibel, and I can feel the imaginary steam coming out of my ears again. My blood is boiling, coursing through my body at maximum speed. How does he have this effect of getting me so riled up? Maybe it's because he says the most outrageous things in the calmest voice I have ever heard. That must be it.

"Alright, alright," he says, raising his hands in mock surrender. "Look, let's be cordial here. I answered one of your questions, as promised. I think that was pretty decent of me, don't you? I'm trying to be nice. All I ask is that you please do the same. Now, I would like for you to go up to your room. It's late, and you need to rest. It's been a busy day, and you have a lot of new information to process. And if I'm being honest, you look a little tired... and ill. A good night's sleep will do wonders. I'll wake you up tomorrow, and we can continue this lovely conversation... maybe I'll even answer another question. We'll see. So, come on, don't pout and go to bed." He ends his monologue with a bright, patronizing smile.

How do I respond to that? Is he *babying* me? Like, "Oh, such a pouty little child, stop throwing a tantrum, go to bed, you need some sleep." Who the hell does he think he is, talking to me that way? That whole monologue was the biggest load of bullshit I have ever heard. I mean, seriously? He's fucking unbelievable. Who even is this guy? What does he want from me, for fuck's sake?!

"What the—" I start to say, but Beth interrupts me.

"Tal, let's go to our rooms. I'll walk with you." She gets up from the table, leaving her plate of uneaten pasta behind. She slightly sways while standing up but quickly steadies herself, walking over to me with a tight smile. Reaching out her hand and grabbing mine, she hastily leads us out the door.

I don't have the energy to fight him and Beth simultaneously, so I unwillingly stumble behind her as she pulls me away.

"What the hell was that?" I ask as she walks me down the dimly lit hallway.

She sighs and shakes her head. "There's no use, Talia. Just go to your room and try to calm down. Tomorrow, we can chat some more." She tries to give me a light-hearted smile.

There's no use.

"You keep saying that! '*There's no use.*' What does that mean? And I don't have a room here. My room is far, far away from here! What are you even talking about?" I implore. I try not to yell at her, my voice sounding strained and exhausted. Why is she acting like this? I feel the tears start to pool in my eyes as I look at my older sister, who has already looked away.

Beth stops at the door to "her room". "I'll see you tomorrow," she says with another tight smile before heading in.

Before she closes the door, I grab and stop it. "Where is Dad? If he's here, why wasn't he eating with us?" I ask as a last attempt to have at least one question answered.

Beth stares at the floor for the longest time before finally lifting her gaze to meet mine. Her expression is empty, but her eyes glisten with unshed tears. "He doesn't get to eat," she whispers, her voice barely audible. With a sudden, forceful motion, she pushes my hand from the door and slams it shut.

I stand there, frozen, staring at the door in stunned silence. Her words reverberate in my head, each one sinking deeper.

He doesn't get to eat.

Chapter 2.2

I STAND THERE FOR what feels like an eternity, staring at the door that was slammed in my face. My mind races, torn between opening it to press for more answers—any answers that make sense—or just walking away. *He* hasn't come by to lock Beth's door yet. I assume he always does, but honestly, I don't know. Not knowing anything has become a common thread for me nowadays. I don't know where I am, why I'm here, why Beth is acting this way, or what's going on with my father. It's probably best to leave Beth alone for now and think about what to do later.

I walk over to the other door and begin knocking, hoping my father will respond this time. The last time I knocked, I thought I heard something, but it might have just been Beth from her room. I continue knocking, harder each time, until it feels like my knuckles are about to bleed.

"Dad?" I ask eventually. "If you're in there, please, please, answer me."

Nothing.

"Please, just one sound... just so I know you're okay," I plead. "Or at least... alive," I mumble inaudibly.

"Talia, go to your room. Come on now, I thought I asked you to do this a while ago," *his* voice booms throughout the hallway.

Whipping around in his direction, I glare at him. "I don't have a room here," I snap.

"Okay. Go to the room you woke up in, then. Let's call it that, for now," he states, completely unfazed.

I open my mouth to retort, but he raises his hand in that dismissive gesture—a we're-done-here signal. The cold, disturbing look in those blue eyes cuts off any of my potential comebacks. There's something so dark and chilling in those eyes, something that makes my stomach twist. As I instinctively cross my arms over my chest, I can feel goosebumps appear. This is the first time I've exemplified real weakness since meeting him, and it makes me cringe. But I can't help it. To be honest, he truly scares me. He has all the control, all the power. No matter how hard I fight it, I can't deny that my family and I are prisoners, and *he* isn't. Therefore, I decide not to push him any further today. I've done enough for one day. Tomorrow, I'll try again.

Without another word and with as much casualness as I can muster under the circumstances, I swiftly turn and head toward the ladder leading up to the concrete box. I hear the jingle of keys as he locks Beth's door, and then his footsteps as he walks down the hallway. By the time I reach the top of the ladder, I hear the heavy thud of the steel door closing behind him, locking us in.

I sit on the bed I woke up in not so long ago, though it feels like an eternity has passed. Time has no meaning here. At least I know how long I've been here—only about two days, he told me. Not that long, yet too long for my liking. Especially since I was knocked out.

I contemplate going downstairs and trying to talk to Beth through her door again, which leads me to wonder why he didn't lock my trapdoor. I saw a lock on the outside of it earlier. I wonder why he locks them in but not me. It's not like any of us can get out of this hellhole anyway. Seems like an odd precaution. I can't help thinking about potential reasons why he doesn't lock my door, but none come to mind.

I know I won't be able to sleep anytime soon due to my anxiety and insomnia—not the greatest combination for sleep. Also, considering everything that has happened today and all the new information, my mind can't stop racing. I have too many thoughts churning in my head and not enough time to think them all. Or maybe I do have time now that I have been kidnapped. However, the last thing I want to think about is my sister and father being locked in rooms downstairs. It's upsetting and infuriating to think about.

Don't get worked up again.

I sigh and run my fingers through my hair, only to realize how greasy it feels. It's then I remember I haven't seen a bathroom anywhere around here. As if on cue, the urgent need to pee hits me. Wonderful. Slowly, I get up from the bed and climb down the ladder. As I turn, I realize I'm not as afraid as I was the first time I descended these steps. My eyes scan the hallway, and my gaze lands on a door right in front of me that seems to blend into the wall. The only thing that stands out is the door handle. The handle is small, with no keyhole—clearly not locked from the outside.

How did I miss this before? I was so focused on staying alert, trying not to fall into some horror movie cliché, yet here it is right in front of me.

I walk over to it, push down on the handle, and open the door. Sure enough, it's a bathroom. How convenient. I can't help but wonder again why I didn't notice it earlier. I guess I was too preoccupied with avoiding danger, too busy looking around instead of straight ahead. Great, now I'm the cliché. I walk in and close the door behind me, noticing there's no lock on the inside either. Well, it is what it is. As far as I can tell, there aren't too many visitors here anyway.

I can't help but wonder what Beth and Dad do if they have to go to the bathroom. How long do they stay locked in those rooms? Does he let them out in the morning, or at least for meals? Then again, my dad doesn't get to eat, apparently. So when does he get to leave the room? Do Beth and Dad have any way of contacting *him* if they need to go to the bathroom or if there is some kind of emergency? Maybe they have bathrooms in their rooms? That's a possibility. Considering I'm the only one located in what seems like the attic, they could potentially have bathrooms in their rooms. I didn't get to see Beth's room today, but I'll check it out tomorrow when he unlocks it. I'm hoping today wasn't a one-off case of me spending time with my sister.

The bathroom is surprisingly nice, full of thoughtful amenities. A toothbrush, toothpaste, shampoo, moisturizer, and a variety of other toiletries sit neatly in a cupboard to the left of the sink. It's almost too considerate, and that's what bothers me. I don't want to think of *him* that way. He's holding us captive; he's not kindhearted. I use the toilet, take a scalding shower, and brush my teeth. I wish I could change into clean clothes, but I haven't seen a closet anywhere. Judging by Beth's appearance, I'm guessing there isn't one.

After finishing a subdued nighttime routine, I climb back up the ladder. I sit on the bed for a moment and realize I'm too wired to sleep. So, I lay down anyway and start singing "Home" by One Direction quietly to myself. It's always been a song that calms me; it helps rein in my emotions and clear my mind.

I sing out loud quietly, with the melody playing in my head. My eyelids start getting heavy, and my eyes close. Somehow, while humming the song, I manage to drift off.

· · · ● · ● · · ·

"Scrambled eggs work for you?" he asks while grabbing a carton of eggs from the fridge.

We are currently back in the kitchen room area. He woke me up this morning by banging very loudly on the ladder and yelling, "Time to wake up, sweetheart." Long story short, I nearly puked this morning. Beth and I are watching TV as he makes us breakfast. She put on *Parks and Recreation* and convinced me to watch it with her.

I give a curt nod in reply to his scrambled eggs question.

"Oh, I love scrambled eggs!" Beth exclaims as if she's won the lottery. She appears to be in a much better mood this morning.

I didn't get a chance to look at Beth's room this morning because once I got downstairs, the steel door was already open, and he was already in the kitchen. I could see him and Beth chatting and laughing while he was looking through the fridge and Beth was leaning on the kitchen island. Every few seconds, he would look up from the fridge to flash Beth a smile. I observed them for a while. They looked comfortable together. Beth looked light and happy; her whole face lit up as she babbled away about something I couldn't hear. I would say they were flirting if I didn't know any better. It's unsettling to think about, but it's positively what it looked like. However, once I came in, Beth rushed over, gave me a quick hug, and sat down on the couch. His face immediately spread into a dark smirk once he saw me, and he asked me if I slept well, to which I responded with a quick nod and went over to sit on the couch.

"You're not a morning person, are you, Talia?" he asks now.

I make a disgusted face and slump deeper into the couch. "I am a morning person. I just hate it here," I reply.

"Why?" he asks, and he sounds serious. He looks genuinely confused, and it makes me want to laugh. Humorlessly.

"Why?" I repeat, dumbfounded. "Well, let's see... the biggest reason is that I'm being held here against my will. That seems pretty high on the list. And the room I'm forced to sleep in is dirty and cold, and the hallway is dark and disgusting," I say, my tone derisive but serious.

"I guess." He nods and shrugs slightly. "It all depends on your attitude. You can walk around her and sulk, or you can accept it and be like Beth," he continues calmly.

"Accept it?" I echo incredulously. "You want me to accept the fact that I've been kidnapped and am being held captive?"

I'm getting angry again now, and I hear my voice rising. Somehow, he always knows the right thing to say to push my buttons. It's not what he says but the way he says it. His "calm and kind" tone while saying the most outrageous things. It infuriates me to no end.

"Let's not start this again," Beth jumps in, turning away from the TV and looking between both of us. "I didn't sleep well, and I don't want you yelling at each other again."

She makes it sound as though we are having some sort of family disagreement. As if we're a *family* arguing about *what's for dinner*.

"Why didn't you sleep well?" he asks her, again using that soft, caring voice that irritates me to no end.

"I don't know—I had a bad dream and couldn't go to sleep after," Beth answers unconvincingly. Is she hiding something? And is she hiding it from him or me?

I shake off the nagging feeling. "So, are you going to tell me where my father is?" I ask. I don't ask him or Beth specifically. I just continue staring at the TV, letting the question hang in the air for either of them to grab it.

"You know where he is," he says, unfazed. When I don't respond, he adds, "You can go see him after breakfast if you want."

"How very generous of you," I reply sarcastically while still staring at the TV. At least I'll get to see my dad. I try to hide it from him and Beth, but I get filled with a sudden jolt of joy and hope at the prospect of finally seeing my dad.

"It is, isn't it?" He grins and tilts his head slightly as if this is a fun, playful game.

I roll my eyes and lower them, giving him a cold glare. "I thought I told you that I don't appreciate banter. Especially with you," I say icily. I don't want him getting any ideas.

"Right, right." He waves his hand at me dismissively and turns around to the stove. "Icy, serious, no-fun Talia. I got it."

"Correct," I respond before turning around to look at the TV again.

I think I can hear him chuckle, but I don't look over to check.

"Breakfast will be served in two minutes," he announces after a few minutes.

I groan but get up from the couch as Beth eagerly jumps up and runs to the dining table. I roll my eyes at her enthusiasm as I walk over slowly and rigidly.

"Luke, do we have any orange juice left?" Beth asks in a chirpy voice.

"Of course, darling." He smiles and walks over to the fridge, retrieving the orange juice.

"Thank youuu." Beth giggles.

This interaction makes me want to puke. I literally have to swallow it down.

"Let's get this over with so I can see Dad, okay?" I say through my gritted teeth with a tight jaw.

Beth's smile falters, and he shoots me a weary look from the kitchen.

"Breakfast is meant to be enjoyed. Haven't you heard it's the most important meal of the day?" he asks in a condescending tone, yet still with that hint of charm that I despise.

"Bullshit," is all I mutter, without looking up from the table.

I'm so done with his games. He thinks he can get me to open up and swoon over him, like he obviously somehow convinced Beth to do? Not a chance. That's not happening with me. At this point, I can't even tell if Beth is pretending in order to survive or if she's genuinely brainwashed. Does she actually like him? Because that flirtation in the kitchen earlier seemed authentic to me. I guess she could simply be a phenomenal actress. She's got me convinced, and I've known her my whole life. But there's this awful feeling gnawing at my gut, telling me she isn't pretending. That this is real. And nothing frightens me more than that. Because if she truly has some sort of feelings for him, I'm screwed. I will never get out of this hellhole.

Thankfully, breakfast ends quickly. Beth barely touches her food again, pushing around her scrambled eggs and bacon without actually eating much. I, on the other hand, finish mine and almost ask for seconds. Surprisingly, I still have an appetite—though I doubt it'll last. I bet if I were here as long as Beth, I'd lose my appetite too. I decide to take my plate to the sink and wash it. I'm not interested in owing this asshole any favors, no matter how small. Plus, at home, everyone cleans up after themselves, so it's just what I do.

"You don't have to do that," he says once he sees me washing the plate.

I stay silent while I scrub it and dry it off. I turn around, putting my hands behind me on the counter. "So, my dad?" I question. I hate that I say it with so much hopefulness. I don't want him to sense any weakness in my voice or demeanor. But I am too excited to see my dad and see how he is. I feel like an overzealous kid. I feel like jumping up and down. Obviously, I can't do that.

"Sure," he replies disinterestedly. He walks over to the sink, and I flinch away when his hand brushes the side of my arm as he reaches to turn the water on. He gives me a (faux) confused look, and I notice a hint of a smirk underneath.

I quickly move even farther away, walking toward the steel door.

All of a sudden I remember something and turn around to face him. "I was wondering if I can have my phone to text my friends and mom that I'm okay?" I ask, trying to sound casual and subtle. It's worth a try, right? Maybe it's not. It's stupid, of course. But I *have* to try. The worst thing he could do is—

He scoffs and looks over at me, an amused look on his face. "Come on." He shakes his head while chuckling. "I think I've done enough to accommodate you. I'm letting you see your dad, for god's sake."

I decide not to push it any further. Because, yes, he is letting me see my dad. I don't want to lose that opportunity. I might try again later. I will not give up on trying to do *something*.

"You're right. Can we go do that, then?" I ask in my most amicable manner while walking over and standing by the steel door.

"Is this really necessary?" Beth asks suddenly. Her high-pitched voice pierces the silence of the room, and my head automatically jerks to look at her, giving her a baffled look. What the hell is her deal?

"Beth, she wants to," he says while turning the water off and drying his hands.

He strides over to the door and stops way too close to me. "Let's go then." He raises his eyebrow as he gestured for me to proceed.

I try to contain my excitement and act aloof as I stride out of the room and to the door where my father allegedly is. I stand patiently, arms crossed, face furrowed, as he walks over slowly with the keys.

Beth runs out behind him, but she pauses by the steel door, looking at us from a distance. I squint due to the dim lighting and see a distressed look on her face. Whatever. She's irritating me. However, I get an uneasy feeling from her earlier outburst and current behavior. What is so troublesome about me seeing our dad? I simply want to know that he is okay, and I have missed him so much. Her behavior confuses me, and I no longer want to think about it. Instead, I shift my focus back to *him*, jiggling the keys.

"Are you going to open the door?" I ask impatiently, glaring at him.

He quickly looks over his shoulder to glance at Beth. She sinks to the floor with a grunt and puts her head between her knees. *What is her deal??*

I shake my head at her and tap my foot impatiently, anxiously. My nerves are all over the place, mostly from excitement but also from a creeping trepidation developing irrationally inside me. My anxiety builds with every passing moment as we stand unmoving.

"Fine," he says finally, sticking the key in the lock and turning it. He opens the door slowly and doesn't move.

Neither do I.

I feel stuck in place. I look over at him.

With a bored and borderline annoyed expression on his face, he motions for me to enter the room.

When I still can't move, he sighs. "Do you need a special invitation? I don't have all day. Get in there before I change my mind," he says in an exasperated tone.

I. Still. Can't. Move. *What is wrong with you?* I'm terrified, is what it is.

A thousand thoughts and questions swirl through my head. But one sticks out above all: the door has been open for at least a few minutes now, so why hasn't my dad come out on his own?

With another roll of the eyes, he grabs my arm and shoves me through the door into the room.

I close my eyes and take a deep breath. The air smells stale and filthy. There's no other way to describe it—just wretched. I open my eyes slowly, taking in the surroundings. The room looks almost identical to the concrete box upstairs, except there's an open door leading to a small bathroom. Thank god. At least he has a bathroom. I scan the rest of room, and my eyes land on the bed, where a disfigured figure is curled up. My father.

I take a step closer and inhale deeply, trying to calm myself. With that done, I walk over to the bed with assurance, trying to mask the tremor in my hands. My god... he looks entirely worse than Beth. His appearance is... deathly. Curled into a ball, his body seems like a sick illusion, no longer the broad-shouldered, muscular man I remember. Beads of sweat cling to his bald head, yet his lips are blue. His skin is almost transparent, tinged yellow, and covered in an array of scratches and bruises. His eyes remain shut. No sign that he's even aware I'm here.

I look over to the door, which is still ajar, but nobody is standing there.

I kneel, leaning slightly against the edge of the bed.

"Dad?" I whisper, my voice breaking. My hands tremble as I put one of them on his arm, trying my best to avoid touching any scratches or bruises. It's impossible.

I shake him lightly. "Dad?" I whisper a little louder, my voice still quivering. "It's Talia."

I hear a whimper. So inaudible, I could have imagined it.

But, suddenly, his eyes flutter open. Unbearably slowly, as if it's physically painful to do so. He makes eye contact with me. Or at least I think he does. The eyes are settled but distant, without a hint of recognition. He stares for a couple more seconds, eyes completely dead, before closing them again. There is no other movement from either of us as I kneel there, hovering over him, unable to comprehend.

After some moments, I get a surge of anger from somewhere deep within. Jumping up from the floor, I run out of the room. I see *him* standing to the right of the door, leaning casually against the wall and looking bored.

"What the fuck have you done to him?" I holler, raising my hand to slap him.

Unfortunately, he grabs my wrist and twists me around so that I am uncomfortably positioned with my back against his front.

I gulp with panic and disgust. He doesn't budge an inch as I try to squirm out of his tight grip. One of his arms holds my wrist across my chest, while his other is around my torso, holding me close to his chest. I feel his breath on the back of my neck as he leans forward. It's sickening.

"I gave you what you wanted," he snarls in my ear. "You asked to see him, and I gave you that. I never promised anything else. I don't owe you shit," he continues, pressing his mouth closer to my ear. I can almost feel his breath going through my ear canal and into my brain.

I try to shake my head, shake him away, but his positioning makes it impossible. I go stiff, trying not to puke, shiver, or show any sign of weakness.

"I will let you go in a couple of seconds, and you won't try this shit with me again. Got it?"

I stand still, paralyzed in repulsion and terror.

"*Got it?*" he snarls again, emphasizing his question by squeezing me.

I manage to nod.

He slowly lets go, and I feel myself falling to the floor. My brain, still in shock and full of terror, no longer has control over my skeletal and muscular systems. I fall to the concrete floor. This time, he doesn't catch me as I fall, and I hit the side of my head, a sharp pain reverberating throughout my whole frame.

"Get up and go to your room. Visiting hours are over," he declares. His voice has slightly returned to normal. I hear him shut Dad's door and lock it.

"What did you *do* to him?" I whisper. My head is spinning, not only from my fearful thoughts but also from my fall. I stay lying on the floor, not daring to turn my head to face him as tears start gathering in my eyes.

He sighs and stays silent for a long time.

"Your father is no longer needed," he eventually says in a monotone, almost robotic, voice. The words ring in my ears and pierce my brain, vibrating throughout my body.

"What do you mean?" I ask quietly, afraid of the answer.

He sighs again. "It means what it means, Talia. Your father is no longer needed. No longer needed *alive*." He emphasizes the last word harshly. "Now, get up and go to your room. That was a nasty fall. You probably don't have a concussion, and you should just sleep it off," he adds dryly.

· · · · ●● · ●● · · ·

In the following few days, I sit upstairs in the concrete box, the trapdoor closed and secured with the bed over it. He tried to come up a couple of times, tried to talk to me, get me to eat. But how can I?

I sit on the bed, staring at the ceiling, the walls, the floor, the sheets underneath me. There aren't a thousand thoughts and questions hurtling through my head. Thoughts aren't pushing against the inside of my skull, threatening to spill out as they usually do. I can only think one thought. One thought that tears apart my insides. One thought that makes me want to scratch out my soul and leave it on this floor to rot. One thought that has wrapped itself around my throat, slowly but surely suffocating me.

One thought...

My father is undeniably going to die, and there is not a single thing I can do to prevent it.

Chapter 2.3

Author's Note: The following chapter was written while listening to the first movement of *Sonata No. 14 in C-sharp Minor, Op. 27, No. 2 "Moonlight"* by Ludwig van Beethoven & *Prelude in C-sharp Minor, Op. 3, No. 2* by Sergei Rachmaninoff. Both are remarkable masterpieces that correspond with the chapter's tone, flow, and narrative. Listen while reading for the full experience.

I STEP ONTO THE dirty, concrete floor of the dimly lit hallway, releasing my grip on the ladder. I glance left and right on instinct. However, there is no one and nothing in sight. I feel a twinge of disappointment in my chest since I was hoping to see Beth in the kitchen. The steel door at the end of the hall is wide open, the bright light enticing me to advance toward it.

Step by step, I make my way down the hallway toward the steel door. Suddenly, I stop in my tracks as a beautiful ambience of melody surrounds me. Someone is playing the piano. I haven't seen a piano around here, though. Who is playing? I can't move or think as I close my eyes and listen to the mesmerizing sound of someone's fingers running across the black and white keys.

I recognize the melody: Sonata No. 14 in C-Sharp Minor by Beethoven. The first movement. The "Moonlight" Sonata—one of my favorite pieces of classical music. I feel goosebumps rise on my skin as I listen to the emotional composition swell to a crescendo. The person playing is clearly troubled, hurting, and in distress. This is evident by their performance. The piano lets you express genuine emotions; it allows them to flow out of your body through your fingers, even if it's not intentional.

I used to play the piano. I was good. Exceptionally good. I was playing it all, from Mozart to Tchaikovsky to Rachmaninoff. I stopped once Beth and Dad disappeared, having no emotions to express. Nothingness is impossible to transform into melody. I lost my passion. Sometimes, on lonely, sleepless nights, I still play to relieve the anxiety and lose myself in the euphoria of the various symphonies. It's not the same.

Where are Beth and Dad?

With that thought and the onset of panic, my eyes fly open. I think back and don't remember seeing any other doors as I walked down the hallway. I backtrack to check.

Turns out I am correct. Where the wooden doors should be, there's nothing but a cold concrete wall. No doors. No way through. Panic continues to tighten in my chest, but strangely, the feeling is distant and dull. I can't focus on anything but the melody, so I turn to walk toward the steel door, following the invisible, indescribable pull.

I approach the steel door and stand in the doorway, trying to figure out where the music is coming from. It is louder now, more passionate, more frantic, and raw. Nevertheless, the person playing maintains a flawless performance. Not a single wrong note. My eyes flow across the room, from right to left, and land on the beige steel door at the far left side. It is open, to my complete shock. I've never seen it open. I figured that it is where he goes once he locks us in. Though I never

*imagined it would be completely agape in front of me. Could it be...
could it be him playing? If so, I loathe myself for loving it so much. I
abhor the goosebumps, the rising heart rate, the warmth, the desire that
is bubbling at the surface as I listen to the melody.*

*Unconsciously, my body starts moving toward the door, toward the
music. I feel as if I am being pulled, a magnetic force overpowering
my body. I force myself to stop in the doorway, slowly trying to lean in
and examine this new area before entering. Fear and panic seem faint
and hazy compared to the intense feeling of the music. As I try to lean
forward carefully, my legs have other plans, and I stumble across the
threshold. Unceremoniously, I end up inside the room.*

*The room is nothing short of striking. It is dark. Even darker
than the hallway I had just been in, although I can see everything
surprisingly clearly. The walls are a rich, deep, dark purple color. The
marble floor is in the same shade of purple, making the whole room
fuse and appear as a grand ballroom from the olden days. There is
nothing else in the room besides a white grand piano standing in the
middle, with an unidentifiable figure sitting on the piano bench. The
figure that has been playing this masterpiece.*

*I stand spellbound, frozen, captivated, my mind blank. I close my
eyes again to avoid reflexively moving toward the figure. I still feel
the dim pulse of fear, confusion, and panic deep inside me. For the
first time tonight, I decide to listen to them. I don't move any closer
but don't move back from where I am, either. Unconsciously, I have
already made my way further from the beige steel door and closer to
the figure.*

*I feel nothing except for the melody, the "Moonlight" Sonata
replacing the blood flowing through my veins. The Sonata courses
through my body, captivating every single cell. I finally don't feel
empty. I feel complete for the first time in months. The nothingness that
has become my way of life is slowly being filled by the sounds that pulse
and reverberate throughout the massive ballroom. I tilt my head back*

slightly, letting my body be wholly enveloped. My brain is an abyss, and the only light that shines through is the music playing.

I am surprised that the figure hasn't noticed me or is ignoring me. I feel a slight pang of discontentment at being unnoticed, but it is a fleeting feeling, like all the others. Any and all feelings and emotions I had before have since dissipated, falling deep, deep inside the abyss of my brain until I can no longer perceive them.

The music stops.

I didn't even notice that the movement was over until I can no longer hear the enchanting rhythm.

I don't dare to open my eyes. I am now silently hoping that I will continue to go unnoticed and the piano player will play on, continuing with the atmosphere created.

And so it continues.

The figure continues playing Beethoven for a while, then moves on to Chopin, and finally—to my great frustrating satisfaction—ends with Rachmaninoff's Prelude in C-sharp Minor. The figure plays the most brilliant and passionate rendition of the piece. I have to say, even though I am good and I have played this piece myself, I dim in comparison.

I open my eyes in order to further engulf myself in this particular piece. As the allegro agitato section approaches, I stare at the fingers moving swiftly, not missing a note.

Nothing can compare to what I am feeling at this present moment. I can't help but let out a quiet gasp at the technique.

The music stops abruptly.

The figure starts to turn in my direction ever so slowly.

I quickly look down at the marble floor and freeze in place. I am no longer immobilized by the melodies; this is a different sort of frozen. I freeze cold. The music's warmth leaves my body instantly and is replaced by the chilling silence.

There is silence for longer than I expected. The figure doesn't say anything. When I can't bear it any longer, I raise my eyes to make eye contact.

Except that I can't make eye contact. Because... because the figure has no facial features. Completely blank.

But the head still tilts to the side as if looking at me, examining me. I can almost feel the nonexistent eyes burn through me, causing my eyes to widen and my breath to hitch.

From somewhere in the room, I hear a cryptic whisper, "Wake up."

· · · ● · ● · · · ·

My eyes fly open. I'm in bed, sweating and breathing heavily.

I'm in the concrete box upstairs.

"Nightmare?" someone asks from one of the corners.

I flinch, startled and confused, as I look over and see *him*.

"Were you watching me sleep?" I question, trying to cover myself with as much of the sheets as I can.

"Yes. You looked so peaceful for a while, but then you started freaking out, thrashing and yelling. It was odd," he says casually.

"*That* was odd? Not the fact that you were watching a random person sleep?" I ask sarcastically.

He rolls his eyes and shrugs. "You're not a random person," he says after a moment of contemplation.

"Yes, I am. I've been here for what—a week? Out of that week, I was passed out for two days and sitting up here alone for three days," I state.

"You can get to know someone pretty well, even in the span of two days. Even when they're asleep. And by observing a person, you can understand them even better," he fires back.

"So this is you *observing* me in order to get to know me better?"

"Yes." He smiles.

"Then stop," I snap.

"You really aren't a morning person," he muses, still with a smile. "Besides, you should be nicer to me. I'm the one who helped you wake up from your nightmare. Could have just left you to your demons."

"Huh, weird, because one demon still seems to be in the room with me," I retort.

Throwing his head back dramatically, he laughs.

I bite the inside of my lip and clench my jaw to prevent myself from completely losing control.

He lifts his head back up and makes excruciating eye contact with me, tilting his head slightly. "Ask me a question."

"What?" I ask, confused.

"Ask me a question," he repeats. "I will answer."

His blue eyes pierce through mine. It feels as though his eyes are trying to drill through my eye sockets and skull to get to my brain. It feels like he is genuinely, *literally*, trying to get into my brain.

"Uhhh..." This is so unexpected that I have no idea what to ask. After a few seconds of pondering, I respond uncertainly, "I guess I'll just stick with one of my initial questions and ask where we are?"

Honestly, all I want is to ask him if he plays the piano. Because that dream... that dream seems so real, and it is still so fresh and clear in my mind. I want to know if he is the featureless man at the piano because I have this feeling that it is him. But I can't be stupid right now, so I decide to go with the question that could potentially aid my current predicament. I will investigate about the piano at a later time.

He briefly considers the question before responding with frustrating condescension, "Do you mean geographical location? Or, like what kind of building we are in?"

"Both?" I say, still uncertain. *I want to know about the piano.*

He shakes his head. "No. That would be me answering two questions, and I only said one. So, which one will it be?"

I roll my eyes. "Fine. Tell me the geographical location. City, state, country, if you so please."

He sighs heavily as if I've disappointed him. "Pine Barrens, New Jersey." After a long pause, he adds, "United States, obviously."

"Pine Barrens..." I rack my brain for why it sounds so familiar. "Oh, shit!" I remember an article I read a while back. "Isn't it the forest known for the haunted folklore and ghost towns?" I ask. I'm a little excited. Obviously, I'm also terrified but excited because I love spooky legends.

He grins. "Yes. We're actually in one of the ghost towns right now." He pauses, as if contemplating if he should say more. "Technically, we're underneath one," he adds, biting his lip and squinting his eyes. I see he regrets it as soon as he opens his mouth. He's given me more information than I asked for, and I'm sure he doesn't like that.

"Oh," I respond, instinctively looking up at the ceiling. After a long moment of silence, I start to ask, "So we're—"

"Alright, I'm going to go make breakfast," he says at the same time as I start my sentence.

It's clear that the Q&A session is over.

He stands up and looks at me expectantly.

"What?" I ask.

"As much as I would love to move the bed with you on it... again. I think you should get up. For your own comfort," he says with a smirk.

"Oh," I reply, finally realizing what he means. I've been keeping the bed over the trapdoor for the past few days to block it, hoping no one could get in. Clearly, it hasn't worked. "How did you—"

"You're not heavy, Talia. Neither is the bed. I had to be careful, though, to avoid waking you. But you seem to be a heavy sleeper. I simply opened the trapdoor carefully, moving the bed with it, before opening it fully," he replies, shrugging casually.

I'm not a heavy sleeper, but I haven't slept in a few days, so I guess my body knocked itself out. I'm usually a light sleeper; any sound or ray of light wakes me up.

I get up from the bed, moving it until the trapdoor is fully revealed.

"You coming down for breakfast?" he asks as he opens the trapdoor.

On the one hand, I haven't eaten in nearly three days. On the other hand, my father is still dying—whether from starvation or something worse. If I don't eat, I won't survive, and therefore, I won't be able to save my family. Caught between starving myself and being a horrible daughter, I finally settle on being a horrible daughter. I hope my dad can forgive me once I figure out how to get us all out of here.

I nod slightly before he disappears out of view down the ladder.

Closing my eyes and throwing my head back, I breathe deeply before going downstairs.

I shower quickly, brush my teeth, put my hair in a bun, and make my way to the kitchen. The steel door is open, and I see Beth leaning against the counter, talking to him while he's making food on the stove.

"Talia!" Beth exclaims, running over and enveloping me in a hug. "Feeling better?" she asks.

I can't help but roll my eyes at that question. "I wasn't sick, Beth. And no, I don't feel better. Our father is still dying," I respond.

Beth backs away from me without another word and goes to sit on the couch.

"I'm making French toast today," he says, looking up from the stove.

"Good for you," I say sarcastically.

"Good for all of us," he replies with a smile before returning his gaze to the pan.

Asshole.

"After breakfast, do you want to have a movie marathon?" Beth asks, looking up at me hopefully.

"I'm not really in the mood," I reply, still standing by the door.

She tilts her head and pouts, giving me sad puppy eyes.

"Fine," I give in after a couple of minutes. "What did you want to watch, anyway?"

"I don't know... I was thinking like rom-coms?"

I groan. "God, please no." I love a good rom-com, but this is not the time for one. "How about we watch horror movies? That relates better to our current setting."

Beth sighs. "You're so pessimistic."

"I'm realistic," I counter. "*You're* the one living in a fantasy world. I'm honestly in awe of how oblivious and stupid you're acting."

"I'm not oblivious and stupid!" Beth shouts, her face morphing into theatrical anger. "I just like to stay positive!"

"Girls, girls, calm down. Let's have a nice breakfast, and then you can have your movie marathon or whatever. Just have a nice time, yeah? We don't need to be yelling all the time," he says in his usual calm and collected voice while setting the plates down on the table.

Beth sighs and walks over to the table.

I shoulder past her and mutter, "Coward," before taking a seat at the table.

It's immature. But she is acting like a coward. I don't know what she's been through, but how could he have made her so weak, so compliant? I haven't seen him treat her badly—not yet, anyway. In fact, I'm almost surprised he hasn't. Wouldn't that assert dominance or whatever? So, it makes me wonder: Has he always been like this? Before I arrived, did they sit around, eat, watch TV, and do nothing? Sure, we're being held captive; it's not a picnic. But compared to what I've read about or seen in the media, this isn't so bad. Of course, I don't want to stay here. I don't plan to. But he hasn't done anything torturous to Beth and me. Although, he is starving my father. I don't know what to think, what to make of this. Beth's attitude toward him terrifies me deeply. She's so sunny and obedient around him, it's unsettling. It makes me wonder if there's something else going on.

I push the thoughts away as I eat my French toast and try to tune out the useless conversation he and Beth are having.

"Do you play the piano?" I ask all of a sudden. I don't even know where that came from. I mean, I do. I just had a dream about it not that long ago. But I don't know why I'm asking this question right now. I guess it's been on my mind this whole time, and it slipped out.

"Uhhh," he seems taken aback. "Me?"

"Yes, you. Do *you* play the piano?" I ask more confidently this time. "And what's behind that door?" I point in the direction of the beige steel door.

"Aren't you full of questions this morning?" He returns to his usual self with a smirk.

"Well?" I press.

He sighs with evident exasperation. "Behind that door, as you can guess, is another room," he answers.

I raise my eyebrows expectantly, waiting for him to elaborate.

"If you want, I can show you that room after breakfast. It's not a secret. Beth has been in it before," he says.

"I don't think—" Beth starts, her voice quiet and unsure.

"And the piano?" I ask, interrupting whatever Beth was trying to say.

"I don't play the piano. Why are you asking that?" He looks at me with a questioning expression.

"I-I had a... never mind," I reply, losing my confidence. "No specific reason." I look back down at the table.

Out of my periphery, I can see him looking at me curiously for a moment before he turns back to his food.

You're dumb.

We finish breakfast silently.

Beth returns to her position on the couch and resumes watching her rom-com.

He's almost finished washing the dishes when I bring up the conversation again. "So, are you going to show me the room?" I ask.

"Sure," he responds, turning off the water. He dries off his hands and walks toward the beige steel door. Before getting out his keys, he turns to me. "You ready?" he asks.

I shrug and nod, confident and understatedly cautious.

He smirks and pulls out his keys, unlocking the door and pushing it open. "Ladies first."

I walk forward, holding my breath. If this is anything like my dream, I will be horrified. Although, if it is nothing like my dream, I might be a bit... disappointed. I am also concerned because I have never had such a vivid, realistic dream.

Still holding my breath, I take one step after another toward him and the beige steel door. A million thoughts swirl through my head. I can feel them, but I can't discern or retain any of them.

"Are you okay?" he asks.

I must look strange, moving as if in slow motion. But I am so uneasy. This dream really messed me up, and I don't know what to expect. *Get it together, Talia.*

"I'm fine," I snap as I pick up my pace and finally reach the door. I walk right past him and into the room.

I stop in my tracks as soon as I actually register what is in front of me.

Holy. Shit.

The room is precisely how it was in my dream, except for one small detail. Instead of the grand piano in the middle of the room, there is a huddle of people. They are all in a circle, engrossed in a whispered conversation.

He clears his throat from behind me before speaking loudly, "I would like to introduce Talia to all of you. She is Beth's seventeen-year-old sister."

The people in the huddle all turn around simultaneously to examine me. That's what it feels like: examination. I can feel every one of their unnerving eyes studying every part of my body. It makes my skin crawl and my blood pump furiously. I shudder involuntarily.

"Talia," one of the men says, stepping toward me. "It's certainly a pleasure."

I take a step back and end up bumping into something. Or rather *someone*. I didn't realize he was standing so close behind me.

"Talia insisted on exploring today," he says from behind me. "She wanted to know what was behind the door. So I guessed this would be as best a time as any to introduce you."

Although I am currently pressed directly against him, I'm unable to move away. The sight in front of me is too unsettling.

I guess now that there is more than one man around, I should start referring to *him* as Luke. I really don't want to personify him, to give him that much humanity, but he is undoubtedly much less alarming than these other people.

I scan the crowd, and my eyes land on an all too familiar face. My heart skips a beat, and I choke on my breath. My limbs quickly lose feeling as I stumble back even further before completely falling into Luke's—already outstretched—arms.

"Natasha..." I'm able to wheeze out slowly and shakily right before I lose consciousness.

Chapter 2.4

It has been days.

Days since I found out about Natasha and why I am here.

Days of me lying in bed, utterly void of feeling and emotion and movement. Complete and utter numbness. While Luke sits beside me.

When I came to after passing out from seeing Natasha, I found that Luke had brought me up to bed. Since then, he has not left my side except to bring me food and help me down to the bathroom. He has been talking a lot, explaining everything to me in detail, nonstop. He talks and talks, and then we sit in long periods of silence. Then he talks again. And then silence follows once again. It is a never-ending cycle that has been my life for numerous days now.

But I am unable to move, speak, take care of myself. Or do anything resembling normalcy.

The nothingness and emptiness that enveloped me before is nothing compared to now. I'm slowly tumbling down into a dark abyss with no end in sight and no way out. I am gone, with no one to save me.

"Talia." Luke comes up the ladder, carrying yet another tray of food.

He has to physically spoon-feed me these days. When this started, he didn't understand, and he was hesitant. But now, he has to shove the food down my throat in order for me to survive.

I get it.

I don't fight it.

I just can't do it myself.

· · · · ● ● · ● · · · ·

"You're awake, thank god! Are you okay?" Luke asks in a worried yet relieved tone.

My eyelids flutter, eyes barely open. Everything seems out of focus and dizzying. I close my eyes.

I am numb. I try to open my mouth, but I'm unable to. I try to move my hand, my foot, anything—but I am unable to.

"You don't have to talk right now. I'm just relieved you're okay. Just let me talk—explain things to you? I—they gave me permission to tell you things. I will tell you," he rambles.

I stay still without opening my eyes. I can hear everything, yet I cannot react. Conscious but unable to move. Essentially paralyzed.

"I guess I'll start with why you're here... you wanted to know that. That was one of your questions when we first talked... I just have to—I'm just going to tell you without stopping, and you have any questions... well, stop me?" He pauses for a moment.

I can tell he's looking at me, waiting for some sort of acknowledgment. But I give nothing. I physically can't.

So he continues after a while, "Anyway, I just—well... you're here for a reason. That man that spoke to you earlier, before you lost consciousness, he is our so-called 'leader.' He's important. He makes the decisions. He's the one who decided that your father is no longer needed..." he trails off.

If I could feel my heart right now, I bet I could feel it breaking and crumbling at those words. But I don't feel anything. Fortunately, probably.

"He—your father," Luke takes a deep breath. "I'm so sorry, Talia; he passed away yesterday." *He pauses for what I assume is a reaction from me. When none comes, he continues,* "It happened while you were still sitting up in your room. Beth doesn't know. I will tell her soon, I promise. I just couldn't bear to see her face. I couldn't tell her. I'm so sorry for that. I really am..." *he trails off again. Waiting for a reply?*

Nothingness. I am nothing.

Emptiness. I am empty.

"This man, the one you saw earlier, his name is Mark. He's... well, he's my father. I-we have to listen to him. If we don't, the consequences aren't... pleasant. He can be kind to the people he cares about, but... not always. Anyway, I digress. There's a bigger picture. My father is in charge of an organization. Some might call it a 'cult,' but I despise that word. I don't think of us that way. I prefer 'organization.' Anyway, that's not the point. We save people, we help them, we make them better. And eventually, they are able to join the community. That's what's happening to you and Beth. We have people everywhere, all over the Mid-Atlantic and Northeastern regions, in every city and town. They track, they report. Washington, D.C. is a big one, just like Philadelphia and New York City. Plus the suburbs of those cities. That's how we found your family. One of our people studied your family, and they saw what your mother did to your brother and how she treated the rest of your family. We had to save you. Unfortunately, we couldn't save all of you. I'm so sorry for the trauma you've had to endure, thinking your father and sister were either missing or dead. I can't imagine how horrible that must've been for you."

He pauses for a moment to take a deep breath.

I can sense his eyes on me again. At least, I think I can. It's my "sixth sense" speaking.

I wish I could react to the word-waterfall coming out of his mouth, but I still can't. I'm not even able to open my eyes.

Nothingness.

"Now you know why you are here," he continues. "For your own well-being. Your mother was tearing your family apart, mistreating you, and what she did to your brother... well, you know, I don't need to tell you about that. I just wish we could have saved you earlier and not caused you as much pain."

· · · • • • • · · ·

"Talia, I made some soup. You doing okay?" Luke asks as he sets the tray on the table next to me. He brought a table and a lounge chair up here so that he could feed me and sleep here sometimes. He barely leaves.

However, I still cannot respond. Over the past few days, I have been able to at least sit up with his help. I still barely open my eyes. And when I do, I want to close them immediately. There is nothing for me to see, and all it does is make me dizzy and sick.

He kneels beside the bed and helps me sit up. All I can do is fall forward a bit as he sets me up in a sitting position. I'm basically a rag doll.

"Beth told me you like chicken noodle? I made you some," he continues. "Here." He brings the spoon to my lips.

· · · • • • • · · ·

"There are a lot of people like you, Talia. We have saved so many. Some of them are now out in the world, working as scouts—searching for people like you and your sister. Broken families. People who need help." Luke pauses. "Your father didn't want to be part of it. He fought us and didn't want to listen. We tried for six months to convince him,

but in the end... Mark had to make the tough decision. I won't say I agree with it, but I have to follow what Mark says. I don't have a choice. I believe in what we're doing, Talia. Our organization is helping people get out of these dreadful situations, such as your family. We heal them, and then they can help even more people. I know not everyone understands this, but I hope you can at least try to. You seem special... at least to me."

It's been hours of this, or days—the constant stream of talking and explaining. I can't tell time anymore. I haven't responded, and I don't think I will anytime soon.

Nothingness.

Luke takes a deep breath. "I wish you would talk to me so I could at least know you can hear me. I miss you pestering me with questions... because now, I can answer them. But you're not asking anymore. Mark says we need to give you time to process everything, and of course, I agree. I just wish you would say something... " he trails off, presumably not knowing what else to add.

I assume he's done talking for the time being, so I begin drifting off. All I do is drift in and out of restless consciousness these days. Haunting nightmares from which I can't scream and brutal reality from which I can't wake up.

Suddenly, Luke starts up again, "Talia, I hope you're listening. This is important for you to hear. All of this information. I want—I won't go into too much detail until you come back to normalcy... I don't know if you can process all the details now. But I still want you to be listening. Mark means well. He means well for you and your sister. As long as you let us explain, and listen to us, and understand. It can be hard at first... when my dad first started telling me all of this, it was odd to me as well. He wanted me to have a customary childhood, so he sent me away to live with my mother's grandparents in Paris. They don't know anything about all of this... my mother prefers to keep it separate from them. They also live in a different country, so it doesn't impact them. But I lived with them until I was eighteen, and then I wanted to go to college in the United States. I wanted to be a chemical engineer. I'm smart and probably could have been good in that field. But once I got back here, my father finally opened up to me about th—all this. He didn't push me into it. But I knew it was my calling and legacy to be part of this organization."

He pauses again, taking a breath, then continues, "I don't regret it. Yes, sometimes I wish I could've had a more normal life with a proper job and proper friends... but I know this is where I'm meant to be. Our organization is doing good work, and that's what matters. There are so many people who need saving, families like yours, and I've pledged my life to helping them. Talia, I hope you know I never meant to hurt you—physically or emotionally. I hope you can accept my apology if I ever made you feel unsafe around me. I know that's possible when you're with someone unfamiliar. You must have felt fear, confusion, and anger. But I'm sure those feelings will fade once you learn and understand more about us. Once you're able to get up and talk again, you can meet other members who have been through exactly what you're going through right now. They'll help you. We all will."

••••••••••

Luke comes back empty-handed after taking the mostly-full tray of food back downstairs. I couldn't have more than a few spoonfuls of soup, and I couldn't chew the bread or anything else he brought up.

He helps me lie back down carefully to keep me from falling. He's been so gentle with me. It perturbs me. I don't want to feel like he is caring for me. I don't want to have those feelings. Although, feelings in general are so distant and alien to me at this point. I don't know if they are actually there or if I'm imagining that they are. Maybe I'm making them up because I don't know how to feel anymore—phantom feelings.

"I'm going to sit here, okay? Just like I usually do. If you need anything, I'm here," he murmurs, and I can hear how exhausted he sounds. It's almost as if he is afraid to break me. Like if he says words in a higher decibel, I will shatter like a dropped piece of glass.

It infuriates me.

Maybe my feelings are coming back after all?

· · · ● · ● · ● · ·

Luke is back with more food and more spoon-feeding. It seems like it's been days that I've been here, with his relentless pestering.

After he manages to feed me a couple of spoonfuls, he sits back down in his chair.

"I thought about it, and I think it's time to address your most prominent question. At least, I assume you have this question. You've been getting better, I think. You're able to sit up with my help, and you're able to eat more. I wish you would open your eyes though, so I can know you're awake and listening..." he trails off. I'm assuming to look for any sign of perception from me.

He doesn't deserve a response. Though even if he did, I'm incapable of giving one.

"Anyway, I guess I'll just go right ahead and say it, with the hope that you've been hearing and processing everything. I think... well, so, Natasha." He pauses, taking a deep breath. "I assume you're wondering about Natasha. Why she's here and what she has to do with all of this..." he trails off again.

It's so irritating how he's still expecting a response from me. It's been days. Does he not have critical thinking skills? Leave. Me. Alone.

He continues, "This could come as a shock. I know you and her were—or are—close. She helped you through the disappearance of your sister and father after we saved them. And that had to do with the fact that she is part of our organization. You might have thought it was a coincidence that you met her, but it wasn't. She was meant to find you because we wanted to save you as well. So she found you, she helped you, and when it was time, she saved you." He pauses again, uncertainty filling his voice toward the end. He sounds nervous. Almost... uncertain, or even scared?

I can hear a deep breath, a loud swallowing sound before he continues, "She's a wonderful woman. I'm sure you know that. She's so important to this organization and to my father. She's—" He pauses again as if unable to form the words.

Just spit it out already!

"She's my mother," he finally declares, his voice booming through the small attic room.

Wait... WHAT?!

If I could, I would be positively freaking out right now, hyperventilating and all. I might possibly be screaming internally, but I'm not sure.

What. The. Ever-loving. Fuck.

Did he actually just fucking say that Natasha is his mother?

•••••••••••

"What did you just say?" Luke asks as I hear him come over and stand next to my bed.

My eyes flutter open.

It's been five days of me floating in this state of nothingness. Or so he's told me.

"Natasha is your mother," I repeat in a raspy, inaudible, emotionless voice.

He looks me over, concern etching his face. "Is that all you remember from what I've told you?" He hovers over me like a helicopter.

Using all my strength, I raise an arm and push him slightly away from me. "No. I remember more," I mutter, with a hint of annoyance and a lot of fatigue. I'm already tired simply from opening my eyes and speaking a few words.

I'm getting some feeling back in both my brain and my body. I won't go as far as to say I feel better, but I feel *something*.

I try to sit up but end up falling back down.

He makes a move to help me up.

"Don't," I murmur, trying to raise my arm again, but it simply flails and falls back to my side this time. I guess I've already used up all my energy.

"Talia, don't be like that. I'm trying to help you..." He backs away slightly. "Yes, Natasha is my mother. I know you might feel betrayed. I hope you remember everything else I told you, and maybe you have questions... I'm here and willing to answer them. You don't seem to have a lot of energy, so maybe not right now. But you spoke for the first time in five days, Talia. I think that's progress."

He looks me over, his eyes trailing along my body and settling on my face. I suddenly feel very exposed and uncomfortable.

I close my eyes again and try to collect my thoughts. "Beth," I croak out.

"Beth is okay. She hasn't come up to visit you, but only because I told her it's best for you to rest up. I didn't want her to come up here and worry about you," he says calmly.

"Beth," I croak out a little louder.

"She's fine. Don't worry about her. She's eating dinner and watching TV right now. Maybe she'll visit you tomorrow if you're feeling better," he says gently, his voice laced with concern. "I think it's best for you to keep resting. You're doing better. You couldn't even open your eyes or speak a few days ago. Look at you now. This is very good, Talia. We might actually be able to have a real conversation tomorrow."

"Beth," I rasp out again, with every last ounce of power left in my body. It doesn't come out as any more than a raspy whisper.

He doesn't respond this time.

I know he's still in the room. Probably sitting in that chair and examining me.

I try to pull up the covers over my head, but my arms don't work, and I end up letting out an inaudible sigh of defeat before drifting back off into the abyss.

••••••••••

For the first time in days, I wake up and my eyes open easily. I feel truly awake. Not dazed, confused, or tired anymore. But I take it slow as I rub my eyes and carefully sit up in bed.

Luke isn't here. Thank god.

"Talia, you awake?" comes a voice just as I hear someone climbing up the ladder.

Spoke too soon...

"Oh, wow, you're awake. You've been asleep for twenty-eight hours. I was getting worried because you seemed to be making progress, and then you wouldn't wake up for so long. I even checked your pulse a few times. But you seem better now." He gives me an apprehensive look.

I internally shudder at the thought of him checking my pulse and touching my skin. "I'm better," I mutter, not making eye contact.

"Are you hungry? It's technically lunchtime, but I can make breakfast if you want. Beth and I had omelets for breakfast. I can make you one too? What do you like on yours?"

"I'm good."

"Talia, you have to eat. It's important to get your energy back. Come on, you don't want to end up the way you were five days ago," he says, concern lacing his voice once again.

"I don't think it was the lack of food that led me to be that way," I say. My voice is still quiet and raspy. I guess that's to be expected after being semi-comatose for five days.

"You were just in shock. That is completely acceptable, given the circumstances. It happens. We've seen it happen to many people. But now, you have to start eating and getting your energy up. Not

138

all at once, but you have to start somewhere. You can't stay in your room forever," he states.

"This isn't my room."

"For the time being, it is. Wait ten minutes, and I'll make you a nice omelet. I'll ask Beth what you like. Don't try to stand up, or you might pass out again. Be mindful," he says sternly.

I roll my eyes, but the only thing it does is agitate my headache. "Ibuprofen, too."

"What?" he questions.

"Ibuprofen."

"Why do you need ibuprofen? What hurts?" he asks, coming closer to me.

I lean away from him, a tiny amount, so as not to get dizzy or fall over. "Headache," I respond.

"Okay, I'll bring you food and ibuprofen. Now, stay here, don't do anything reckless. I will be back shortly," he says sternly again before making his way back downstairs.

I plop back down on the bed. My head is pounding, and my whole body aches. It feels like I've been in a car crash. Which I actually have been in before, so I have authority to say that. The positive thing is that I finally have feeling back in my body. Although now I'm wishing I didn't because it hurts like a bitch.

"Talia, you are so important. Don't forget that. You are important to this organization, to my father, to me..." he trails off. "You can do a lot of great things. Just try to get better, and don't give up. Take it one day at a time. Don't push yourself, but try to get better."

Remembering Luke's words makes me shiver. How am I supposed to get out of here? And now that I know Natasha is involved in all of this... shit. Natasha knows everything about me. I told her everything—my deepest secrets, my worries, my thoughts, my feelings. I trusted her. I was a fool. *Brainless and Reckless* should be the title of my autobiography—if I live long enough to write one. Considering everything Luke's shared with me, it's not looking like

I will. It seems like I don't have much time left in this world, unless I plan to join this cult. If I do, maybe I'll have a chance of surviving. But honestly? A life of fear and torture doesn't sound like much fun. "We save people"—what kind of bullshit is that? Did he think I'd believe that?

Hah. As if.

I'm foolish, but I'm not *that* idiotic. Every kidnapper and killer has likely made up an excuse in their head to validate their actions. This is just another one that Luke, Mark, Natasha, and the rest of their cult made up. Pathetic is what they are. Yet they definitely still terrify me. I don't know what I'm going to do. *What do I DO?*

Seriously though, what in the world am I going to do?

Chapter 2.5

IT'S BEEN THREE WEEKS since Natasha kidnapped me from D.C. and brought me here. I know this because all they do around here is talk. They're always explaining things. They don't call it "kidnapping," though; they call it "saving." But... same shit, right? There is no denying that I've been brought here and am being held against my will. So, I'm sticking with *kidnapping* as the correct term, even though they haven't physically harmed me. They've been accommodating, almost too friendly, which still doesn't change the fact that I can't freely leave.

Luke has been even more than hospitable—frustratingly so. He doesn't leave my side, like he's afraid I'll slip away if he takes his eyes off me. And yes, that's precisely what I want to do, but he doesn't need to know that. Maybe he already knows, which is why he's constantly around me, like a shadow that won't even leave me at night.

I've been able to slowly start leaving the attic room. I can go downstairs to eat, use the bathroom, and attend the creepy purple room for their "meetings." I try my best to tune out the meetings because I couldn't care less, and I refuse to be brainwashed. So, I don't even know what they are about. Beth is in the meetings too. Apparently, she's been going for a while. She seems to enjoy them, but she still looks so sickly. I can't help but wonder if she's really happy or if she's just pretending. Either way, she's always giddy, annoyingly so. It bothers me more and more as time goes on. I was just starting to get used to her flirtatious behavior with Luke—though, okay, I'm not used to that either. Truthfully, it disgusts me. But watching her ramble on and connect with these people takes me to a new level of rage.

"Are you hungry?" Luke asks.

Currently, I'm reading a book called *Lock Every Door* by Riley Sager. It's an intriguing read so far—a thriller/mystery that's been on my to-be-read list for a while. Apparently, they have a library here, and ever since I accidentally told Luke I used to love reading, he keeps bringing me new books. "Used to" being the key words he missed—meaning, before I got kidnapped, before my life became this. I hadn't meant to share anything personal, but Luke has a way of getting information out of me without me noticing. I hate it.

But I do enjoy reading. I missed it. There's always a silver lining, right? Reading makes me feel like I'm escaping reality, even if it's for a little while. It takes me into a different world, a different life, a different perspective. Reading has always made me feel that way, even before I was trapped in an underground dungeon full of psychopaths.

I roll my eyes. "We literally just had breakfast. Can you leave me alone and let me read?" I ask in an irritated tone.

"I'm good. Just keep reading, then," he says calmly. He settles back in his chair and keeps doing his Sudoku.

He. Never. Leaves.

He sits in the chair constantly, and I can feel him surveilling me every now and then. It's immensely disturbing and maddening.

"I wish you would leave, though," I grumble, looking back at my book.

He doesn't respond, doesn't look up from his Sudoku.

I set my book down beside me and glare at him. "Where is Beth?"

"She's at a meeting," he responds, still not looking up.

"What am I not there?" I suddenly sit up straighter, glaring at him harder, anger spiraling through my body.

"It's a meeting for members only. You still don't want to be a part of our organization, so you weren't invited," he responds in a bored tone.

"Since when is Beth a *member*?" My voice rises a few notches.

"Potential new member."

"What the hell does that mean? What is this—a fucking sorority? *Potential new member.*" I am yelling now and standing up from my bed. Ready for confrontation.

He finally looks up at me with a slightly annoyed, yet still uninterested, expression. He sighs heavily in exasperation. "I don't know what you want me to say." He shakes his head like a parent does when disappointed at their kids' behavior.

"What is your *ISSUE*?! Just say words! Say *something*! Why the hell are you coddling me?" Before he can respond, I speak again, "I don't *want* you to say just anything. What I want is for you to tell me the truth for once. Seriously, stop lying to me. It's not like I'm going anywhere, anyway." My voice is quieter and shaky toward the end.

"I have been nothing but truthful with you, Talia," he says calmly. HOW IS HE ALWAYS SO CALM?! It's driving me mad.

"Then tell me. What is going on with Beth? Why is she acting the way she is? Why does she look the way she does? Why can't I recognize my own sister anymore?"

He sighs, yet again. "Because she has been saved, Talia. Of course, you're not going to recognize her anymore. She's a different person with a different perspective on life. We got her out of your horrible household and helped her. Most importantly, she let us, and now she's so much better."

"Yeah, yeah," I respond sarcastically. "All I'm hearing is that you took advantage of a vulnerable girl. You kidnapped her and brainwashed her into believing your bullshit," I spit out the words

I've been keeping in since I first got here. Since I first saw Beth, since I first saw Luke and all of these people.

He rolls his eyes. "You can believe what you want to believe. I just hope you open your mind and see the truth..." he trails off. "Sooner rather than later would be best."

"Is that a threat?" I hiss, raising my eyebrow and glaring at him even more intensely.

"Not at all."

I cover my face with my hands. Rage is boiling inside me, threatening to spill out like molten lava from a volcano at any moment. "You are impossible to talk to," I mutter.

"I've heard from many others that I'm actually a great conversationalist," he replies. I can hear the amusement in his voice.

I snap my head up to him. "I'm not trying to have a *conversation* with you. And I *don't* understand why you think I'd want to banter, or whatever the hell you call it, with you. We are not friends. We are not acquaintances. We're *nothing*. You're literally holding me hostage! Seriously, where are you getting this idea that I want to spend time with you? Why are you always here? Just lock me up and leave me alone. That would be better than this. Why do you keep asking how I am? Why can't you understand that I don't want to talk to you? I have no interest in that whatsoever. All I feel for you is burning hatred. You're an immensely vile person. You're an accomplice in my kidnapping, and you think it's okay because you're 'saving me,' or whatever twisted justification you have. None of this is fucking okay! You are holding me against my will and threatening me with death—oh no, not directly, but look at what happened to my dad when he refused to join your psychotic cult! So now, why the hell do you think we can just have a normal conversation? How delusional are you? How fried is your brain that you think that's even possible?" I gulp in a breath, still seething with anger. No words could fully describe the rage bubbling inside me. There need to be new words invented to capture what I'm feeling right now.

Luke's face is stone-cold, his eyes narrowing at me as he sets down his Sudoku. He makes no move to stand up. I can't read him at all. "Are you done?" he asks, his voice still calm but with an edge to it.

"I could continue, but I think you got the gist," I spit back.

"That's good. I'm glad you got that out. I've been waiting for it," he responds.

"You're abhorrent."

I think I see him wince or hurt flash across his face at my words. But he gathers himself very quickly, and I no longer see anything but an emotionless expression. "Nice vocab word."

I shut my eyes. "Get the fuck out."

"I don't think I will."

I take a deep breath, trying to calm myself. "GET OUT!" I scream. The deep breath didn't help.

"No. I'm staying."

"Well, then I'm leaving." I get up from the bed and make my way to the trapdoor.

He gets up swiftly, grabs me by the waist, picks me up, and drops me back down on the bed. Surprisingly gently. However, that is not the point.

I stare at him in horror. What the hell was *that*? "Are you out of your mind?" I ask, still in shock. My whole body is rigid. He touched me. He touched me. He manhandled me. This is a new level of low. I can't start putting it into words. The waves of repulsion, of feeling violated.

"We're both staying here. Calm down and continue reading your book. We were having such a nice time before this."

A short, hysterical laugh escapes me. "Wow, you really are delusional."

His expression flashes with something I can't place. "Read the book."

• • • • •• • • • •

"I simply want to know what is wrong with you or what they did to you in order for you to make this decision?" While cooking pasta, I decide to confront Beth—who is calmly watching T.V.—about her joining this cult.

"It's for a good cause. And once you get to know everybody, you can see that they are all good people. You have to give it a chance, Tal," Beth responds pleadingly.

"Yeah, they're so great! They killed our father," I say, with a thick layer of sarcasm. Yes, I'm trying to cover up my emotions through sarcasm. But who doesn't do that? It's a well-known and well-worn coping mechanism.

Beth shakes her head. "They didn't kill him."

I give her a sideways glance. "Well, not directly, I guess. Not physically. But they starved him. I consider that to be murder."

"It wasn't their fault. Mark had to do it."

"You're saying it was Dad's fault?" I let out a shaky, exasperated breath. "Jesus, Beth, you're so brainwashed. I don't even know how to talk to you."

"I'm not brainwashed!" she exclaims.

"You keep telling yourself that," I snap.

"Can you stop being a bitch for like a couple of minutes?" she snaps back.

"Nope," I reply with a fake smile and turn back to the stove.

I hear Beth throw her head back against the wall and groan. "I don't remember you being such an annoying brat. No wonder Mom had to call Trevor to deal with you."

"Nice one." I hide my hurt expression by continuing to stare at the pot of pasta.

"I hope Trevor has left Mom by now. He deserves better than having to spend any time with her," Beth changes the subject.

I don't respond. I can't fathom what to say to her or what to say in general.

"Silent treatment, really? Be a grown-up, Talia. Can we not have a normal conversation?"

I sigh and answer without turning to her, "No, we can't. Not when you're like this."

From the corner of my eye, I can see her roll her eyes and fall back into the couch. "You're acting like such a child right now. I'm eighteen, you know, I can make my own decisions. This is the decision I made."

"That's where you're wrong. Because you didn't make this decision, it was made for you, and you were led to believe that you're the one who made it all by yourself. *That* is what I hate most... the fact that you genuinely believe you made this decision when you had nothing to do with it. You were manipulated, and you still can't see it."

Beth stays silent.

"It kills me," I whisper. I know she can hear me.

She stands up from the couch and walks toward me as she speaks, "Why can't you accept it? Just accept it. Become part of the organization. I promise you, you will feel so much better. You will understand the cause, and you will want to help others. Just like they helped us. Some people are even worse off. Trust me." She sets her hand on my shoulder while saying the last words.

I want to shake her hand off, but she's still my sister, and I love her more than anything. So, I force myself not to move as much as I would like to at the moment.

"Just give in. Let them care for you. Let them in."

At this point, I can't help but glower at her. I turn to face her fully, removing her hand from my shoulder and giving her a pointed glare. How can she say something like that? Something so unimaginably senseless as "give in".

Fucking *give in*. That's what she wants me to do.

Unbelievable.

"Do you even know what you're saying? You're asking me to give up on my life. You're asking me to give up on fighting for my life—for our lives. I can't do that, Beth. Not while I'm still sane. There is absolutely nothing you can say to change my mind about this. I will keep fighting for us. I will keep pushing back. I will keep believing that we can get out of this mess. Those assholes won't get me, no matter what. I am not *giving in*. There is not a single chance in the world of that happening."

Beth doesn't say anything else. She simply stares at me with an emotionless expression. I've been seeing a lot of that lately.

I turn back around and turn the stove off. "Pasta is ready," I mutter.

• • • • • • • • • •

"I decided this would be a good time for us to talk, Talia," Mark announces as I walk into the daunting purple room.

Luke told me his father wanted to "have a chat" and led me over to the purple room, closing (and I heard the lock click) the door behind him as he left me alone. With Mark.

"What will this conversation entail? Because if you're once again trying to convince me to join your cult, I will once again decline. Do you think I will change my mind once you've talked to me? Luke and Beth have already endlessly chattered on about this bullshit, and there is nothing you can say to change my mind. So, I would recommend you not waste your precious time."

Mark doesn't respond immediately, just giving me an ominous smile.

"Natasha!" he yells suddenly, making me flinch. Not only at him yelling but also at her name.

And surprise, Natasha steps into the room from the far-right corner. I hadn't noticed the other door before, which probably leads to yet another room. I suppose I should've considered how people got in here, but in my defense, that door has always been closed, and I've never seen anyone come through. Until now. It makes me wonder how big this place really is. Do all of these people live down here?

"Pulling out the big guns," I snicker, rolling my eyes, trying to keep an apathetic exterior. I can't fall apart right now. Not in front of them.

"Don't be like that, dear. We both know this isn't like you," Natasha says in a soft, caring voice.

What a duplicitous bitch.

"Imagine thinking you still have the right to talk to me after everything you've done," I respond in a cold and sarcastic tone.

Keep it up. Don't break down, Talia. You got this.

"I haven't done anything, sweetie. Nothing at all, besides help and save—"

"Don't you dare fucking say you saved me," I hiss through gritted teeth. "I've said it before, and I will continue saying it: all of you are the scum of the earth. After everything you've done, you should be rotting in prison. And I'm not just talking about what you did to me. I'm talking about Beth and my father and the numerous other people you kidnapped and murdered because of your delusional beliefs."

All they do is stare at me. Mark's smile is unfaltering. I'm beginning to think he might be a genuine psychopath. There is undoubtedly something wrong with this man. Natasha has a minor look of perplexity reflected on her face, but overall, she looks as calm and collected as ever.

"Take a seat, Talia. Let's talk." Mark gestures toward a table in the left corner of the room, one that I have never noticed before. I need to improve my observation skills.

My eyes flicker to the table momentarily and then back to him. "I'm not interested."

"Take a seat," he repeats while walking toward the table himself.

Natasha follows close behind. I wonder if she has also been brainwashed. I wonder if Mark "saved" her as well, however long ago, and then went as far as making her his wife. If that is the case, I can't help but feel extreme pity. However, I also wonder if she has as much to do with this as Mark, without any sort of manipulation. Deep down, I want to believe that she is not a bad person. That she didn't do all of this to me willingly. That she didn't have a choice. It's a dangerous mindset, but it's what I have to believe for the sake of my sanity.

"Talia, take a seat, darling. We need to have a real conversation. You need to hear us out, and then you can leave."

"I've heard enough from both Luke and Beth. But thanks for the offer." I'm going to stand my ground.

"We can stay here all day. It's up to you," Mark states casually.

I raise an eyebrow in a challenging way. "Fine by me."

"We might as well start talking," Mark continues, his voice steady, "because there's no way you can leave until we've had this conversation. You can stand by the door if you want." His demeanor is resolute, icy—disturbingly calm. A sinister aura surrounds him. It's almost inhuman, this coldness. I'm not sure if it's just his exterior or if that's who he really is inside. That's what scares me the most. Because while I can put up a façade, try to remain composed, I'm still tearing apart on the inside. What alarms me, and what I know deep down, is that Mark doesn't bother with a façade. This is just him.

This man that is holding me captive doesn't have an ounce of humanity.

It's more terrifying than anything else.

· · · · ● ● · ● ● · ·

"How did your conversation with my dad go yesterday?" Luke asks.

We're sitting in the upstairs room that they keep insisting I call "my room" (never going to happen). I'm reading yet another book, *When She Returned* by Lucinda Berry. Luke is doing Sudoku, as per usual. I'm not saying I'm getting used to this, but it's becoming increasingly routine. Deep down, this unsettles me. The fact that this is starting to feel normal and habitual. Even comfortable? Deep down, I hate it. I hate every part of it. Every shriveled-up cell of it. However, I can't help but feel this ray of established familiarity shine through.

"Your mother was there too," I state.

"Oh?" He raises his eyebrows. "And...?"

"It didn't go any differently than any conversation you and I have had." I shrug.

Of course, they weren't going to convince me. No matter what Mark and Natasha say, I remain tall and strong. I'm secure in my position. I will not give in to their brainwashing. I will not "give in", period.

"Shame," Luke mumbles.

"I want a phone," I say out of nowhere. This is not something that I've been thinking about. But then again, it doesn't hurt to ask randomly. The worst he can say is "no", right?

Luke looks up at me with a quizzical expression. "What?"

"You heard me. I want a phone. I'm not asking for a phone to text or call or to have internet access—although I miss social media. I just want a phone so I can, like, play games on it and—I'm bored like ninety percent of the time here... unless I'm reading. So, I would like a phone."

Luke looks confused and skeptical for a couple more seconds, but then he shrugs. "Sure."

"Seriously?"

"Yeah, why not. It won't have service or anything. But I can't deprive you of your games, can I now?" He smirks.

I laugh.

...Where the hell did that come from?

Did I seriously just *laugh* at something he said?

What is wrong with me? What is happening?

Luke's smile gets wider, and his eyes have a disconcerting sparkle to them.

Shit.

"I think this is the first time you've genuinely laughed at something I said. Like, not a condescending or sarcastic laugh," he comments with an amused smile.

I try to make my face an emotionless mask. "Don't get used to it," I mutter.

But his smile doesn't drop as he shakes his head in amusement and returns to his Sudoku.

After half an hour of silence, he speaks again, "It's your birthday in two weeks."

I peel my eyes off the book and look at him inquiringly. I can't help but scrunch my eyebrows and glare. How does he know that? "How do you know that?"

"February fourteenth, right? Valentine's Day. You're turning eighteen?" He avoids my question.

But I press on, "Do you have, like, a file on me? How do you know this?"

He laughs. "I don't need to have a file on you to know your age and birthday. Anyways, my mom told me."

Ah, Natasha. Thank you. What a great lady.

I roll my eyes, looking back at my book.

"We will celebrate," he continues.

Is it not registering with him that I'm trying to ignore him? I feel like I have made it pretty clear—many times.

"I'd rather not."

"Why?"

I think my response over for a second. "There is nothing to celebrate in my life currently."

I could say that I've been kidnapped and am being held captive, which is why I don't want to celebrate, but even I'm starting to get tired of bringing that up. Everyone's aware. Never in my life did I think I would spend my eighteenth birthday in an underground bunker, a prisoner of a cult whose members are trying to force me to join them.

"Every birthday is important. Every age is important. You can still have a nice time. We can decorate the room. And we don't have to invite anyone who makes you uncomfortable. It can be just you and your sister... or you, me, and your sister. Whatever you're comfortable with."

"That's not much of a party."

"Well, you don't like most of the people here, so I apologize. But, yeah, it won't be much of a party."

"I don't like anyone here."

"I Iuh?"

"You said I don't like 'most of the people here,' and I just want to clarify that I don't like a single person here. I just want the record to clearly reflect that."

He smiles with amusement once again. "Noted."

"How old are you, anyway?" I ask.

Why did you ask that? Why do you care?

"Look who wants to have a conversation now." His smile gets wider.

What am I *doing*?

I glare at him. "Whatever." I look back to my book, embarrassed and confused by my own actions.

"Nineteen."

"Wait, really?" I ask.

I'm a little intrigued now. I thought he was at least twenty. I mean, he told me he joined this cult when he was eighteen. So that means he's only been part of it for a year? I don't know why, but I expected him to be older. He looks older, too, not that I have ever looked at him too much or examined his facial features. I guess the way he talks to me makes him seem older.

"Yes. Why are you so surprised by that?"

"I don't—I just thought you were older," I mutter, shaking my head. What is wrong with me? Why am I having this conversation with him? *Shut up and read your book.*

Thankfully, he doesn't say anything else.

I'm definitely getting a little too comfortable, and I couldn't be more appalled by that.

Chapter 2.6

It hits me with the force of a beehive falling from a tree—hard, sudden, and painful.

It hits me in the middle of the night.

My father is dead.

He is dead. I will never get to see him again. I will never get to talk to him again. I never even got to say goodbye. I don't even know what they did with his body.

It hits me so hard that I can't breathe. I try to gasp for air, but the invisible hand around my throat simply grips tighter. *Calm down*. I'm unable to. It feels like I'm sinking into molten lava—my whole body burning in place, and soon, there will be nothing left besides an imprint of where I used to be.

The tears start pouring down my face as I try to free myself from the invisible death-grip around my throat while simultaneously trying not to drown.

Do you ever start crying uncontrollably, and then all the other pain in your life bubbles up and you sob even harder? Well, that's what happens now. My mind jumps from my dad's death to the fact that I'll probably never see Trevor again. I'll never see my best friends, or even my mother (who, to be honest, I don't miss, but still). I'll never have a normal conversation with Beth again—the real her is gone, and I don't know how to get her back.

My father is dead.

I was barely conscious, in a shock-induced comatose state, when Luke first told me my dad died. So I guess I didn't fully process it until now. It never fully hit me with all the other cult absurdity going on. But now it has, and my soul aches with devastation and sorrow.

My father is dead.

The waves of it keep hitting me, over and over again. It pulls back and then hits again with greater force each time. Wave after wave, each other stronger than the next. I can't stop it. I can't control it. And I can't breathe.

I can't breathe.

I sit on the bed, unable to move for a long time. Tears and snot stream down my face.

Then, I start clawing at the sheets, the bedposts—anything I can grasp—trying to rid myself of this suffocating feeling. I rock back and forth, scratching at my neck, my wrists, my whole body. I see blood. Skin caught under my nails, blood dripping onto the bed, but I can't stop. I want to tear myself apart until I no longer feel anything.

Even if it takes physically tearing myself apart for it to happen.

"Talia, what—" comes an annoyed voice from the trapdoor. It opens. "Talia—" it says again as the ladder squeaks. "Talia, what the hell are you doing?!" the voice shrieks.

Beth runs over to the bed, which is now situated at the right corner of the room instead of in the middle (the way I like it, over the trapdoor). Luke insisted on it being away from the trapdoor so that he doesn't have to move the bed each time he wants to climb up here.

"What the hell are you doing?" Beth grabs both my wrists and holds them apart roughly.

I can't help but smile at her.

She still cares. How nice.

The horrid feelings stop. I'm in euphoria. Spinning and smiling.

"What is wrong with you? What are you doing?" I can hear Beth's distant voice yelling.

But it's okay. She can't pull me out. I want to be there. In this state of undeniable bliss. I want to stay here forever. I close my eyes so that I can enjoy it further. Beth's angry and worried face was getting in the way of my dreamland. I think I'm going to call this place Sevritulem. That's a good name for it.

My father is dead.

He is. There is nothing I can do about it. Sevritulem is not a place for sorrow or despair. It's a place of happiness and sunshine. *That reminds me of Michael and how he used to be my sunshine.* No. I can't think about that. Not now. Not here. In Sevritulem, there's no father, no Michael, no Beth. No one. It's a place for me alone, and I'm content. I want to stay here forever.

I feel a faint pain on the left side of my face. Strange.

Then, more pain on the right side of my face. Odd.

Then again, even more pain on my left. Ouch.

Suddenly, my eyes jolt open and I'm staring into the dark.

As my eyes adjust, I realize I'm in the concrete box room, sitting on the bed with Beth in front of me.

"Talia?" she questions quietly. She seems panicked and worried. Why?

"Did you..." I choke out.

"I had to slap you. I didn't know what to do. I'm not a freaking doctor. It probably wasn't a good thing to slap you. You probably shouldn't do that... but it worked, right? You closed your eyes, and your whole body was convulsing. You were saying things I couldn't understand..." she trails off. "What happened? Did you have a nightmare?"

I want to go back to Sevritulem.

"No..." I respond unsurely. Was it a nightmare?

My father is dead.

I don't feel it.

I think that's a good thing.

"Oh my god, Talia, I need to go get you bandages. You are bleeding all over!" Beth exclaims. "I don't know if I should leave you alone. Will you be okay? Don't go back to sleep. I'll be right back," Beth rambles on while backing up.

She quickly stumbles down the ladder, and I hear her opening the bathroom door. She returns a few minutes later, carrying multiple first aid kits.

I'm fine. I don't need this. I don't even feel it.

"Say something," she requests.

"What?" I croak out. I don't even recognize my own voice. It sounds so distant and... broken.

That can't be me.

·········

"Talia, how are you feeling today?" Luke climbs up the ladder and enters the room.

"I'm fine." I sit on my bed, reading a book, not looking up.

"How are your wrists and neck feeling?"

"I'm fine."

He sighs and sits down in his chair. "You've been saying that for two days now. Talia, I'm genuinely wondering how you're feeling. What led you to do this? I want to know. I want you to feel like you can tell me..." he trails off. I can feel his deep blue eyes perusing every inch of my body, lingering on the bandaged parts.

I don't look up. "I'm *genuinely* fine."

I miss Sevritulem. I've slowly and surely slipped out of it in the past two days. I now feel like I'm eighty percent in the present, and feelings are coming back. Everything hurts. Emotionally.

"Talia, please."

I snap my head up and glare at him. "What do you want me to say, huh? You killed my father. I have nothing to say to you. So, I'm going to stick with: I'm. Fine. Leave me alone. I'm not interested in your pity or whatever else you have to offer."

"I'm not pitying you, I—"

"Yeah, yeah, you *care*. That's what you keep saying. But trust me, I'm not buying into that. It's honestly funny to me how hard you're trying. Why don't you give up already? It's obviously not going to work on me. I'm not as weak as Beth," I interrupt.

"Wow, nice," I hear Beth's voice come from my left.

Turning my head around slowly, I now see that she's standing by the entrance to the trapdoor. I didn't hear her climbing up.

"Thanks for that, Talia," she continues. "Weak, really?" Her voice breaks at the end.

"Well, there's no point in me trying to cover it up or lie to you. You heard it, right? I stand by the statement," I say quietly, wishing I could take the words back as soon as they leave my mouth.

Her face falls and I recognize the hurt look. "Right." She scurries back down the ladder without another word.

"That was uncalled for," Luke jumps in. His voice is still calm but with a hint of disdain.

"That's your opinion."

"Beth loves you so much, and you just hurt her feelings. That wasn't kind. You should apologize," he continues.

I give him a look that says "are you serious?" and then return to my book.

Frankly, I don't know how much longer I will be able to survive like this. Because I am surviving, I'm not *living*. This doesn't feel like living. It feels like surviving from day to day, and I can't find a reason for doing so any longer.

Luke keeps talking about something. I'm not listening. It's probably more information about the cult—he likes to keep me updated on their exploits. My book still rests in my lap, the first page open for the last two days. Focusing on anything feels so out of reach at this point. Thoughts keep swirling in my mind: about Dad, about the rest of my family and friends, and about how I no longer want to be here. I'm not sure if "here" means this room, this underground complex, or maybe even this world.

Luke leaves soon after, realizing I'm not planning to engage. I spend the rest of the day staring at that first page, contemplating my life. What could I have done differently? It's obvious once I think about it: I never should have trusted Natasha. But then I consider the circumstances that led me to that trust.

Fact: I was supposed to go to the grocery store with Beth that day. But I had a terrible day at school and a mountain of homework, so I yelled at everyone before locking myself in my room. If it had been Beth and me who got kidnapped, my father would still be alive. Sure, I'd still be miserable, but maybe I would have been more easily brainwashed into joining the cult. Would that have been such a bad thing? Before Beth and Dad were taken, I was so much purer, more innocent. I wouldn't have acted the way I do now.

My thoughts shift to how I acted when Beth and Dad went missing—my frenzied spiral into hysteria, my behavior, my complete disregard for everyone and everything around me. I began sleeping around and drinking, doing drugs, avoiding my friends, and leaving town for days at a time. If I hadn't done all that, I could have been more productive in searching for Beth and Dad. I could have been more proactive with the police or the FBI. I could have had a better support system, and maybe that would have kept me together and prevented me from being utterly broken.

My mind circles back to the fact that if I hadn't spiraled so out of control, I never would've met Natasha during one of my miserable nights out. If I hadn't been a complete mess, I could have saved my family. I could have saved myself.

Could have.

How I wish I could end all of this now. Yet I owe it to whatever family I have left—and more importantly, to the shattered pieces of myself—to at least try to keep fighting. In this wrecked state, it feels nearly impossible. I'm entirely lost, detached, drowning in the mess I've created. I can't help but blame myself for this predicament. I am responsible, at least for some of it.

I feel so completely defeated and demolished.

· · · ● · ● · ● · ·

Michael is singing "this is my trying" by Taylor Swift.

I join in at the second verse.

"Okay, stop that now. I'm going to cry," Kate says, wiping under her eyes and laughing. She waves her hand in front of her face, and I can see her tearing up.

"I thought you said that I'm a terrible singer." Michael grins.

"Well, yes. But even you can't make this song any less of a masterpiece. Also, once Talia joined in with her angelic voice, it sounded phenomenal. And gut-wrenching."

I stand up and give an exaggerated bow. "You're very welcome."

"Honestly, Michael, how did you land such a beautiful and talented gal? She can sing, she can dance, she can play the piano... I'm in awe. She could do so much better," Kate muses.

"No, I couldn't," I respond immediately, giving Michael a fond look and walking over to sit on his lap.

"You could. But I'm glad you choose not to." He smiles up at me.

I give him a quick peck on the lips. It's still enough for Kate to say, "Keep your PDA to yourself," and turn away, making a mock gagging sound.

"You two are so disgustingly lovey-dovey, it makes me sick." Kate scowls. "I'm so jealous."

I laugh wholeheartedly, and so does Michael. I have never been happier. Life is so perfect, and I have no idea how I got so lucky. I have found the most amazing guy in the world, who makes my whole world light up whenever he is near. Like my own personal sunshine. Someone I can share everything with and never feel judged. Someone who, even at fifteen years old, I could see the rest of my life with. There aren't words to describe this feeling. It's like a constant feeling of indescribable euphoria. However, I have also never felt as grounded as I do now. There isn't a moment I want to miss with him.

"Sing something else. Just Talia this time around, though," Kate requests.

"More Taylor?" I grin at her.

"Is there anyone else?" she sasses back.

I laugh again. Yes, our obsession with Taylor Swift is extensive, but that shouldn't be news.

"Can I borrow your guitar?" I turn to Michael.

"How could I forget she plays the guitar, as well! What a multi-talented queen! Seriously, Michael literally never let her go," Kate exclaims.

I just keep laughing. Could I get any luckier? Honestly, there has to be a luck barometer breaking somewhere.

Michael passes me the guitar and I tune it quickly.

I get up from Michael's lap and stand in the middle of the living room as if it were a stage. "Alright, lady and gentleman. This is a song that I—that Taylor Swift wrote, but I will be performing. If you know the words, please do sing along!"

I start strumming and singing "Better Man" by Taylor Swift.

Kate joins in for the chorus.

During the bridge of the song, Kate is basically yelling, so I have to stop.

"Why'd you stop? I was just getting into it," she complains.

"Maybe a little too much," Michael remarks.

"Shut up. I can't help it. It's another masterpiece."

I sigh contently. I'm so happy, I can't contain it. If this were a musical, I would burst into happy-song at this very moment. It's not, though, so I restrain myself. It's not like I've had a hard life or anything. Honestly, my life has been severely, boringly average (to a certain extent, with some bumps along the way). But I can't complain about that, right? I definitely can't complain about it from now on because everything about my current existence is perfect. I wouldn't give it up or change it for anything else. I feel complete. Invincible.

"Is Grace coming over?" I ask. She was supposed to be here hours ago, but of course, she has to spend every second of her life with Brad. They have been that couple since essentially kindergarten. I couldn't see it any other way, though; she and Brad are inseparable. A unit. Sure, they've had their fights and "breakups", but they are two people who are meant to be together. I hope the same applies to Michael and me.

"She said she'll be here..." Kate trails off, looking at her phone, "thirty minutes ago. Yeah, so she and Brad are definitely... yeah. They're so annoying. You all just make me feel like the most single person ever. I hate it," Kate complains.

"Tom just texted me that he's here," Michael says, standing up from the couch and walking over to the front door.

"Hey, man!" Tom greats Michael. Tom walks into the living room with his usual light-hearted, bubbly smile. "Hey, Kate, and hey, Sparkles." He comes over and gives me a hug before walking over and taking a seat next to Kate. "So, are we playing guitar—or piano—and singing, or what?"

"Actually, we were just finished with that," I say. "But I can play something else if you so desire."

"I would, yes," Tom replies with the same sassiness. "How about some Queen?"

"I'm switching to the piano for that," I say, hanging the guitar back in its place. "Lady and gentlemen, blah blah blah, sing along because I know you know this one," I say, taking a seat on the piano bench.

Michael comes back in and takes a seat, never taking his eyes off me.

I smile—the permanent type of smile—and turn to the piano. I start playing "Don't Stop Me Now" by Queen.

After a moment, I turn around to give Tom a pointed look, and he immediately joins in.

"Don't stop me now. Don't stop me now," he sings.

"Thank you, Tom!" I say before continuing to sing.

By the second verse, Grace and Brad arrive and join in immediately—coming into the living room, already singing. Kate and Grace stand up and start dancing around the living room as Michael picks up the guitar and starts playing along with me.

We all continue singing together. Singing and laughing. I love them all so much.

I feel so complete.

· · · ● · ● · ● · · ·

The next morning, I'm sitting beside Beth in the kitchen.

"I'm sorry for what I said yesterday. You're not weak. I really am sorry about saying that. I wasn't thinking clearly," I mumble, not looking up and stirring my oatmeal.

Lately, I haven't been hungry at all, and I've noticed that I've lost a fair amount of weight. My cheeks are starting to hollow, and my cheekbones are becoming more prominent. This morning, I looked at myself in the mirror and didn't recognize my own face and body. So frail and sickly.

"Whatever, Talia, I know you didn't mean it. You're going through a lot and haven't been yourself lately," Beth replies.

You did mean it, though.

"Yeah. Right," I mutter, staring at my food.

"Anyway, you want to do something fun today?" Beth changes the topic.

I look up at her questioningly.

"Apparently, there is like a whole arcade room built down here. Luke gave me the keys to the room!" Beth jingles the keys in front of me.

I frown. Why would he do that?

"There's like video games and karaoke and stuff... and a bunch of arcade games," Beth continues excitedly.

"Why would he give you the keys?" I ask.

She rolls her eyes. "Why can't you just be excited?" She asks in an annoyed tone.

I continue frowning.

"Actually, Luke told me that he is doing this for you. He doesn't want you to be upset, and he said he heard you singing—"

"He heard me singing? When?" I ask, shocked and flustered.

"Yeah, and he said you sounded lovely. He said he'd never heard a voice like that. I told him that I already knew this. And then he asked if you play the piano, for some reason... and I said that you do. So then he gave me the keys and said we could make a day of it. There's apparently a piano and other instruments in there." Beth shrugs. "We can have fun like we used to."

"Piano?" I ask. The last thing I want to do right now is anything that reminds me of my old life. Playing the piano, singing, and having fun will only give me a false sense of reality. That is the absolute opposite of what I currently need.

"Yes, what about it?" Beth asks, interrupting my thoughts.

"What?"

She frowns. "Um... okay. Anyway, do you want to do this or not?" Her voice sounds soft but has a slightly annoyed edge to it.

On the one hand, if I keep rejecting and disappointing Beth, I will lose her. I already feel us drifting farther and farther apart—even farther than when we were actually apart for six months. Now that we are together, confined in an underground complex, we're even more distant than when we were separated by physical miles.

On the other hand, I need to stay clear-minded. Having a fun, carefree day will not help me stay focused. I need to figure out my next steps to get us both out of here. I have made up my mind that even though I feel shattered inside, I will fight for my life.

However, I would never leave here without Beth. And for her to leave with me, I need to mend our relationship. One day of "fun" can't hurt, right?

"Sure." I offer her a fake, soft smile.
One day of fun can't hurt.

Chapter 2.7

THE LONGER I WALK through this underground maze, the more dread builds up inside me. The endless, dim hallways and steel doors are disorienting and nauseating. Each steel door offers a new beginning before it opens, leading to an identical dim hallway—one after another. I feel like Theseus, and hopefully, I will be able to slay my own beast like he did. For now, though, I feel lost in this labyrinth, with no escape in sight.

"He said it's right after this door," Beth states.

"How many keys are on there?" I ask, trying to sound casual. I wonder if Luke has removed the keys that might actually help us get out. Probably.

"I don't know." Beth looks at me quizzically. "Why?"

I shrug and smile, stopping at the door. It's not exactly easy to approach Beth with my plan to escape from here. She's already invested in this cult and its members. I hope my real sister is still somewhere in there, but for now, I don't want to push it.

"Ready for some fun?!" Beth shrieks, pushing the key into the lock.

"You know it," I say, in the best "excited" tone I can muster.

Beth turns the key and pushes the steel door open. She sprints inside without hesitation, with wide eyes and a joyous smile. I follow cautiously.

I have to admit, this is incredible. The room is filled with arcade games on one side and more mature gambling games on the other. There are slot machines, too. Half arcade, half casino. The farthest back wall is where the piano stands: a beautiful—and expensive—Steinway. Around the piano, on the wall, hang other instruments: guitars, a trombone, a saxophone, violins, and so on. There is a stage in the middle of the room with microphones, a DJ booth, and a karaoke machine.

This really is something, but I don't want any false sense of reality to set in, so I push down all the feelings and walk over to Beth. She is standing near the huge flat-screen TV.

"Do you want to *Just Dance*?" Beth asks, all hyper and joyful. She's practically jumping in place with excitement.

"Sure." I give her another fake, soft smile.

The following hours go by in a flash. That sounds cliché, but after being cooped up in a concrete box for weeks, it's surprising how much fun regular activities seem.

"See! You're having fun!" Beth exclaims abruptly while we're playing some old arcade game. "Why don't you play the piano? We can sing and do a concert like we used to."

I'm trying to figure out how to work this game, so at first I don't process her words clearly. I'm bent on winning at least once. "What?" I ask distractedly.

"Do you want to play the piano and sing? Like we used to?" Beth repeats.

I freeze. No. I can't do that. Over the past few hours, I have already been having too much of a good time. I can't let myself fall even farther down this rabbit hole. "I don't think that's a good idea," I murmur.

"Why not?" Beth asks, her voice confused and slightly disappointed.

"I just... we're having enough fun, right? It's—I'm not really in the mood for that," I respond, trying to hide my actual reasoning.

"Okay, I guess..." Beth trails off, giving me an odd look.

I smile again, trying to lift the spirits and alleviate any confusion or suspicion.

"Anyway, I'm going to go play *Mario Kart*. Come join me if you want." Beth shrugs.

"In a bit," I respond.

As she walks away, I let out a deep breath I didn't even know I was holding.

This is going to be harder than I thought.

• • • • • • • • • • •

"How was your day?" Luke asks as he climbs the ladder and sits down in his chair.

I raise my head from the book and glare at him. "Why are you here?"

"Is that any way to respond?" He raises an eyebrow.

I roll my eyes and frown. "Did you need something?"

"I was simply wondering how your day went. I did arrange all of it for you."

"That's very considerate. Thank you," I reply sarcastically.

He sighs overdramatically. "Can you please have a conversation like a normal person?"

"Not with you, no."

He leans his head back and sighs deeply again. After a moment, he picks up his brain-teaser's book and starts flipping through it.

Thank god he didn't feel the need to respond to me and continue this excruciating back-and-forth that he usually insists on having. What I can't understand is why he keeps coming into this room. Why does he give me no privacy whatsoever? I have never seen him in Beth's room. So why does he insist on constantly coming up here?

Luke's brows are furrowed in concentration, and I return to reading my book. I would feel much more comfortable getting lost in the book if he wasn't in the room. He always puts me on edge and makes me anxious, so much so that I can't properly concentrate on reading.

After ten minutes, I decide that since I can't concentrate on reading, I might as well play a game on my new phone. Yes, he did indeed give me a phone, as I requested. Of course, I have already tried calling, texting, setting off the emergency call, and going online—alas, none of it worked. My hope was that he would mess up and that I could somehow get access to the outside world. But the world is working against me. It's okay, though; I'm not losing hope yet.

I settle on playing *Temple Run*. It's a classic and just the type of mindless entertainment I need right now.

"Enjoying your new phone?" he asks as soon I unlock the phone.

I lift my head and give him an annoyed look.

"Silent treatment?" he asks after I don't respond.

I lower my head back and start playing the game.

"*Temple Run*?" he asks after a few minutes.

I focus on the game and don't respond. How much more irritating can he get?

"I like that game too," he continues.

Apparently, a lot more.

"You know, if you actually talked to me once in a while, like an actual conversation, you could feel much better. Maybe even better about being here, or whatever it is that's bothering you. I can be like your personal therapist."

I pause my game and raise my head at his last words. Personal therapist? Pfft. "That's funny," I respond.

"How so?" He furrows his eyebrows, looking slightly offended and hurt.

"You? Acting as my personal therapist? The only person I trust less than you is your mother." I laugh, but it's sharp, mocking. "I thought I made it clear to you that I have no interest in being whatever twisted version of a friend you have in mind. I don't want to have conversations with you. I don't want to be around you. But, since I don't have a choice, I guess I'll have to suffer through it. You've stripped me of everything I thought I had. I'm not myself anymore. Hell, I'm not even a person anymore. I'm just... existing in a shell of what used to be. I've been here for what, a month now? It's all a game to you, and you don't realize that you're destroying an actual human being. Fuck! I can't believe I'm giving you the satisfaction of thinking you can get a reaction out of me or that you have any control over me. But damn me to hell if you really believe that I'll ever share something personal with you, you fucked-up, psychotic asshole." I spit the words out, trying to keep my voice level, but the venom creeps in, louder and sharper with each word.

I can see Luke flex his jaw for a second, and something resembling hurt or perplexity flashes in his eyes. However, as usual, he relaxes quickly, and the same calm façade returns.

"I'm upset that you feel this way, but at least you're actually sharing your thoughts and feelings with me. I understand your anger, and I'm sorry, but there is nothing I can do about it. You're the only person who can change your own experiences and attitude," he says calmly, with a slight smile.

Anger boils inside of me at his tone and body language. I want to scream at the ceiling, I want to claw my skin off, I want to lunge and rip his larynx out, I want to make myself disappear forever.

Instead, I close my eyes and try to take deep breaths. I can't let him get to me. I can't let him have that control.

"You want to talk some more?" he interrupts my calming thoughts.

I open my eyes. "I would like some dinner," I respond calmly.

Luke gives me a weird look and eyes me suspiciously for a minute. But eventually, he sets his book down and gets up. "Alright, I'll make chicken parmesan. Be down in half an hour."

I nod and sit back in bed.

POLINA QUINN

Alone for thirty minutes. Who would've thought that a mere thirty minutes alone could give me this much joy?

•••••••••••

Days stretch into an endless blur—a monotonous cycle of sleep, food, books, and phone games. And, of course, Luke is there at every turn. I'm still trying to figure out what his deal is. It's not like I can escape anyway. It's been a week since my "day of fun" with Beth, and she keeps inviting me to join her again. But I can't do it. Maybe I sound dramatic, but I know I can't keep distracting myself with all this fake fun. I have to focus on what really matters.

After weeks of contemplating all of my options, I have finally come to a conclusive decision.

"My birthday is in a week." I lift my head from my book, finally getting up the nerve to talk.

"Yes, it is," Luke states with a slightly confused expression.

"I wanted to ask you something about my party if you don't mind," I approach my question cautiously.

He nods as if giving me the "go-ahead".

"Well, I, um—so, I was wondering if, um—if you could, like, um—"

"Jesus, Talia, spit it out," Luke groans in frustration.

I'm nervous. What if he sees right through me?

"Okay, fine," I snap. "I was wondering if you can invite like... everybody?" I finally get the words out. I dread the further questioning.

"What do you mean?" he asks.

I collect myself again before responding confidently, "I mean, invite everybody in your cu—organization. To my party."

"Why would you want that?" He furrows his eyebrows. "The record clearly reflects that you don't like a single one of them," he mimics my words from last week.

I roll my eyes. "Well, I changed my mind. It's not that I like them all of a sudden now. It's just..." I trail off, not knowing how to approach this exactly.

"What?" Luke asks, seeming very intrigued.

"Just invite them, okay? Just... just invite them." I sigh, hoping that he won't prod with more questions.

"Alright, I guess." Luke shrugs. "I'll let everybody know they are invited. Anything else, princess?" Luke asks with a smirk.

I roll my eyes again. "Yes, actually. I would like to ask for you to never call me '*princess*,' ever again. Unless you want to be puked on, of course." I give him one final glare before returning to my book.

"Funny," he responds with sarcasm, returning to his brain-teasers.

What an asshole. Calling me princess, what the hell? It's as if everything I say to him goes right in one ear and out the other. I have told him multiple times that I have no interest in having conversations with him, or banter, or whatever he wants to call it. So why is it so hard for him to get that through his thick skull?

I sigh heavily and drift off into my world of thoughts.

I hope I made the right decision.

· · · · · · · · · · ·

Today is the day. Ugh, that sounds so cliché. But it's true. It's *the* day.

My birthday! Eighteen!

However, more importantly, today is the day I make the big announcement—my decision. I am so nervous. I shake as I put on the clothes Luke brought me yesterday. He went shopping and bought me a lot of new clothes. It disgusts me to put them on because he bought them, but I also can't keep wearing my old jeans and sweater forever. Plus, he actually has objectively good taste, and I look nice. Not that I have anyone to look nice for, but I can argue that it's nice to look nice just for yourself.

"You ready, birthday girl?!" Beth exclaims as she climbs up the ladder. "I'm so excited! Eighteen! I can't believe it. My baby sister is turning eighteen years old."

"Shut up." I roll my eyes good-naturedly and grin. "You're less than a year older than me."

"Ten months is basically a year. And you'll always be the baby," Beth states.

I grimace and stick my tongue out at her.

She laughs.

I miss this. I wish I weren't in this hellhole and could actually enjoy these moments with my sister. I wish I weren't stuck, being held captive. I wish I could have a normal life and be able to enjoy these moments without thinking if I'm going to be alive in a year. Or if I'll even be alive tomorrow.

"Come on, hurry up, it's time to go. You can't be late to your own party." Beth climbs up into the room and grabs my arm, ushering me to the ladder.

"Who says I can't?"

"It's rude."

"It's called being fashionably late," I state as I wrestle myself out of her grip and go back to put my shoes on.

Beth groans and throws her head back. "Come oooooooon. Hurry up! I want to go and have fun."

I feel my nerves start to sizzle again as I finish putting my shoes on and finally start descending the ladder. Beth is fidgety, jumping up and down with excitement.

"You need to calm down," I say sternly—with a hint of amusement—as we walk down the hallway.

"Actually, I think you need to get on my level," Beth responds as she skips through to the steel door and into the kitchen.

"Is the party in that room?" I ask, pointing toward the beige steel door that leads into the purple room.

"Yes, yes, come on!" Beth rushes toward the door and flings it open, running in without waiting for me.

I make my way to the door slowly and enter the room.

"HAPPY BIRTHDAY, TALIA!" A chorus of strangers erupts around me, their voices too enthusiastic and jarring. Beth stands at the front of the group, beaming and laughing.

"Happy birthday, sis!" Beth exclaims again.

I find all of this disturbing and irritating. Not to sound bitter and ungrateful, but right now, that's exactly what I am. What do I have to be thankful for? A room full of people who are complicit in my captivity? What's there to celebrate? Being trapped in an underground maze with no escape? Or maybe that I'll probably never see my friends or family again? Yeah, I'm sticking with bitter and ungrateful.

I do feel a pang of guilt, though. Beth is so genuinely happy, so delighted. I don't want to ruin that for her. She's been through so much—things I'll never fully understand. I don't even know what happened to her before I was brought here. But from the way she looks, it's clear it wasn't anything good. She seems a little better than when I first saw her, but there's still a shadow in her eyes from whatever happened to her. Every time I try to ask, she changes the subject or shuts me down.

The crowd starts to disperse, people mingling and laughing while I stand awkwardly in the doorway. I stare at them, the weight of it all pressing on me, and I feel the urge to cry. How did I end up in this hellhole? But I swallow my tears, shoving the hurt deep inside. I can't let them see. Not now. I'll cry later, when I'm alone, like I always do. With a forced breath, I take a few steps into the room.

The decorations are elaborate, over the top. The dark purple walls are lined with gold streamers and other various shiny decorations. A long buffet table stretches across the middle of the room, laden with more food than a crowd could possibly eat. The ceiling and floor are covered with a vibrant sea of balloons in every color. Arcade games are set up along one of the walls, as well as a karaoke machine, and a few people have drifted in that direction. The right side of the room features a DJ booth and a makeshift dance floor, where some are already swaying with drinks in hand.

I keep looking around, distraught that I don't get to spend this day with people I care about. I can't bring myself to appreciate any of this, knowing the truth behind it.

"Do you like it?" a voice asks.

I snap out of my thoughts and look to my left.

Luke.

"It's... a lot. I can see you put a lot of work into this," I respond.

"So, you don't like it?" he questions.

I shrug. "I didn't say that." I turn around again and examine all the decorations adorning the walls.

"Are you going to keep standing by the doorway, or are you actually going to do something? This is your party, after all," Luke's voice is soft and hopeful. It makes me nauseous.

"I'm taking it all in."

"Alright. Would you like something to drink or eat? I made a lot of stuff."

I turn to him with a disbelieving look. "You made all the food?"

He laughs, throwing his head back. "Well, unfortunately, food delivery services do not deliver to underground structures located in a ghost town in the middle of a forest." He makes eye contact again. "So, yes, I did make all the food by myself. Nobody else here is really qualified enough to make food," he adds.

Arrogant asshole.

"What makes you qualified?" I inquire.

"You usually like the food I make, right? I cook practically all your meals daily, and I've never heard you complain. I thought that was qualification enough," he responds, with a shrug and a smug look.

"Maybe I'm just polite."

He laughs again. "I definitely wouldn't accuse you of being that."

Asshole.

After I don't respond, he speaks again, "So, any food or drink for you?"

I give him a disinterested look. "I'll manage on my own, thanks." I start walking away from him toward the long table. But then I stop. "Actually..." I turn back around.

He raises an eyebrow. "Yes, princess?"

I visibly gag, and he laughs. My gagging was not an overreaction, more of a genuine response to him calling me that.

"Can you grant me my birthday wish and never call me that again?" I snap, narrowing my eyes.

"Sure." He chuckles. "Is that all?"

"No, I actually have a question."

He walks up closer to me. "When don't you? Go ahead."

I muster up all my courage and ask, "When would be an acceptable time to make an announcement?"

"An announcement?" He scrunches his eyebrows.

"Yes. I have something to say to everyone here."

"Um..." he trails off, looking uncertain. "I would say to do it soon before everybody gets trashed. Some people are already getting rowdy, and they've only been here for thirty minutes."

"Rowdy?" I repeat, grimacing.

He shrugs. "What kind of announcement is this?"

I gather my lips into a straight line. "Guess you'll just have to wait and see. Do you mind rounding up everyone around the DJ booth?"

"Right now?" he asks.

I collect myself. "Might as well get it over with now."

He shrugs again and walks away, going toward a group of people.

I let out a deep breath. The worst isn't over yet.

I walk over to the DJ booth and ask the DJ if he can switch off the music for a couple of minutes and hand me the microphone. He smiles and says, "Of course, birthday girl". It's creepy that they all know who I am, yet I have no idea who any of them are. It sends a cold shiver through my whole body. I'll get to know them better soon, I guess.

"One, two, three, check?" I faux-test the microphone, trying to relax my thrumming nerves.

I hear some people laugh as they all gather on the dance floor in front of the DJ booth. Everybody is staring at me, and I feel my anxiety and fear start to build up. All these unknown eyes trained on me, waiting to hear what I have to say.

"Get on with it, birthday girl!" someone shouts.

I cringe internally. If one more person calls me that, I swear I will lose it.

"Uh, right. Hello, everyone. My apologies for the interruption. I have a quick announcement to make, and then you can get on with your... partying."

They all stand and stare at me. It is dead silent, and all I hear is my shallow breathing and rapid heartbeat. I feel my hands shaking, my foot tapping, the sweat forming on my upper lip, the heat on my face, the swirling thoughts in my head. I am so mortified I almost want to drop the microphone, run away, and hide from all these people. Away from this horrifying cult and their prying eyes, looking into my soul, examining my whole body.

"Alright." I take a shaky breath. I'm going to make it short—no dancing around the subject, no long speech, no stuttering. I take another deep breath as I see everybody's impatient faces. "I have recently come to a decision, and I thought it would be appropriate to announce it at my birthday party. With all of you gathered here," I say emotionlessly, trying to hide my voice's shakiness, uneasiness, and dread.

"Spit it out, Talia," Beth yells from the front. "I want to sing karaoke."

What follows are agreeable hums and nods. They turn their attention back to me after a second of murmurs.

I take one final deep breath and close my eyes, not wanting to make eye contact with anyone as I say this. This is the one of the hardest things I've ever had to do, and it takes every last ounce of strength and courage to keep going. I push aside my feelings of self-love, reasoning, survival, and pride. I push them far away into the abyss and leave myself a blank slate. I don't need them anymore. After I say this, I don't need them. I don't need anything. I will be empty—everything drained from my body. Only a mold left of what used to be. Nothing more than the shape of a human, with a hallow inside. Nothing more than a physical presence.

I keep my eyes closed as I push everything down into the abyss and fall away into nothingness. Forever falling now and never to return.

My whole body tries to fight me. as I breathlessly spit out the words—

"I agree to be part of your organization."

Chapter 3.0

"THREE WEEKS OF TRAINING—DONE!" Beth exclaims, bouncing on her toes. "I still can't believe you agreed to join. I mean, I knew you would eventually, but I'm so happy!" For the past few weeks, Beth has been practically vibrating with excitement and enthusiastically shouting every word in my face.

These past three weeks have been my "training" to become a full-fledged member of this cult—or uh, *organization*. Today is the first time in about two months that I get to step outside. Outside, as in *outside*—fresh air, the world beyond these walls. To say I'm anxious would be an understatement. Of course, five other members will be going with me, and Luke has designated himself as my personal bodyguard—"to make sure nothing happens to you" (direct quote), which really means "to keep you from escaping."

Training has been... interesting, to put it mildly. There isn't a specific word I can use to describe it. It mainly consisted of learning the history of the organization and self-defense/combat skills. I also had to learn a whole script of how to talk people into going along with my efforts to save them. In other words, I had to learn how to trick people into going along with the organization's delusional ideas.

"Yeah," I respond while stirring the pasta.

"Are you ready to go out into the real world for the first time in forever?" Beth inquires.

"Sure." I shrug. "Haven't you been outside?"

Beth shakes her head, her face reflecting sadness. "Unfortunately, I was assigned a high position as soon as I joined. Which means I'm more of a desk person. But I don't get to do much. Sometimes, I end up doing paperwork, but it honestly feels pointless. I don't feel as important as they claim I am." She looks severely disappointed. However, in a few seconds, her face soon lights up again. "But I'm super excited for you to tell me all about it! I mean, I don't even know what's up there and what they do when they go out there. So, like, you have to tell me everything. Remember every detail. I will be waiting. Is the pasta almost ready?"

"Yeah, like two more minutes." I sigh and stop stirring, getting the sauce out of the fridge.

"Where is Luke, anyway? What time are you supposed to be leaving?"

"He said at three p.m. It's two-thirty right now. So I guess I have to eat quickly." I sigh again and turn the stove off, draining the water from the pot and stirring in the sauce.

"I can't believe you made me chicken parmesan with pasta. You are an amazing sister." Beth grins while setting the table.

"I'm okay." I smile.

"The bestest. I do miss Trev, though. He is definitely the superior sibling."

I laugh. "Tell me about it."

"Rude bitch." Beth gives me a mock glare, her lips twitching with a smile.

"Looooove youuuu," I drawl out, with a genuine laugh—my first genuine laugh in a while.

"I miss Trev," Beth repeats with a sad sigh.

I ignore her comment and serve the pasta. "I have less than fifteen minutes to finish eating. And I still have to pack my to-go bag," I stress instead.

"Right, right. Let's get to it." Beth starts on her food.

Beth is slowly starting to gain some weight and essence back. She doesn't look deathly anymore, and her appetite has definitely drastically increased. I wonder what the change has been, but I won't question it. I'm just happy that she is eating and looking much healthier. I hope that this will be permanent. Furthermore, I hope that it progresses into even better changes. I want my sister back.

"This is probably one of the best meals I have ever had," Beth chirps contently while rubbing her stomach. "Seriously, I'm pregnant from how good this was."

"I'm glad." I gather our plates and set them in the sink, planning to wash them later. "Alright, I'm running late, so I have to hurry." I dash back upstairs to grab the supplies Luke said I might need: bug spray, toiletries, a mini umbrella, extra clothes, and a few other things. I haphazardly stuff everything into the backpack he gave me and rush downstairs, racing down the dimly lit hallway, past the kitchen, through the beige steel door, into the purple room, and finally stop by the third steel door. I haven't earned the privilege to open this one yet. Luke is already standing there, scowling at me.

I have gained enough status for the beige steel kitchen door to always be open into the purple room, but I don't yet have enough privilege to move freely around the underground complex as Beth does. I wonder why Beth has never tried escaping with the freedom she is given. I would have tried millions of times already. But whenever I bring it up, she shushes me or walks away without another word. And the topic is closed. I always wonder what horrible things have happened to her before I got here to make her this way. It terrifies me.

"Late," Luke remarks. "Everybody else already went up."

I roll my eyes. "I'm like two minutes late. All of you are super uptight and need to chill."

"Have you learned nothing in training?"

I sigh and wonder how my pride has made it out of the box that's hidden deep inside my inner abyss. It's not supposed to come around anymore. It doesn't belong here, in this shell of a body. I'm not supposed to be feeling things, especially not pride. I lost that freedom when I agreed to be here voluntarily. "I'm sorry. I really am. I'm sorry for letting everyone down. I promise I will be early next time," I say in an almost robotic voice. I try to add sympathy to my tone so that he doesn't suspect anything.

"It's okay, Talia. This is your first trip. I was just trying to give you a hard time. Nobody is mad." Luke smiles lightly and holds the steel door open for me. "You've packed everything I told you, right?"

I nod.

"Use words," Luke requests sternly. "When we're out there, sometimes I might not see your little nods or shakes, which could have a detrimental impact. Life or death. Remember to use words."

"Yes," I reply.

"Good." He smirks. Obviously overwhelmed with even this slight amount of power over me.

I hated training. It was so stupid, and most of it was common sense: "Don't get caught," "always stay together," "never give up information about the organization, no matter what," "use words to communicate, not gestures," etc., etc. Dumb.

"I'm sure you know that a lot of the people in our organization do not trust you yet," Luke states as we walk down one of the numerous hallways.

"I'm well aware," I respond.

It's a bit disappointing that they do not trust me yet. But it's also completely understandable. To be fair, I don't trust them either. So why would I be mad they didn't trust me (yet)? I'm entirely okay with proving myself until they do.

"It's going to take some time." Luke uses his kind, caring voice as he speaks. I despise when he does that. It makes my blood boil.

I feel anxiety rise in my chest as we approach a staircase leading to what I assume is the outside—the world I haven't seen in roughly two months.

Today is March ninth. Three weeks and two days have gone by since my birthday. It's hard to believe I've been down here this long. I got captured on January tenth, just a week after the winter term began. At this point, I'm never going to catch up on schoolwork. It's weird that I'm thinking about schoolwork. Almost funny. Almost. Because in reality, it's probable that I'll never get out of here, never graduate, never go to college, never get a job, and never live the life I imagined. And yet, here I am, thinking about schoolwork. Tragic.

"What are you thinking about?" Luke asks as we walk up the steps.

I give him a look that says *"don't even start with me right now"*.

He nods. "I just want to make sure you are focused. We need to focus and not have our heads up in the clouds. So get your shit together," he says rather harshly.

Ah, yes, another rule from training: "always stay focused". As I said, stupid.

"I am focused. Don't you worry," I respond, my voice dripping with bitterness.

Shove it all down, Talia. He is the boss. You have to listen to him. Shove it all down, down into the abyss.

So I do. And I hope Luke didn't catch my bitter tone.

Thankfully, he didn't. Or he chooses to let this one slide. We silently walk up the seemingly endless stairs and finally reach a massive steel door. It's even bigger than all the ones down below.

My heart is racing.

Will I get to see sunlight? Will I get to breathe in fresh air? Will I get to feel the chill and breeze of early March? Will I get to see the trees and birds and other wilderness? It all seems overwhelming and I start getting dizzy.

I almost fall over, but the voice inside my head screams at me.

Focus.

Focus.

You need their trust. Do not show signs of weakness. You are a soldier.

Focus.

So I do.

· · · · · · · · · · ·

"Hey!" A guy struts up next to me as the group walks in a straight line through the woods.

Once Luke and I exited the underground prison, the fresh air and sunlight hit me like never before. I choked, blinking against the brightness, feeling blinded for almost five minutes before I managed to regain my composure. The air is brisk, but the sun is brilliantly bright today. It's just sometimes hard to see it through the thick trees. I have no idea where we're going, but one of the older members is leading the way. I guess I'll find out when we get there. It's not like I have a say in anything anyway.

"Hi?" I frown, looking over at this guy who just appeared next to me. I quickly turn my head back around to stare straight in front of me. Who is this dude, and why is he talking to me?

"I'm Alex," he continues with a huge, unsettling smile.

"Talia," I respond. I'm hoping he stops talking to me now, but I predict he won't.

"Is this your first time going out? I remember when it was my first time. It was a month after I was saved and after I passed training, of course. I've been part of the organization for about a year now. It's really great. I get to go out almost every week now. They've given me more responsibilities, and I'm hoping to become a group leader soon," he rambles on and on.

I side-eye him briefly, without turning my head, and don't respond. What could I possibly say?

"You're not too talkative, are you?" he asks, still with that stupid grin.

I shake my head. He needs to stop talking. I see Luke glance back at me from the front, and he narrows his eyes slightly as he sees the guy next to me. I shift my backpack uneasily and maintain eye contact until Luke turns his head back to the front.

"Is Luke your friend?" the Alex guy asks.

"No."

I have a feeling he doesn't hear me as he continues speaking without missing a beat, "He's a nice guy. A little scary sometimes. A real intense vibe. Don't think I didn't notice the glare I just received from him. But it's probably just because I'm talking to you. You're not dating him, are you?"

I stop in my tracks and whip my head sharply toward him.

Alex also stops, and the smile falls off his face as he watches my angered expression.

"Absolutely not. Never say that again. Never speak those words," I snap.

Alex seems taken aback by my tone. "Oh, I-I'm, um, s-sorry," he stutters. "I didn't think..."

I glance at the group in front of us. They didn't notice us stopping since I was walking toward the back. They're walking slowly, so I jog a few steps and catch up. Alex does the same, and trudges next to me. I can see him in my peripheral vision, glancing at me sideways—trying to be inconspicuous—every few seconds.

"What do you want?" I finally ask, sighing heavily and still not looking at him.

I see him fully turn his head toward me, and a small smile starts to form on his face again. "I was hoping we could be friends," is all he says.

"Why?" I ask, frowning.

"Well..." he trails off, scratching the back of his head. "It doesn't seem like you have too many friends here, and I—I don't mean this in an offensive way at all, by the way. I don't have many friends here either. Most people are much older than me, or just old in general. So, like, when you came around, I thought maybe we could become friends. You just turned eighteen, right? I'm nineteen, so you're closer to my age than anyone."

"Luke is nineteen, and my sister is almost nineteen," I state. I don't know why I felt the need to point that out, but this Alex guy is irking me.

"Yeah, but your sister has kind of a different position than anyone else. She doesn't really get to go out on trips, and when she attends meetings, she sits in the front because she is the secretary and has to take notes. And Luke is... well, like I said, he scares me a bit. I don't mean that in a bad way—and also, his dad is the leader of the organization, so it's not like I could ever by friends with him. I don't know if that makes sense."

"It doesn't," I respond shortly. However, it does make sense to me. I get it. I wouldn't want to be friends with Luke either.

The guy sighs. "I just thought it would be nice to have a friend around here. Not everybody is super friendly, and it doesn't hurt to have someone to talk to and help out with stuff."

I finally turn my head around to look at him. "Look, Alex, is it...?" I trail off. He nods. "Yeah, Alex, look, I—well, I don't really think I need friends. I'm just—" I can't tell him about my plan to escape, can I? "I'm not a very social person, and I don't think I can be of much help to you," I finish.

Alex's big smile returns. "That's okay! You don't need to be social to have friends, Talia. I can still be your friend, and I wouldn't need or want anything in return. Friends don't expect any favors or help. It's more of a mutual respect and trust that builds a friendship. Friendship isn't built on keeping score." He shrugs. "I think we can still be friends, that's all I mean. Of course, only if you want to. And we don't have to be friends right away because, like I said, friendship is something that needs to be built."

This guy sure knows how to ramble on and on about nothing.

However, at this point, I don't think I can get rid of him easily. I give him a tight smile. "Sure."

"Fantastic!" he exclaims loudly, making me slightly flinch.

I look toward the front of the group and see Luke turn back again and give me a glare. What is his problem? Am I not allowed to speak with other people?

"Talia, do you mind coming up to the front? I would like to brief you on what we will be doing today," Luke semi-shouts to me.

"Looks like duty calls." Alex shrugs, still with the huge smile plastered on his face.

"Right." I nod and walk faster to catch up with Luke. "What," I say as I come up to him.

"I see you made some new friends," Luke says in a frighteningly low and deep voice.

I frown. "Is that a problem?"

He purses his lips before shaking his head. "Of course not. I want you to have friends in the organization. I encourage it. It'll make the transition and journey much better for you. Friends are always great," he says, still with a slight edge to his tone.

"Okay..." I frown deeper. "You wanted to brief me about today?" I try to change the odd subject. I'm really not trying to make friends with anybody here.

"Right, yes." Luke shakes his head again. "Today, we are going to one of our safe spots. Each group in each region has safe spots assigned to them. You are obviously a part of this group. My group. Our safe spot is a little outside of Trenton. So we'll walk for a little while until we reach our car, and then make the trip from there. A safe spot is a place where our scouts take the people they saved before these people get to come to the complex and join us. We will be making this trip every week, and everybody has responsibilities. I haven't decided where you will fit in yet, but for now, just stay by my side and observe. Ask me any questions, and keep an eye out for how things are done. And if you see anything out of order, let me know. You'll be like my right-hand gal, for now."

What a long-ass speech with little content. I swallow my disgust from having to be around Luke for such long periods of time, before responding, "Alright then."

This is going to be much more challenging than I had presumed.

Chapter 3.1

"So, when we get there, you have to be very careful and not spook them. These are vulnerable victims," Luke says as we walk toward the "safe spot".

I try my hardest not to roll my eyes.

Yes, these are vulnerable victims, that I can agree on. But the reasoning behind *why* they are vulnerable victims is where Luke and my opinions diverge.

"I hope you are taking all of this seriously because it is. These are actual people who have been through various traumas. You need to try to find the empathy inside you, as hard as that might be."

I bite my lip to prevent a scowl from forming on my face.

Yes, all these people have been through traumas. And there might even have been multiple traumas throughout their lives. But the most prominent trauma for them right now, in my opinion, is that they got kidnapped by a cult. Understand

And I *do* have empathy. Loads of it, for that matter. Not that Luke would know anything about it. He's given me no reason to empathize with him. Empathy comes from understanding, and I don't understand his or the organization's actions. I can empathize with the victims because I know what it's like to be terrified, to feel trapped. But I won't sympathize with the organization's "cause."

"I need to know we are on the same page," Luke urges.

"Of course." I nod tightly.

Someone help me.

I hold my breath as we keep walking to the safe spot. I can't help the knot in my stomach as we get closer. I can only imagine what these poor people are going through. I've been through some of it, although I'm sure this is much worse. Where are they even being kept? What is this "safe spot"? What must they be feeling?

"Be careful. They could try to attack you. It has happened before. They are vulnerable and frightened. Keep your eyes open," Luke continues with his tedious lecture.

I actually do roll my eyes this time. "Really? Because I was planning on keeping them closed," I reply sarcastically.

Shit.

Bad, Talia. Bad.

Push those emotions down into the abyss. Be empty. Be nothing.

Luke raises an eyebrow in amusement. Thank god he isn't mad, only amused. I can deal with amusement.

"Sorry," I simply say.

He shrugs and nods. "Watch yourself," he warns, but it's more lighthearted than anything.

I shudder involuntarily as we approach a lonely storage yard. Storage unit after storage unit jammed next to each other. It looks ghostly, like a graveyard. A graveyard full of metal and lost souls. It looks massive, yet miniscule. Vast yet cramped. It's hard to explain. Maybe it's my own emotions coming to the surface as I examine the storage units before me. They are all the same. Yet, each one is different. Each one has a story and secrets hidden within.

In some way, storage units remind me of people. On the surface, we all look the same. Though we may differ in color (whether it be hair, eyes, or skin), at our core we're all the same. Sure, some of us have been chipped away over the years and have more scratches, but we're all still human. Inside, we all share the same basic structure:

organs, cells, blood. Some people are bigger, some are smaller—like storage units.

However, once you really look into the soul and mind of someone. Once you open the door, *that's* when you see the real distinctions. All the previously hidden secrets inside are revealed. Some have big secrets, some have small ones, but we all have them. Maybe it's just one secret, just a solitary box in the storage unit. The uniqueness is hidden within, both with people and storage units.

Although it's more than just opening a storage unit door. You have to dig deeper—look inside the boxes, sift through the contents, and make sense of what you've found. The same goes for people. It's not simply about ripping open a body and peeking inside. It's about peeling back layers, digging deep into the mind, into the soul—that's where you uncover the true uniqueness. And similar to a storage unit, not everyone is privy to what hides within.

And yes, you can always dye your hair and wear different clothes, just like you can paint a storage unit and decorate it to your liking. But at the end of the day, it's still a storage unit. It might catch someone's eye more than the others, and it might get more attention and admiration, but it's still simply a storage unit—same as the others.

I don't know if any of that makes sense, but storage units remind me of people.

"Unit eighty-eight," Luke speaks, shocking me out of my thoughts.

Is that where they keep their victims? I shudder, venom pulsing through my veins. Maybe I shouldn't be so judgmental. I'm one of the bad guys now. I'm part of the problem. I'm part of the reason these innocent people are here, hidden in a storage unit. They all look the same, yet one of them hides a terrifying secret.

"Can I stay behind?" I ask. Quietly. Mostly to myself. I'm not sure if he even hears me.

I don't want to go to Unit 88. Right now, Unit 88 is like any other unit. I don't want to open it. I don't want to find out its secrets. I want to keep it the same as every other unit. It's like finding out that a random person you're sitting next to on the subway is a serial killer. Before, it was simply a person sitting next to you. And now, you're thinking he might murder you.

Theoretically, I know there is a possibility that I have encountered a serial killer. Same as I theoretically know there are currently innocent victims in Unit 88. I guess my point is I'd simply prefer to live in the safe denial. At least when it comes to this.

"No," Luke responds plainly. "You're coming in. You have to learn." With that, he starts walking forward without another glance in my direction.

After closing my eyes for a few seconds and taking a deep breath, I re-open my eyes (taking Luke's advice—see, I can follow orders) and follow him into the wretched (un)known.

· · · · · · · · · ·

"You have to tell me everything. Oh my god, this is so exciting. Please, please, sit down… I made dinner. Tell me everything," Beth exclaims at the top of her lungs and lunches toward me as I enter the kitchen.

"Honestly, Beth. It's three a.m., and I am tired. I had a rough day. Can we please not do this right now? I want to go upstairs and sleep," I reply with a yawn. "Forever, preferably," I add, muttering to myself.

"Uh, yeah, sure. I guess. I understand you had an overwhelming day. I'm just so excited to hear the details. Did you see any of the people who got saved? Did they come here with you? Where are th—"

"Can you please leave your questions for tomorrow and let me go to sleep right now?" I snap.

"Uh... sure? Go ahead." Beth steps aside from the door and lets me through. "Good night and sweet dreams."

"Night," I reply with a tight smile and a nod before I enter the all-too-familiar, dimly lit, musty hallway. Oh, how I've missed this hallway, especially after the day I've had. It feels almost homey now—the smell, the look, the feel—everything is recognizable to me. I tried to fight it, but this is my home-base now for however long.

I get up to my room and lie down in bed without taking off my dirty clothes. I couldn't care less about that. As gross as it sounds.

"You okay?" I hear a voice from the door.

Fucking Luke.

I don't move from the bed, continuing to stare at the ceiling and trying to disassociate from the world. From this room. I wish I could go to my Sevritulem place.

"Beth told me you flipped out on her," Luke continues. Why does he never stop? Why does he never understand when to leave? Why does he insist on torturing me with his conversations until I break?

"Can you leave? I want to sleep," I decide to answer because he won't leave until I do. I might as well get this over with as soon as possible.

"Can we discuss today?" he whispers.

"Can we discuss today tomorrow?" I counter.

"Talia. This is serious."

"Please, leave me alone." I turn to my right side and curl in on myself, squeezing my eyes shut and willing the overpowering thoughts to fall into the abyss. Unfortunately, I cannot control everything that falls into the abyss. I can crowd down my emotions, feelings, and actions, but not my thoughts. They soak my brain and drown my peacefulness. They bounce around like a five-year-old in a bouncy-castle and refuse to leave even when I deflate. Even when my whole body is shutting down, the thoughts refuse to leave me alone.

"Alright. Tomorrow, then," Luke finally agrees.

Thoughts swarm me like bees in a beehive as I hear Luke descending the ladder.

One tear. Two tear. Three tear. Four tear.

Stop. You are strong. You are better than this. You can handle it.

I try to push away the thoughts and listen to the voice. But the voice is so far away and hard to focus on. It's like being in Times Square during New Year's and trying to find someone calling your name. The voice feels like it is getting farther and farther away, no matter how hard I try to run toward it.

You are strong.

No, I'm not. The thoughts overpower the voice once and for all.

I fall into a restless sleep. The nightmares revolve around my thoughts. So, I guess they aren't nightmares at all. They are a representation of my reality in a slightly alternate—but no less terrifying—way.

· · · ● · ● · · ·

"Rise your beautiful self, and let yourself shine like the morning sun of a summer's day," Beth sing-songs as she climbs up to my room.

"I didn't know you started to experiment with drugs," I grumble sleepily. Well, not sleepily, more like exhaustedly. I got maybe two hours of sleep.

"What?" Beth questions, sounding confused yet still somehow chipper.

"Nothing."

I hear Beth pause at the top of the ladder. "Oh, well, anyway. I want to hear all about yesterday, and I made breakfast. Luke said he will join us today," Beth continues with her cheery demeanor.

"Read the rotten room, Beth. I'm not in the mood, and I'm not hungry. What time is it anyway?" I mutter, hiding under the duvet.

"It's one in the afternoon, sweet sister. Get up." Finally, I detect a hint of ridicule in her voice. Thank god. "If you're not hungry, you can just sit at the table while Luke and I eat. We've been waiting for you to wake up since eight in the morning."

"You were waiting for me to have breakfast?"

"Yes. I like to eat as a family..." Beth trails off. Realizing her mistake, I assume. "Uhm..." She coughs and clears her throat. "Please get down to the kitchen in ten minutes. I'm starving." I hear her going back down the ladder.

Sigh.

Ad astra per aspera.

Sighing again, I get up from bed, feeling the discomfort from sleeping all curled up and restless in yesterday's filthy clothes, no less.

I head downstairs to the bathroom to shower quickly and wash away yesterday's dirt and guilt. The dirt comes off easily, but unsurprisingly, it doesn't make me feel cleaner. I throw my hair up in a bun, not even glancing in the mirror. I know I'm a wreck, there's no need to see it. A sweatshirt and sweatpants are all I can muster before I trudge to the kitchen.

· · · · ● ● ● ● · · ·

All the days seem to bleed together lately.

It's been a week since I've gone on that diminutive expedition into the outside world of horror, and I refuse to go again. Luke doesn't push it. He says it's understandable that I need time. He says the first time seeing how it is, is very hard. He says he was the same way his first time. I find it hard to believe.

It's not like it's any better down here, in the underground world of horror. But at least I can pretend down here. At least down here, I don't have to face anyone, and I can pretend to be in my own world. Alone. Alone is better.

Beth comes up sometimes, bringing food, drinks, gossip, and games. However, I don't feel like participating in her cheerful charade anymore. It's exhausting, and frankly, it's also disturbing.

I've concluded that they must be drugging her. It is the only logical explanation. I might be sounding insane right now, all conspiracy-ridden and hollow-feeling inside. Which is precisely why I can't understand why Beth is acting the way she is. Like nothing is wrong. Like everything is dandy. Up in the clouds, rainbows and butterflies, fantastic. It's sick. They must be drugging her.

"Writing in your diary again?" Luke's voice drifts up the ladder, followed by his footsteps.

I raise my eyes to glare at him as he comes up. "Well, I did ask for one for a reason."

Yes, I asked for a diary—or a journal, whatever you prefer to call it—so that I can write down my thoughts and not completely lose my mind in this hellhole.

"I still don't understand why you specifically asked for this one. It's not like anybody is going to go snooping around your room and reading your diary."

Yes, I asked for one with a lock that opens only with a combination of my choosing. It feels safer in this kind of environment. It's true what they say: "Better safe than sorry." And I'm sure I would be sorry if anyone reads this diary since I would most likely end up like my dad.

"Feels safer this way," I respond truthfully.

"Hmm." He nods and takes a seat on the chair across the room. "Having a lot of thoughts lately? You know, some say that it's good to talk it out."

"Yes, I've heard of that," I say, without looking up from the page.

There's a pause. "Well, I'm here."

I opt out of glaring this time around and simply roll my eyes. "Yes, you are."

"Here to talk, or chat, or just listen," he continues.

"Not interested. But thanks."

More silence follows. I hear Luke get out his crossword (or Sudoku), though I don't hear him open it.

"You know..." he starts.

I close my eyes and take a deep breath. I know something stupid is about to follow.

"What is it is now?" I ask, trying—and failing—not to sound irritated.

"This guy, Alec, I think his name is. He's been asking about you. Asking people, asking me, asking Beth. Asking around about you, you know?"

I falter and finally look up at Luke. He is staring intently at me with an indiscernible expression.

"You mean Alex?"

"Right. Alex."

"What's he been asking?"

"Well, you know, just asking about you. How you are, why you aren't around, why you haven't been coming outside anymore, where you've been staying. Stuff like that," Luke's expression stays stone-still and unidentifiable.

"Okay?" I give him a confused look. What is his point in telling me all of this?

"It just looks to me that he took an interest in you."

"So?"

"So? Are you—I mean, did you—are you interested?"

"No."

As if I have time to think about some random kid named Alex, who I met once, while I'm stuck being part of a cult living in an underground complex somewhere in the woods of New Jersey.

"Okay, well, he seems to want to hang out with you or something."

"Okay, so? Why are you telling me this?" I ask. This conversation is odd, even by Luke's standards.

"I just thought it was strange. You just met him that one time, right? I don't know. I thought you would like to know." Luke shrugs nonchalantly, finally looking down at his crossword.

"I don't care about any of that."

"Alright then, good."

"Good?" I question.

"Yeah, I meant just like... okay, cool. Just letting you know."

"Okay..." I put down my journal and lock it. "I'm going to go make myself a sandwich, and you... you can stay up here and keep doing whatever." I stand up from my bed and make my way to the ladder.

Luke doesn't say anything or make any moves. As I descend the ladder, I hear him sigh loudly, followed by the rustle of paper.

I walk into the kitchen and see Beth making food.

"Hey, what are you making?" I ask, walking toward her.

She jumps a little and turns around. "Oh, hey, you scared me. I'm making a grilled cheese. You want one?"

"Sure, sounds good." I sit at the table and put my feet up on the chair next to me. "I was also going to ask you something if you don't mind."

"Of course, I don't mind. What's up?"

"I was going to ask where people usually hang out around here. Or, like, *do* people hang out around here? Is there a place or room where people spend time? Like a rec room or something?"

Beth pauses and gives me a peculiar look, but she's smiling softly. "Yeah, there is the arcade place we went to a while back. A lot of people hang out there. There is also another room with pool, darts, and fun board games. I can take you there after lunch?"

"Oh, I was just asking. You know, for future reference."

"Come on! It'll be fun. And I forgot to tell you this, but this guy named Alex has been asking about you for the past couple of days. He's cute, and I'm sure he'll be there. By the way, you never told me you met a cute guy. He seems to be interested in you." Beth wiggles her eyebrows, grin widening.

"So I keep hearing," I mutter.

"What do you mean?" Beth asks, turning away from me to get the cheese out of the fridge.

"Luke mentioned that Alex asked him about me," I say, standing up and going to sit by the TV. "What do you want to watch?" I change the subject.

"I'm really into this show called *The Good Place* right now. If you want to watch, I'm only on episode three."

"I'm not going to start watching a new show from episode three. Let's just watch *New Girl*." I find a random episode and click play.

Beth finishes making the grilled cheeses and sets the plates in front of us, before plopping herself down next to me on the couch.

"Oh, I love this episode!" Beth exclaims as she settles down.

I grab my plate and start eating my sandwich as the theme song begins to play.

Honestly, I have no idea what I'm doing anymore. I'm sitting here, eating a grilled cheese, watching a random episode of *New Girl*, acting as if everything is normal. But nothing is normal. I'm a prisoner in an underground hellhole and part of a cult now. How fucked up is my life? And here I am, sitting comfortably on a couch next to my—also prisoner and part of a cult—sister. And my sister is laughing, telling jokes, gossiping, acting cheery and peachy.

What even is "normal"? I looked it up: *conforming to a standard; usual, typical, or expected.* The problem I have with this definition is the word *conforming*. Because yes, living down here has become the standard. It's usual now. It's typical. I know what to expect each day. I spend my days in my room alone, or with Beth, or with Luke. But *conforming*? That's what I take issue with. I don't want to conform to this life. I won't. So, no, I will not act normal. I won't *be* normal—not in this place. I will not conform to this hellhole or these dreadful people.

"...have fun?" I hear Beth ask.

I turn around and focus on her. "Huh? What?" I ask, confused.

"I said, are you ready to go have fun?" Beth asks in her cheerful and excited voice.

"Uh, yeah, sure. I guess?" I respond. Is it really fun, or is it coping?

"I'm so excited you're finally going to meet everyone! This is great. You're finally assimilating. I'm so happy! I swear to you, it'll be great. The people here are actually very nice, and I'm sure you'll get along with them," Beth says, leaping up from the couch and running to put our plates in the sink.

I restrain my eye roll. I have decided to deal with the fact that Beth has lost her mind, but it's still too much sometimes. There is no other explanation for why she would be acting this way. They're brainwashing and drugging her. That is the only logical explanation.

"Alright, are you ready to go?" Beth looks at me, practically jumping up and down.

"Sure. Let's do this," I say, slowly and unsurely standing up from the couch.

I'm not exactly comfortable leaving the perceived safety of my little, ugly, dimly lit hallway—the one nobody ever visits. It's not safe anywhere down here, but it feels safer in this small corner of the underground where it's just me, Beth, and sometimes Luke.

No, I don't feel safe around Luke. I don't trust him. I don't like him. I barely tolerate him. But he's not much of a threat anymore. I know he won't physically harm me—or at least, I hope he won't. He hasn't shown any signs of physical violence so far. So leaving this "safe space" feels like a risk. And not the thrilling kind. Walking into the purple room feels okay, but the closer we get to the steel door on the other side, the more my anxiety spikes.

Push it down. Don't feel. You are part of the organization now. As long as you don't do anything stupid, they will not hurt you.

Then why the hell am I exceedingly petrified?

Chapter 3.2

"Talia?!" someone calls out in surprise as we enter the recreation room. It's almost comical how much I'm shaking and sweating. I have put so much effort into avoiding these people—keeping to myself, not talking or interacting with them. Yet here I am, about to spend time with criminals. Yes, criminals. Whether they're kidnappers, accomplices, or just bystanders, they're all complicit in this cult's illegal activities. Every last one of them.

There's still so much I don't know. How have they not been caught? Why aren't we seeing more news coverage about people disappearing? Is there any news about me? The coverage of Beth's and Dad's disappearances stopped about a month after they were taken. How are these people getting away with it? How has no one connected the dots?

Or maybe some of them have been caught and are staying silent. Or the authorities are keeping quiet about it. Are the authorities even aware of this cult? Fuck the authorities. They've done nothing for my family. But I have to believe they're looking for me. I have so many questions—most of which will probably remain unanswered. Maybe it isn't so bad that I'm here. Perhaps I can gather some inside information to help me escape. That is, if I survive long enough.

"Hi," I say flatly, trying to fake a smile. It comes out as more of a grimace due to my currently high anxiety levels and overall elevated stress. I do a small wave, which could not be more awkward. All the people in the room stare at Beth and me as we make our way over to an empty table.

"Board game? Chess?" Beth asks as I sit and wipe my palms on my leggings. I uncomfortably take a look around and see everybody still staring. Not a single familiar or friendly face. Not that I expected one.

"Chess," I respond. I haven't played in a while. Dad taught Trevor, Beth, and me when we were just kids; we were all obsessed with it. I never figured out if we were actually any good, but I suppose I was good enough to win almost every time.

"Ah, someone is looking to reclaim her title as Chess Queen." Beth giggles.

"Oh, I don't think I ever lost that title, Pawn." I smirk.

"I'm a pawn? Hah! As if. You wish you were as good as me. I am definitely the King," Beth replies loudly as she goes over to the cupboard and gets the chess board from one of the top shelves.

"I guess we'll find out soon." I laugh at her absurdity.

"Talia?" I hear a quiet, yet chirpy, voice come from the door we just entered through.

I recognize the voice to be Alex's.

Shit.

Isn't this kind of why I came here, though? He's been asking about me. I was intrigued. I don't know. Now I want to leave. Shit.

"Talia?" he asks again, closer this time.

"Alex," I finally respond, turning my head around to look at him.

He's smiling his whole face off as if he is overjoyed. It's slightly disturbing and causes a flicker of annoyance in me.

"It's so cool that you're here! I've actually been asking around about where you've been hiding out. But now you're here! Are you here with Beth or Luke?" he asks, standing near the table now.

"Beth," I reply. Did he not just see or hear her?

"Ah, gotcha. Sister finally dragged you out of your hiding place." Alex keeps smiling.

"I wasn't hiding. I prefer to stay in my room. I prefer peace and quiet," I say a bit defensively.

"That's okay. I like peace and quiet too sometimes. But it is nice to, you know, be social. Spend some time with other people. It's good for your health," Alex says.

"My health?"

"Yeah. Emotional health, mental health, even physical health, I would say. You have to spend time with other people sometimes."

"For my health?" I smile slightly and then try to bite my inner check to prevent it.

"Yep. Maybe you can try coming here a couple of times a week? For some interaction and human contact. Some gossip, some games, some socializing." Alex shrugs, still with that stupid smile on his face.

I nod. I think I've had enough "socializing" for the day.

Beth finally comes over to the table. I could see her purposefully staying away from the corner of my eye. She was hanging out by the shelves, chessboard in her hands.

"Hey, Alex," she says, sitting down across from me. "I would invite you to play a game with us, but I'm afraid chess is a strictly two-person game."

"No worries. I was going to go play some video games with Jeff anyway. Have fun with your... chess," he says, sounding unsure.

I wait for him to walk away from the table. What an odd guy.

"He's nice," Beth says. "And I'm pretty sure he has a crush on you."

I nod and start to arrange the chessboard.

"Do you like him?" Beth prods.

"He's... fine. I don't have an opinion. I don't know him," I respond dryly.

"Well, maybe you should get to know him," Beth says cheerily, with a hint of encouragement.

"Maybe," I end the conversation, and we start the game.

I will definitely not be coming back to this room. The atmosphere is too overwhelming and unpredictable.

· · · · ● · ● ● · · ·

Another five days pass, and Beth and I have been going to the rec room almost daily. We also go to the arcade if we get really bored.

I'm starting to recognize people now. I still don't know most of their names, and I have not talked to any of them, except for a "hi" or "how are you" here and there.

It hasn't been as terrible as I expected it to be. Nobody bothers us. We play chess and other board games, or we play arcade games and sing karaoke. It's not awful. It's not normal, either. It's not a routine. I would hate to have a *routine* in this place. That would mean I'm *conforming*, and I refuse to do that.

I still stay in my room most of the day—reading books, playing games on my phone, and writing about my thoughts and experiences in my diary. It's strangely comforting. But it's even stranger how comfortable I'm starting to feel around the other members of the organization. As I said, I haven't spoken to them yet, but Beth keeps me updated on gossip, so I probably know more about them than they assume. Maybe they know more about me than I assume. They probably do.

"You've been here every day this week." Alex comes up behind me as I'm playing *Pac-Man*. He's been trying to talk to me all week. It's currently Thursday. Avoiding him has been complicated since he always seems to find me. I think Beth has something to do with it.

"Yes, I have," I respond, concentrating on the game.

"I would hate to distract you from your game, but I wanted to chat for a bit." I can hear his smile through his voice.

"About what?" I ask. How do I say "I'm not interested" nicely?

"Just... chat. You know, like, talk? About... stuff?" he says hesitantly, sounding less cheery.

"Alright. Talk."

He's quiet for a while. So quiet that I think maybe he left. "Um," he starts. "Did you hear that Natasha is pregnant?"

"Beth told me a couple of days ago," I reply. Beth did tell me that Natasha is carrying another child. Let's hope this one isn't satanic. However, it is Natasha, so the child is most likely doomed (same as Luke). Poor little child. He didn't do anything to deserve to be carried in the womb of the devil. Surprisingly, though, I didn't freak out when Beth told me. I guess this shows how far I've come. Or how numb I've become.

"Aren't you—or *weren't* you friends with her?" Alex asks, coming closer and standing to my right. I can now see him out of the corner of my eye, but only if I focus on my peripheral vision extra hard.

"No," I respond coldly. I try not to think about those times when I loved Natasha and considered her a mother figure. It's definitely none of Alex's business.

"Oh, that's just what I heard..." Alex says more quietly, probably confused and taken aback by my bitter tone.

I stay silent. I'm not in the mood for this, especially after his previous question. And I really want to focus on my game and not be bothered. Why does he insist on staying around me? It's not as if I'm a joy to be around.

"I guess this is why nobody should listen to gossip. Sorry if I offended you by saying that," Alex says softly.

I lose the game and finally turn around to look at him. He looks upset, slightly scared, and nervous. I almost feel bad for making him feel this way.

"Look, it's fine. I just don't want to talk about it," I try in a nicer tone.

"I understand. I'm sorry. Let's talk about something else?" he offers.

"How about we go play another game? Together," I suggest uncertainly. I can't tell why, but Alex has a calming presence. Although his constant pestering frustrates me. It's a bit of a paradox. He doesn't make me feel on edge like everybody else around here does. I'm not anxious or angry around him, well, most of the time. He is certainly too clingy, but he seems nice enough. Why not give him a shot and hang out for a bit? It couldn't hurt (I hope).

"So," Alex starts. "Fancy going bowling?"

I let out a light laugh. "Sure."

Couldn't hurt.

· · · • · • · • · · ·

March twenty-fifth.

I have been hanging out with Alex a lot.

Mainly at the arcade.

He's nice. Fun. Funny (sometimes). Overall, a fairly good time.

Though, that's not the point.

It's March twenty-fifth. Two and a half months of being stuck in this underground snake pit. I still don't have a clear plan of how to get out, but I've realized I'll need some allies. I can't stay down here forever. Luke hasn't pushed me to go on any more "trips" to "save people," but maybe it's time to go again. It would give me the chance to meet more people, with the added bonus of getting outside. I've been looking too pale lately, almost sickly. I need some sunlight and some Vitamin D. The last thing I need is to get sick down here.

"So, have you given any thought to what we discussed yesterday?" Alex asks as he sits across from me, reading a book about humans. Literally, he is reading a book about how humanity came to be. He says it's actually interesting, and he's recommending that I read it next. For right now though, I'm reading this intense mystery novel and loving it.

"I was actually just thinking about it." I smile.

"Yeah? So you're thinking about going outside again? I know last time you got upset, but I think you were just scared because it was your first time outside in so long. It was probably a lot of pressure, too, and that one woman attacking you didn't help. You can stay a little behind this time, but I think it'll be good for you."

"She didn't *attack* me. She grabbed onto me and... sobbed. I think she was just scared," I defend, feeling a twinge of sympathy for the woman. I can't shake the feeling that it's partly my fault she ended up in that situation. I have no idea what happened to her or to any of the others. I feel awful. "But yeah, I think it's time I try again. Luke says it's fine if I don't go, but I feel bad about not doing my part for the organization. They give me food, shelter, all this stuff, and I just sit around doing nothing. I need to help out somehow, like everyone else." Lying has never been more challenging. I try to sound composed and sincere, to make it seem like I mean what I'm saying.

"Of course, I understand. But I don't think you need to feel obligated in any way. Mark is very understanding. And I'm sure Mark and Luke would never pressure you into anything you don't want to do. Take all the time you need." Alex smiles and gets back to his book.

"I think I'm ready. It's been over two weeks since I've been on that first trip. I can do it," I say. It seems more like I'm convincing myself rather than Alex. But, well, I need to convince myself as well. The first time was traumatizing enough, and I will have to live with that guilt forever. However, I need to do this again to get my life back. I need to get out of here.

"You'll be great! And I will be right there by your side," Alex says without looking up from his book.

"I hope you're more attentive when we're actually out there."

Alex laughs loudly while closing his book and looks straight at me, folding his hands on his lap. "I'm all ears... and eyes."

I roll my eyes half-heartedly, closing my book as well and looking at him. I think about it briefly, debating if I want to spend more time with Alex. Tilting my head slightly, still unsure, I ask, "You want to go see a movie? I heard they have a great theatre room here."

"Like a date?" Alex asks, smirking.

I frown. "A movie. No date."

He shakes his head and stands up from his seat. "Alright, let's go."

I also stand up, and we start making our way out of the rec room and to the theatre room.

"Oh, and by the way, I'm only going to watch it if it's a horror or thriller movie. I don't really enjoy watching anything else," Alex says as we walk down the hallway.

I smile slightly.

This could work out after all.

Chapter 3.3

"ROUND TWO. DO YOU feel ready?" Luke asks.

We stand by the door that leads to the outside. I was late again, so everybody is already waiting outside. It's so nerve-racking to go outside again, knowing what's waiting for me once we get to that storage yard. It's horrifying, honestly, and I don't know if I can go through it again.

But I have to.

I force a tight, closed-mouth, barely-there smile. "Yes, I'm ready," I respond.

"Alright. Talia, you got this. I believe in you." Luke smiles—his "genuine", kind smile, which pisses me off— and then he pushes the door open.

The flood of light and cool air rushes in like last time. But the first step outside feels different this time, warmer, which makes sense since it's late March now. I like it. The warmth of the air settles my nerves a little and puts me in a better mood. It's funny how something as simple as sunshine can make a difference. Seasonal depression is real. But no matter how much the March air soothes me, the heavy weight of dread never really lifts. Not while I'm here, surrounded by these people. I just need to make it through this day. One day at a time. I won't think about tomorrow until it comes.

However, as we tread down the path, Luke by my right side and Alex on my left, the anxiety deepens. This time, it's worse. Last time, I didn't know what to expect. I was an innocent victim going toward something that could possibly set me free. However, this time, I know what we are heading toward. I am an accomplice. I am willing to put myself and my plans of getting out of here before the other innocent victims. There is no way I can help these people who are currently trapped in a metal storage box. There is no way I can make them feel better because I can't even force myself to do so. Nevertheless, I am an accomplice to this crime. I *chose* to go this time around. No one forced me to go again; everybody understood my "freak out" last time. They accepted it. But I chose to go this time, knowing what is ahead—knowing the horror, distress, and fear that awaits.

"How are you feeling?" Alex comes up behind me and scares the living hell out of me. I hadn't noticed that he fell back and I was walking so quickly. On a side note, I wish people would stop asking me that particular question.

"Slightly anxious, but overall okay. How are you?" I ask, feigning pleasantry. Ales is a good guy, and I don't feel like hurting his feelings today. I'm choosing to be nice today. At least toward Alex.

"I'm great! I'm excited that I'm being trusted by the organization more and more lately. They have been so great to me," Alex responds excitedly.

I can't help my disgusted look at his words. Great job, Alex. A kidnapping and murderous cult is giving you more and more responsibilities. Maybe you'll get to kill someone on your own sometime soon! How exciting!

"That's great," I deadpan, fighting to revert my expression into something neutral.

Maybe even with a glint of a smile?

No, that's asking too much.

"I'm excited for new opportunities. I have been underground for so long, doing paperwork and shit, same as Beth. I'm happy they're letting me go outside now," Alex continues.

"Sounds great," I say, nodding, trying to tune him out while simultaneously staying engaged enough that he doesn't get suspicious.

"And you're feeling okay about today's trip?" he asks.

Trip—a grossly understated word for what we are doing.

"Sure." I shrug and force a tight-lipped smile so that he believes me.

"Good, good. I was getting worried about you," he says with a gleaming smile of his own. His smile seems genuine, but I'm glad my fake one did the trick.

"Worried?" I question.

"Yeah... you've been... well, kind of pale and thin lately?" It's almost as if he's asking me rather than making a statement.

"I'm always pale," I respond.

"And thinner. I worry a lot. The underground complex isn't the best place, and even over the past year, I have seen some people completely lose it," Alex continues. "Are you eating? You're not feeling sick or anything?"

I give him a strange look, which, by the look on his face, comes off as more of a glare. "I'm eating," I reply, probably too harshly. But it's also none of his business. Who asks something like that? First of all, it's rude. And secondly, I barely know this guy.

Okay, I haven't been eating as much. Sue me. I'm under a lot of stress, and the anxiety and mood swings I've been having have not been helping with my appetite. Sometimes, I skip breakfast. And lunch. And sometimes dinner. But I feel fine. Not eating for a couple of days won't kill me. I simply have had no appetite lately due to my current situation and location. Can anyone blame me? But I'm fine. I'm fine.

I'm fine.

"Good," Alex smiles. "I—I want you to be okay. You're a good person, and I enjoy spending time with you."

I frown slightly. This is getting too uncomfortable, too intense. But I force myself to participate in the conversation. Alex is a nice guy. I remind myself of that. "You're a nice person, Alex," I say, somehow feeling like my words came out wrong, too forced.

Alex smiles again, nonetheless. "Thanks," he replies cheerfully, adding a small skip to his step.

He holds on to the straps of his backpack as we go uphill in complete silence. I am thankful for the silence. Every once in a while, it looks like Alex is about to say something, but then he doesn't. He keeps a smile on his face and a bubbly exterior as we make our way to the van.

· · ● ● ● ● ● ● · ·

This time is worse than the first. I never imagined it could get worse, but somehow, as we approach that godforsaken storage unit, the weight in my chest intensifies. The knowledge of what's behind that door makes everything harder. The knowledge that I am an active participant in the kidnapping—and possibly, the torture—of innocent people. True, I don't know if they're all innocent; some of them might not be. But no one deserves this.

"You're shaking. Are you okay?" Alex asks, looking over at me with concern.

I glance down at my hands, which are trembling, and it's like my whole body is shaking in sync. Nausea churns in my stomach, and dizziness clouds my thoughts. I didn't eat breakfast. That must be why. But I can't faint right now. Not here, not in front of them. I push the feelings down, burying them deep in the abyss, like I always do. But it's an abyss—it can never overflow, no matter how much I shove inside. Right? Right. I suppress the tremors, swallow down the rising nausea, and force a smile.

"Yeah. Just a bit tired and nervous?" It comes out as more of a question rather than the confident statement I was going for.

"Nothing to be nervous about." Alex gives me his signature smile. "We're helping people, remember? This is a good thing."

"Right. Yeah," I respond, trying to sound convincing.

Push it all down, Talia. Down, down, down.

Luke stops at the front of the line and turns around to face everyone, raising his voice over the chatter. "Alright, listen up. We have a trickier situation this time around. One of our scouts saved a seven-year-old girl. She's in shock right now and tends to lash out if anyone gets too close. The scout managed to sedate her, but we need to proceed with caution. The saving mission didn't go exactly as planned, so her parents have already contacted the authorities. Plus, there are more people to handle than usual, thanks to some mishaps on the scout's end. So stay alert. Are we clear?"

His words hit me hard, and what really stings is the nonchalance in his voice, like this is just another ordinary day at work. I fight the urge to laugh, the absurdity of it all making me feel detached. Alex shoots me a quick, puzzled glance, while everyone else nods in agreement with Luke.

Luke's voice brightens as he wraps up. "Alright, let's get these people to safety, then we'll celebrate a birthday!" He pulls out the key to the storage unit, a twisted excitement in his eyes.

"Birthday?" I question in a whisper, looking over at Alex.

"It's Mark's birthday today. There is always a huge celebration that lasts for days sometimes. At least that's what I've heard," Alex whispers back as we hear Luke pull up the door to the storage unit.

I nod. My head starts spinning for two reasons. First of all, people start moving forward to enter the storage unit. Second of all, fuck, Mark's birthday would have been a perfect opportunity for an escape. Everybody partying and drunk? Fuck, fuck, fuck. Why have I been putting off my plans?

Stupid bitch.

Thanks. Alright, Talia, focus on one thing at a time. Right now, I have to get through this trip, and then I can think about the plan.

"Talia," Luke calls over to me. I notice Alex and I are the only ones left standing. Everybody else is already inside the unit. "Alex, please follow the rest. Talia, I need to speak with you," Luke continues.

Why does he feel the need to address me as if he is my parent? Every time he tries to speak with me, I feel like I'm a child who broke my mom's favorite vase, and now she's calling me downstairs because she found out about it. It also annoys me in general that he is making me stay back as if I am some kind of nuisance. Like he has to have "a talk" with me so that I don't act out or do anything stupid.

"Are you okay?" Alex makes sure again, without even turning to look at Luke.

"She will be fine, Alex. Go inside," Luke commands in a rather distastefully bitter and protective tone.

I don't say anything as they both stand and stare at me. Am I supposed to respond?

To hell with both. "I'm fine, Alex. Go ahead," I finally say while maintaining eye contact with Luke. He is standing rigidly, glaring at me and giving Alex enraged glances.

It feels like one of those standoffs in movies—the silent, tense stares, the anticipation. Good guy versus bad guy. It's all a bit comical, but I suppress the urge to laugh again. I can't decide if I'm the protagonist or the antagonist here. Luke is definitely not a protagonist in anyone's story. Maybe we're both antagonists. Maybe we both suck. Honestly, what's the point of all this? I can't figure out my stance in life anymore. I don't even *have* a life anymore. It's funny, I used to joke about dying—dark humor, I know—but maybe it's not a joke anymore. Ugh. No. I'm just kidding. Sort of.

The standoff feels surreal, and the silence stretches on. This is so bizarre. Is Luke planning to speak? Because Alex has already walked away, and we're still standing here.

I decide that I will be bold today. "So, why are you keeping me behind?" I ask.

Luke seems to blink and descend from his infuriated trance. His face settles back into its usual self, with the slight smirk and ulterior motives hidden behind every facial feature. "Right, yeah. I just wanted to see if you were okay with going inside? If you want to stay outside for today, that's fine too. I don't want you to be overwhelmed like last time. You can take it one trip at a time. I wanted to let you know that it's not necessary for you to help out inside right now if you are not comfortable," he says all in one breath. He then proceeds to examine my face, like he always does, for any signs of how I will respond.

I take a deep breath. Clearly, I'd rather stay out here and avoid a repeat of last time. I'd rather do anything than go back in there. But I've come this far, and I promised myself I'd push through. I owe it to these people—to regain their trust, to prove I'm still part of this. Lately, my mind has been in constant turmoil. On the one hand, I want to hold on to at least some of my beliefs and values. On the other hand, I told myself I'd push all that bullshit deep into the abyss, shut it out, stop caring. Turns out, it's not as easy as it sounds.

Why did I think I could easily let go of everything I've ever believed in and stood for? Lately, it's been a battle just to get out of bed, to function like a normal person. I've dealt with depressive episodes and self-harm before. I suppose most teenagers go through it at some point, to varying extents. But during these months in captivity, it's all gotten worse. The mental chaos has intensified, dulling everything else inside me. I have lost the will to do anything. I could sit and stare at a wall for hours, and the noise in my head never quiets unless someone stumbles upon me and forces their cheerfulness into my hollow shell. Empty, empty, empty. That's all I am now.

Nothingness.

"You've been silent for a while. I'm going to take that as you don't want to go in? So, you can just stay outside, and we'll all be out in about twenty minutes. You can be like a lookout." Luke shrugs, but I see some concern on his face.

It's funny how I can still discern emotions on other people's faces when all I feel is a whole lot of nothing. And I'm sure it shows on my face.

Luke turns around to go into the storage unit, when I once again do not respond.

"No, wait! I want to go in. I want to try," are the words that come out of my mouth. I guess my tongue decided to solve my indecisiveness on its own without any help from me.

Luke stops walking and slowly turns around to look at me again. "Oh, alright then." He looks startled and confused yet also excited and slightly amused. So many different emotions, in a span of a few seconds, flash across his face. I wonder if my face shows anything? Or does it simply show the emptiness of what has become of me?

"It's just... I want to try and help out, you know?" I try to make it sound logical and convincing, though none of what I'm saying is truthful. "I feel like I haven't been pulling my weight. I've been selfish by taking food, water, clothes, and shelter without giving anything back. I think if I do something useful on this trip, maybe I can start repaying you for everything you've done for me, everything you've given me." The words leave my mouth, but I don't actually acknowledge them. It's as if my body is moving on autopilot, my facial muscles forcing words that haven't even passed through my mind. How is it that my tongue is speaking, even when my brain hasn't processed the thoughts yet? I guess I've been "faking it till I make it" for so long that my whole body's gotten used to it. Maybe I've truly become an antagonist.

Luke scrunches up his face for a second and then relaxes again. "Talia, you don't owe me, or anyone else around here, anything. We do all of that because we care for you and your well-being. There is nothing you have to repay. The only reason you should be doing this is for yourself, and only if you want to. Take as much time as you need. However, if you feel ready, I am glad you have come to that conclusion so quickly." He smiles slightly but makes no other move.

I take another deep breath to steady myself. "I am ready, Luke. I need to, and I want to, help," I say quickly before my tongue, or anything else, tries to make up its own words.

What's that saying? All in or nothing?

I guess I'm all in.

Chapter 3.4

BEAUTY IS SUBJECTIVE.

I used to think about it a lot. It's something everyone interprets differently, like a personal definition that varies from person to person—your mother, your friend, your partner. One person might find someone unattractive, but that doesn't mean they aren't beautiful in someone else's eyes. I don't think there's anything wrong with not finding someone attractive. But it's a different thing entirely to call someone ugly or disrespect their appearance. After all, in someone else's dictionary, that person might be the very definition of beauty.

It's upsetting how much power we give to appearances. We tear people down, often without realizing the damage we're doing. When we put someone's looks under a microscope, we make them feel like they need to change—when actually they never needed to at all. It's fine not to find someone beautiful according to your definition, but the tragedy lies in vocalizing it, in turning your thoughts into words that could crush someone else's self-worth.

I can't help but think there's no such thing as a beauty standard. How could there be? Every single person is different. In some cultures, the classic beauty standard might be blonde, skinny, white women. But haven't we, as a society, moved on from that "standard"? Haven't we started to embrace the diversity and uniqueness of people—men, women, everyone? Or at least, shouldn't we? That's not to say you can't find blonde, skinny, white women attractive. But even among them, there are so many differences. One has blue eyes, one has broader shoulders, one has longer legs, one has fuller lips, one has longer hair—the list can go on and on.

The concept of a beauty standard is just a myth, even in the modeling world. Sure, most people consider models beautiful because they fit into their definition of beauty. But each one of them is different in their own way. So, where is the "beauty standard" exactly? It's nonsense. It would only makes sense if society picks one person to be the definitive standard for all time—but that's never going to happen, not when beauty means something different to everyone.

Why am I thinking about all of this? I don't know. Perhaps I was a sociologist in another life. My mind tends to wander into these musings, taking me away from the present. I guess it's a form of dissociation, a way to escape the world I'm living in and imagine a better one—a utopia that will probably never come to pass, at least not in my time.

I'm back in my room now, alone. It's three a.m., and I can't sleep.

This trip definitely had a better ending than the last one. Which is good, I think. Is the fact that I am becoming desensitized to pain and suffering a good thing? Depending on how you look at it, I suppose. The more desensitized I get, the better I become at handling stressful and horrifying situations while my feelings and emotions lay low in the abyss. However, being desensitized comes with its own consequences. I miss out on happiness and loving things, as well. I become a shell, even more so than I am now. Is that what I want? I'm unsure.

I sit alone in my room, cross-legged, back against the wall, staring at the ceiling. Thinking about the beauty standard and how that used to impact my self-worth. Now, I'm lucky if I shower once a week. And guess what? I don't care neither for myself or anybody else around me.

Luke got me headphones a couple of days ago, so I put them on—desperately trying to drown out the noise in my head.

The first song that comes on is laughably mocking.

"Fine Line" by Harry Styles.

· · · ● ● · ● ● · · ·

"What do you want to sing for the talent show?" Michael asks, laughing, as we sit in my living room.

My friends have nominated me to be part of the talent show this year, and although I hate them for it, it doesn't seem like the worst idea ever. It could be kind of fun, and I get to spend more time with Michael since he will be my backup musician.

"How about... nothing?" I respond.

"Oh, I don't know that one. Who is it by?" Michael asks as he tunes his guitar.

I laugh loudly, and he jerks his head up to look at me.

He wasn't even being sarcastic. He was being genuine.

I laugh once again at his expression. "You're so cute," I say, coming over and kissing him on the cheek. "So adorable."

"What?" He furrows his eyebrows, but I can see a smile peeking through. "How about something by Harry Styles? You like him, right?"

"Love him, yes ..." I trail off, trying to think of a good song for me to perform.

"How about a slow one? What was that one called—the one you cried to in the car for like an hour? And I couldn't stop you and was so close to calling an ambulance because I thought you were having a mental breakdown?" Michael asks.

I purse my lips and glare at him. "Funny."

He smiles that amazing glowing smile that makes me lose my mind.

"It was 'Fine Line'," I finally respond. "And unless you want me to cry for hours on end again, I recommend we don't do that one for the talent show."

"Oh, come on. It's beautiful. Let's search up the music and lyrics," Michael says, picking up his phone and googling the sheet music.

"As if I don't have the lyrics memorized." I roll my eyes.

Michael sets the phone in front of him and starts strumming. "Easy," he says after a moment. "Let's give it a try?" He raises an eyebrow at me.

"If I start bawling, it's your fault," I say, clearing my throat in preparation.

"Let's begin." Michael smiles and starts playing. It's so beautiful, especially when Michael is playing it, so much so that I have to close my eyes and take a deep breath.

I start singing the first verse, and fuck; I'm already tearing up. Don't judge. The first line really gets me, okay?

Michael stops.

"You good, Tal?" He looks over at me with concern.

I blink my eyes. "Yeah, I'm fine. Seriously, I don't know why this song gets to me so much." I laugh it off. "Maybe we should do another one?"

· · · ● · ● · ● · ·

It's funny that now the first line of "Fine Line" carries even more meaning for me. The line describes my life and hits closer to home than ever before. Yet, somehow, no tears threaten to spill over, and I don't get a knot in my throat. It's just... nothing. But the meaning behind it is still tremendous.

Of course, the line can be interpreted in infinite ways, like any line of any song. Depending on your background and current state of mind, lines in a song mean millions of different things to millions of different people. That's the beauty of songs—interpret it as you wish.

I have always found this song to be one of the most depressive ones on the album. It's lyrically and musically superior—but that's beside the point. I've always gravitated toward the sadder songs. The ballads, the tearjerkers, the cries for help hidden within melodies. They've always stood out to me more than the upbeat tracks. To me, this song represents giving up, guilt, losing yourself, and losing your identity. And though the song ends on a note of optimism, isn't that, in a way, the saddest part? Trying to convince yourself you'll be alright, even if it means sacrificing parts of yourself in the process? I've learned the hard way that repeating that mantra—"I'll be alright, it'll all work out in the end"—doesn't work.

Others could interpret this song in a completely different way, maybe even in a positive light. For me, though, it's a cry for help.

That is why, right now, sitting here on my bed in this godforsaken underground complex, I have never related to anything more. I have never felt such a connection. Because, yes, I have given up. Yes, I feel guilt. And I no longer know who I am or what I stand for. And nobody can help me. Nobody can help me build that back up. Maybe not even me. No matter how many times I tell myself: I'll be alright, I can get through this, I will survive.

How far have I come that I don't even know if I can emotionally support myself any longer? How bad has it gotten that I don't even know what some emotions feel like? Happiness? Love? Trust? Hope? They seem far away, and I wish I could bring them back into my mind, back into my emotional safe. However, someone has opened up my safe and stolen those emotions from me. Will I be able to find them? Is that for me to decide?

I listen and listen and listen to this song.

Replay, replay, replay. On a sorrowful loop.

Yet the tears never come. Ones that came so easily before.

I remember when I was thinking about beauty a little while ago. Well, the real beauty is understanding that everybody's perception and definition of beauty differs.

I'm not making any sense today, am I? Or I am, but I can no longer follow my train of thought.

You're not really making sense. You might be losing your mind.

I wouldn't be surprised by that.

I think what I'm trying to say is that everything is connected. The beauty in music, and how we interpret it, can be traced back to the meaning of beauty itself. People find beauty in music. But music, like beauty, is vast and varied. There are so many genres, so many styles, all offering something for everyone. Music gives us an outlet for our feelings, our identities, and our experiences. It can be a release for stress, anger, and sadness, but also for joy and love. That's the beauty hidden within it. Everyone finds their own refuge, their own safe space, and perceives beauty through music in their own way.

I have always been a massive advocate for music being able to solve anything. Music is meant to support us through tough times and encourage us through the good times. I believe there is nothing music cannot solve.

So as "Fine Line" plays in my headphones for the thirty-seventh (honestly, I've lost count) time, I feel it differently. I have felt it differently every time. But this time, the maybe-thirty-seventh time, it feels more distinctive.

This time, it feels less like a threat, less like giving up, and more like a promise. More like... a spark of hope? Hope. The same hope that has disintegrated many before me. Maybe I don't have to give up or lose myself to feel alright again. Perhaps all I needed was a spark.

I get my journal and open a new page.

Hoping that something beautiful will ensue.

Chapter 3.5

"So, Beth..." I try to approach the subject very carefully. We're currently having breakfast. Well, Beth is. I have lost my appetite once again. It has been two days since I've started writing out my plan to get out of here, but I'm definitely going to need help. The thing is, I don't know how brainwashed Beth has been, how unstable they have made her. I don't even know if she wants to leave this place or if she is going to rat me out. I must be extremely careful with her, or everything might be lost.

"What's up, Tal?" Beth asks as she chews a piece of bacon.

The smell of food is making me nauseous. What is wrong with me?

"Beth," I start again. "Do you like it here?"

Smooth...

"Here? The kitchen?" Beth asks, looking up at me with furrowed eyebrows and the most confused expression.

"No, not the kitchen. Well, the kitchen is part of it, I guess. I mean, like, this place. This whole place. The underground complex. Down here," I conclude, sounding like a fool. I have to be more delicate.

Beth scrunches her whole face, even more so confused than before. "Yeah? I guess it's okay. Why?"

I take a deep breath. "I just—well, don't you wish you could like… go outside more?"

"I definitely wish I could. But, unfortunately, my job is down here, and it's not so bad. I'm kind of starting to like it now. I understand that they don't want me to go outside. I don't know why, but I guess they need me here. It makes me feel more important now." Beth shrugs and goes back to her breakfast.

"But if you had a choice, wouldn't you rather spend more time outside?" I try to approach the subject again.

Beth doesn't even look up at me this time. "I don't know. Maybe. But it's not up to me," she responds casually. "What's with the questions?"

"I just wanted to find out if you were interested in… getting out of here," I finally say.

"What? Like for a walk or something?" Beth asks as she cuts her pancake.

"Sure. Yeah. For a walk. Far away."

Beth finally looks up at me again. "What are you talking about?" *Fuck, Beth!! I want to get out of here! Please hear the sub-context!!*

"I want to get out of here," I say. There. No sub-context. Clear and simple.

Beth lets out a loud, short snort-laugh. "You're insane! Funny. But insane."

It's my turn to look confused. "Insane?" I question.

"Yes! How in the world would we be able to leave? More importantly, why would we want to? This place has all the amenities and everything we could ever need. Why are you trying to ruin it?"

"Why am I—are *you* insane? How the fuck am I ruining anything? *THEY* have already ruined everything!" My voice rises as I wave my hands, feeling myself slip into a slightly unhinged state. "How can you be so blind? They're using us, forcing us to participate in something completely illegal. Who knows what else they're involved in besides kidnapping and murder! Which, by the way, are already serious crimes, Beth! And you think we have everything we need? We have no family, no friends, no education, nothing! No *freedom*. How have they convinced you that any of this is okay?" I practically spit out the words. I'm livid—not at Beth, really, but at them. I know it might seem like I'm taking it out on her. She's pissing me off, even though I know it's not her fault. Ugh, I'm a mess.

"Family? *Family*?" Beth raises her voice as well. "Oh, Talia! You mean the dad who's dead, the mom who barely noticed us even when we were with her, and the brother who ditched us years ago? *That* family?" She scoffs. "And friends? Make new ones! There are plenty of people here, and I've made some great friends. Friends come and go. That's how it works. And education? Well, if you ever bothered to look up from your little pit of misery, you'd know they offer classes here. *Anything* you want! Some people are even doing online courses. One girl is studying at Harvard!" She's shouting now, her voice echoing off the walls. "So maybe try opening your eyes instead of blaming everything on the people who saved us from the disaster we were in before." She grabs her plate, storms past me, and disappears into her room.

That went well.

How the hell am I supposed to convince the only person who I'm doing this for to go with me?

What am I supposed to do now?

·········

I have been sitting around the kitchen all day. Thinking, watching TV shows, and more thinking.

I am so lost. The one person I thought I could definitely rely on threw me a curveball and might throw me under the bus soon enough.

Who knows what is going on in Beth's head? How can I trust that she won't snitch on me to Luke, or even worse to Natasha or Mark? I can't trust her any longer, yet I need to convince her to come with me. Because there is no way I can leave without her. She is my sister, and she is stuck here. This situation is so helpless, and I don't know how to convince Beth that this place is awful. There is nothing good here. It is pure evil. All these people, who are willingly part of the cult, are evil.

I wish my dad were still here. He always knew what to say. But they took him away from me, too. They're slowly but surely stripping me of everything I've ever cared about. I don't even know who I am anymore. And the worst part? I have no control over any of it. They hold all the power, and I'm nothing but a puppet dancing on their strings. I've seen what they're willing to do to keep this cult alive—they've already shown me that much. But do I have the same resolve as they do? Would I do whatever it takes to save myself and Beth? Would I kill? In theory, yes. Does that make me a monster? A murderer? I tell myself it would be self-defense, self-preservation. But it's hard to shake the feeling that, in the end, it still makes me a killer. Hypothetically, of course. For now.

I think about Mom and Trevor for a while. I think about Kate, Grace, and Michael. I think about all my friends. I wonder what they are doing right now. Are they looking for me? Have they given up hope? Are they going through their lives with me as simply a deadweight in the backs of their minds?

I think about how all this is at least partially my fault. I trusted a complete stranger (Natasha) with confidential, private information. I was so blind with self-pity and desperation that I let myself be led into a trap. I betrayed my family and my friends to find some solace for myself. And look where it got me.

I go over my escape plans again. They're scattered in my journal, and I know a million things could go wrong with any of them. I'm not stupid enough to believe they are foolproof. Honestly, they're not even good plans. But what choice do I have? One plan hinges on Beth helping me—she has the keys and access to everything. They're so confident in their brainwashing, in her loyalty, that they don't even bother setting limitations. Yet, they never let her go outside. Why is that?

Another plan rests on somehow involving Beth in the next group trip and then making our move. But since she's not allowed to go outside for now, this one falls to the bottom of the list. I wish someone could guide me because I have no clue what I'm doing. I'm not a strategist. I'm not a fighter. I'm a regular teenage girl trying to find a way out. Even as I write out these plans, I know they're flimsy at best.

I can keep writing them out as much as I want, but I doubt they will ever be enough for guaranteed execution.

· · · · · · · · · ·

I stand up from the couch and walk over to the fridge to get some water.

"Hey Talia, are you okay?" someone says from the door to the ballroom.

I jump, turn around, and put a hand to my chest to calm my fast-beating heart. "Fuck, Alex! You scared the shit out of me," I say while steadying my breath. "You can't sneak up on someone in a place like this."

"A place like this?" he questions, walking across the room to sit on the couch.

"Why are you here?" I ask. Is that rude? I didn't think anybody except for Beth, Luke, and I were allowed into this part of the complex. This is "our space". Honestly, I would prefer if Luke didn't show up here either. But it is what it is.

"Rude," Alex remarks lightheartedly, with a soft laugh. "Aren't you glad I'm here?"

I give him an indulgent smile. "Sure. Why are you here, though?" I decide to pursue my rudeness.

"I actually have an important topic to discuss, which I'm kind of nervous about..." he trails off.

I walk over to the couch and sit on the opposite end.

This doesn't sound good.

"Okay, go ahead." I give him a supportive nod.

"Uh... okay, so, well, it's... um," he begins, avoiding eye contact.

"Nice start," I can't stop from saying. Wow, I'm mean today.

He gives me a glare, but I know he doesn't take it to heart. "Okay, fuck, I'm going to come right out and say it," he says. He pauses slightly. "Okay, I'm apparently not going to just say it. Um... alright. Do you like it here?"

I frown. This conversation sounds familiar.

"Here?" I question.

"Yeah, you know, like, here. The underground. Where we currently are..." Alex says without making eye contact with me. He is looking down at his hands and fiddling with his fingers. He seems super nervous, but I can't make assumptions yet.

However, I decide to be slightly bold. "No, I hate it here."

Alex finally looks up at me, and I can't read a single emotion on his face. He clears his throat. "Okay." He nods and takes a deep breath. "So, if you had the ability to leave... this place... you would want to?" He takes pauses between each phrase, which tells me that he is still extremely nervous. However, he is making full eye contact with me now.

I try to discern his facial expression. What is he thinking? Screw it, I decide to be bold again. After a slight pause, I respond, "Yes."

He nods and looks away again.

"Alex, what are you trying to say?" I finally ask.

He shakes his head and looks at me again. "I think you know. But, if you want me to spell it out... I want to leave here. This place. These people." He looks away again.

I wouldn't have heard his following words if I hadn't been intently listening. But I hear them, and it's all I need.

"I want to escape," he whispers.

Chapter 3.6

"To live is the rarest thing in the world.
Most people just exist, that is all."
— Oscar Wilde

THIS QUOTE HAS ALWAYS lingered in my mind, surfacing at odd moments. I wouldn't say it's unique or groundbreaking, but it is beautifully phrased. People are always telling us to "live life to the fullest" or scolding, "Don't waste your youth." From a young age, we're bombarded with the idea that we should live with purpose. Yet most of us end up merely existing. We're told to truly live, but no one ever gives us the chance.

Instead, most parents push their kids into a rigid structure: school, strict schedules, endless extracurricular activities. If they're lucky, maybe there's a gap year to travel, a fleeting chance to "discover themselves" before the grind of college and work. But is that really enough? How can we "live to the fullest" when, from the very start, we're molded to fit society's expectations? We're given identities before we even learn to walk and then told, later, to "find ourselves." From an early age, gender roles, stereotypes, beauty standards, and other societal pressures get coded into us. So, once we're grown, how are we supposed to tell where society's constraints end and where *we* begin?

I keep coming back to this quote and what it means to me. Months in this hellhole, alone with my thoughts, have shown me that I don't truly know who I am. I know it sounds cliché, but it's true. What's the point of being here if we're just existing? How do I start truly living when I don't know where I belong? Who am I now? Who am I supposed to be? I have nothing figured out, and yet in less than two years, I'm expected to choose a college major that could define the rest of my life.

Then there's this whole idea of "society." What even is society? Is it everyone on the planet? Is it divided by classes or age groups? My mom used to drill "socially acceptable" behavior into me: "No, you can't wear that—it's inappropriate." "Eat properly; people are watching." "Don't act like that in public." But who decides what's acceptable? And why are there different rules for when you're alone versus with others?

If I look at it through my mother's lens, maybe there are actually multiple societies. In some places, it's polite to burp at the table or sit on the floor to eat. In others, revealing clothing is no big deal. In mine, none of these are considered acceptable. The point it—it doesn't matter. I've had a lot of time to think about it, and I've decided most of these social norms are a way to keep people in cages.

Anyway, I was thinking about the quote and lost my train of thought. I think all of this basically illustrates what this quote means to me.

"To live is the rarest thing in the world.
Most people just exist, that is all."

Most people just exist because, from the very beginning, they are not given a chance to actually live. And most of the time, when people stray out of the box they have been caged in and try to live, they are judged, shunned, and forced back into the "social norms". It makes me furious. People should live however they want to, within the limit of not harming another living being.

I have a lot of time to think and brew over everything while I'm sitting up here, my mind wandering endlessly. My life is filled with silence and philosophical thoughts about social issues and the meaning of life.

"What's got you all furrow-browed?" Alex steps up the ladder and sits down on the edge of the trapdoor, legs dangling down.

"Are we at the stage in our acquaintance relationship where you can enter my room without asking in advance? Or at least knocking?" I raise an eyebrow and put my journal to the side, shifting to a cross-legged position on my bed.

"Relationship? Hmmm, I like that." Alex smirks.

"*Acquaintance* relationship," I emphasize, but smile nonetheless.

"I've got time." Alex grins. "Anyway, I'm sorry for just dropping by. I wanted to know if you had any thoughts about what we talked about yesterday?"

"I've had a lot of thoughts. Not just about that. But that's not important." I shake my head. Stupid. "Uh, yeah, well—when would you want to... do it?" I ask, a little nervous about talking about this topic, even though Alex is the one who brought it up.

"I'm not super sure, but I would like it to be as soon as possible." Alex shrugs, but he looks serious and a bit concerned.

"How am I supposed to convince Beth?" I give an exasperated sigh. It's a rhetorical question, mostly. I cannot give up on her. I can't. But she is making it so damn complicated, even more so than it already is.

"I know you are doing this for Beth, and obviously, I care about her as well. As much as I care about every person who's in the same boat as we are down here. But Talia, you have to be thinking about yourself as well. You have been stuck here for over two months. This has to be an action plan. We can't have ifs or buts. It has to be thought out carefully and done according to our plan without any concerns or setbacks. This has to be done accurately and without doubt. I need to know you are on board with it. Whether it be with or without—"

"Don't say that," I interrupt. "Don't say it. She will come with us, whether she likes it or not. And she is not going to make a fuss about it. She will be on board. No concerns, setbacks, or doubts." I nod at him with a serious look. I will find a way. I am doing this for Beth. This has always been for her and dad. Now that Dad is no longer in the picture, it's only for her. I can't think about the past. It's done.

"As long as you're sure," Alex says softly, he still sounds doubtful and concerned. I hate that voice.

"Alex, I promise I am completely on board. I don't even know what I would have done if you didn't come to me with this. I have been so lost on what to do and how to do it. I am extremely thankful to you. I just need you to trust me." I sigh again, my head spinning. I don't feel well, probably because I haven't eaten in days.

"Are you feeling okay? You sort of look pale and sickly, not to sound rude. Which I probably do. Shit. I'm just trying to be nice and caring." Alex looks down at his dangling feet, embarrassed.

"It's probably the lack of fresh air and the constant anxiety, stress, and fear I feel in this place," I respond immediately. "The life is slowly getting drained out of me," I mutter, more to myself than him.

"Don't worry. This will be over soon."

I give him a tight-lipped half-smile and nod slowly.

It surprises me how quickly I've come to trust Alex. Over the past few weeks, he hasn't given me a single reason not to. Since that first trip, he's been nothing but kind, caring, and supportive. I appreciate it, though at times it can be irritating. I'm not one to trust easily—especially in this place. But Alex seems to be on the same page as me, and I need help. So, for now, I really don't have a choice. I have to trust him and hope for the best.

"You know, it won't happen within the next day or two. Not even within the next week. We need time and planning, and it needs to be thought out carefully, considering everything that can go wrong..." Alex trails off.

"I've actually been writing down some ideas and possible problems and solutions that could come up in my journal. We can take a look together?" I offer while grabbing my journal and waving it in the air slightly.

"Yeah, sure!" Alex jumps up and moves Luke's chair closer to the bed, bending over my journal, which I open to the first page of my planning.

· · · · ● · ● · · · ·

"Leaving your room once in a while and interacting with other people isn't going to kill you," Mom says as she stands at the threshold of my bedroom.

"It might." I shrug without taking my eyes off of my computer.

"Sitting in here and watching criminal documentaries isn't helping anyone, Talia." Mom lets out a long sigh as if she's upset, but really, she just sounds angry.

"What would you suggest for me to do? Go out and drink with friends? Like everything is normal? They're missing, mom. They have been missing for a week. What the fuck do you want me to do? Chill out and have a good time?" I yell at her.

"You don't have to drink or do anything. But wouldn't it just be nice to see your friends? They have been stopping by over the past week. They care about you and want to support you through this."

"I don't want to see them. Or anyone. And I don't want to do anything except to be in my room. Alone." I raise my eyes to look at her, trying to look confident, although my voice is already faltering, and my eyes haven't been dry in days.

"Talia, please don't think you are the only one going through this. I lost them too," mom pleads.

"You didn't lose them, Mom! They are alive. They are out there. And we have to do something. We have to find them! Not just hang out with friends and receive support. We have to fucking find them!"

"Language, Talia, please." Mom shakes her head. "You are not the police or any kind of detective or private investigator. Leave this to the professionals. There is nothing you can do."

I stare at her, not knowing what else to say.

Her face morphs into Trevor's face, then into Beth's face, then it morphs into Luke's face, until finally, it morphs into a disfigured blob and vanishes.

There is nothing you can do.

I'm no longer in my room. I'm in the woods. Lost. I look around. The trees are covering the sunlight, but I can see a meadow, an opening, nearby. I run toward it.

I'm in the underground complex, lying on the floor of my room here, staring at the ceiling. Unable to move.

There is nothing you can do.

The words echo through my head for what feels like an eternity.

They echo on forever, in daylight and in my dreams.

I wake up from another memory-dream. Those suck the most. I never used to have them. I didn't even think they were real. But ever since I've been in this place, I have had these flashes of real memories as part of my dreams. These "dreams" keep reminding me of how good I had it, even at my worst of times. And look at where I am now, all because of my stupidity.

"Wakey, wakey, eggs and bakey!" Beth comes up the ladder and peeks her head through the top. She is looking all cheerful, as per usual.

"You're going to have to run out of these dumb wake-up calls sooner or later and wake me up in a normal way." I press my palms to my forehead, sighing. "And I'm not hungry, by the way. So, no thanks to the *eggs and bakey*," I add, mimicking her voice at the end.

"There's going to be a morning when you wake up and are actually in a good mood. Then you will appreciate my creative wake-up calls." Beth smiles at me. "Let's go to the arcade today. Maybe after lunch? I feel like I can beat you at bowling today, and then we can do some karaoke!"

I raise my head from the pillow. "Uh, yeah, sure. Do you mind if Alex tags along?" I ask. Alex and I have some planning to do, and we can't afford to waste a day.

"Ohhhh, Alex." Beth smirks. "Of course, he can come. What's going on with you two, anyway?"

"Nothing?" I respond, furrowing my eyebrows in confusion at her insinuation.

"Sure, Jan." Beth rolls her eyes, with a smug expression on her face, and starts descending the ladder.

I rest my head back against my pillow and internally scream like I do every morning when I wake up here.

"Talia, I wanted to let you know that the next trip is scheduled in a few days. It's a smaller one than last time, so I hope you're up for it," Luke says as he comes up the ladder.

"Does anybody ask or knock before entering a person's room anymore? I could have been changing or something!" I exclaim in frustration. Seriously, why is everybody coming into my room so casually all the time now? Can I have any privacy?

"Well, you aren't changing," Luke states matter-of-factly. "And I wanted to let you know so that you can prepare physically and mentally."

"And this couldn't wait until I saw you later on in the day? As in, outside of my room?" I snap.

"You never leave your room, so I figured it would be doubtful you would leave it today."

"For your information, I am going to the arcade after lunch. I could have seen you there," I enlighten him in an irritated tone.

"For your information, I have some business to attend to. So I won't be here for the next couple of days, up until the trip. I am here to give you the heads up and then leave," Luke says in his usual calm tone.

I wish I could strangle him without repercussions.

"Thanks for the heads up," I mutter as I try to cocoon myself back into my bed.

"Are you alright?" he asks, his voice sounding full of bullshit concern.

"I wish people would stop asking me that."

I hear Luke prop himself up and sit at the edge of the hole. "I know you have gone through some hard times while you have been down here. But you've been outside twice now, and you seem to be going to the arcade more often. I thought you were feeling better. Though now it seems like you're back to spending all your time in bed."

I stay silent for a moment. "Did I not just tell you that I am going to the arcade after lunch?" I mutter in an aggravated voice. Can everybody leave me alone? I only woke up, for fucks' sake.

"Yes, you did." Luke sighs. "But you don't seem content. You seem depressed, Talia. And I heard you aren't eating and have been less social lately. Does this have to do with the trip, again? Do you need some kind of counseling? Because we have that down here."

What. An. Asshole.

"What I need is for you to leave and let me wake up so I can start this beautiful day," I answer sarcastically.

"Okay." Luke sighs again before I hear him descending the ladder. "Just think about it, okay?" he asks for the last time before I hear him jump down and his footsteps disappearing down the hallway.

"Everyone is so full of shit," I mumble to myself.

Great, now you're talking to yourself. And not just in your head, but out loud.

"Fucking great," I whisper as I hide myself completely under my covers.

• • • • • • • • • •

"I've written some stuff down too. Although I don't think this is the right place to be discussing it," Alex whispers as we stand by the mini bowling alley.

I take a look around and see a bunch of people from the organization around us. Agreed. It's probably not the best place to be chatting about an escape.

Beth dragged me here (forcefully) after she had lunch. Essentially, she dragged me out of bed without as much as a word. And the whole way to the arcade, she was going on and on about all the gossip she had recently heard. As if I care about what goes on in these people's lives.

"You're right. Should we—" I'm about to offer to go back to my part of the complex.

"GUTTER BALL, AGAIN!" Beth exclaims heatedly, interrupting my sentence. She quickly looks around. As she sees everyone staring at her, she adds, "Sorry for the outburst." Her face is a bit pink as she comes over to where Alex and I are standing. "I suck at bowling," she complains to me.

"I agree. Have you hit a single pin over the past half hour?" Alex asks teasingly.

I giggle without noticing.

Beth glares at me and then turns back to Alex. "I barely know you, little boy. Don't get all high and mighty with me." She narrows her eyes.

"Beth gets super competitive, even though she mostly sucks at everything." I laugh.

Alex gives me a side glance, also grinning.

Beth is anything but intimidating, as much as she tries to be sometimes.

"Also, we're the same age," Alex says to Beth.

Beth throws her hands up in the air dramatically and stomps away to the food counter, refilling her soda.

"Hey, Alex!" some girl bounces over to us, too perkily for my taste. She seems preppy and optimistic—I hate that. "And who's this?" she asks, pointing at me while prancing over to us with the biggest smile. It kind of makes me want to punch her.

"This is Talia," Alex responds with a huge smile of his own. I think I've gotten used to Alex, so I don't notice his cheerfulness anymore, and it doesn't bother me as much. But I can only handle so much.

"So nice to meet you! I'm Julia!" She thrusts her hand toward me, her enthusiasm almost palpable.

"Hi," I respond halfheartedly, shaking her outstretched hand. "Nice to meet you," I mumble as I go over to the lane and grab a ball. Beth has informed me, with a swift glare in my direction, that it is apparently my turn to bowl.

When I return from bowling a strike, Alex and Julia are chatting away, making me feel more nauseous than I was before.

"There's a party tonight!" Julia exclaims as I take a seat across from her. "Not everyone will be there—it's mostly people our age. I'm nineteen, by the way. We have a lot of teens down here, so it'll be cool and fun without all the grumpy older folks! Are you coming?" Her eyes sparkle as she talks, her face glowing with energy.

How can anyone be so upbeat in a place like this? It has to be drugs or hardcore brainwashing.

Any brightness I once had has long since faded. Now, there's nothing left but the dull emptiness that's settled into every part of me. Julia, on the other hand, seems to be handling things a lot better.

"Uh... no, I'm not," I respond hesitantly. Mostly because I have no clue as to what she is talking about and no interest in attending any parties around here.

"But it's going to be so fun! Drinking, dancing, singing, everything! You *have* to come!" Julia insists, bouncing up and down in her chair.

Kill me. Kill me now.

"No thanks." I give her a tight-lipped smile, hoping she will leave me alone.

"Come on, Talia! I know it's not really your scene. I've heard about you from Alex and Luke and some others. But I think you will have a good time! It will give you a chance to come out of your shell and make some new friends! I promise everybody around here is super nice, and they will be excited to meet you. If you don't like it, you can always leave," Julia continues.

People like Julia are the reason this organization is getting away with all of this. Her optimistic attitude and blatant disregard of the wrongdoings, is the reason the organization keeps functioning as it is. She is one of them.

"I'm okay not attending." I nod toward Julia and look away to see Beth get another gutter ball. She is not going to be happy.

"Talia's not really a party girl," Alex says softly.

Before my life down here, no one would have ever said that about me. After Beth and Dad went missing, I practically lived for parties. Even before that, I was always there from the first drink to the last laugh. It was everything—being surrounded by friends, the buzz of alcohol, the warmth and love from people around me. But that's all behind me now. Here, I'm the reclusive girl holed up in her room, barely holding it together. Who would've thought?

"There is a party girl hidden inside every girl!" Julia exclaims. "We just have to find Talia's and bring hers' out. Come ooooon," she pleads. "You have to come!"

I stand up from my seat. The last thing I will ever do here is enjoy myself or do anything relating to my old life. "Thanks, Julia. Both for the invite and for being so nice. But I'd really would rather not."

With that settled, I walk over to the water fountain and refill my bottle.

For the continuation of my time at the arcade, I stand next to Beth and don't spare a glance at Alex and Julia.

· · · · ●·● · · · ·

"You were kind of mean to her," Alex says as he splays out on the couch in our kitchen/living room.

"I was perfectly pleasant," I defend myself.

"Oh, really? So that wasn't you trying to be closed-off and rude? Oof." Alex laughs deeply, and I glare at him from the kitchen where I'm making tea.

"Don't you have a party to go to?" I ask mockingly.

"Please, the party doesn't start for another two hours. You can't get rid of me that easily," Alex responds, rolling over to his side.

"Wishful thinking," I mumble. "I'm surprised Julia didn't follow you here," I say a little louder.

"I didn't think you would appreciate that."

"I wouldn't."

"Well then, look at me, such a good friend." Alex grins shamelessly and finally sits up on the couch.

Sometimes, I regret befriending Alex. It's dangerous and always keeps me on edge because I can never be sure if I can truly trust him. But then other times, when I'm making tea, and he's being an idiot on the couch, and we're about to have a Harry Potter movies marathon, I appreciate him. He's not bad and a nice person to have around. He also provides me with the level of social interaction that a person needs to stay sane.

I roll my eyes as he splays himself out on the couch again.

"It's more comfortable this way." He shrugs and grabs the remote, turning on the TV.

I walk over to the couch and sit on the end he is not occupying, tightly squeezing myself between the edge and his feet.

"You're good at bowling," he comments randomly as he searches for the first movie.

"Thanks. My friends and I used to go a lot. It was right beside my house." I shrug.

"You never talk about your friends back home," Alex remarks.

"I'd rather it stay that way," I say quietly.

"Why?" he asks, in his usual caring and concerned voice.

"Alex, please, can we not… it's just—it's hard to talk about them, and it gets me upset," I say, shaking my head and not looking his way as I take a sip of my tea.

"Okay, I understand," he says, and I hear a hint of disappointment and sadness in his voice. "Here, found it!" He clicks play, and we settle in on the couch as the movie starts playing.

Even as the first scene of the movie I've watched many times before starts playing on the screen, I feel the familiar tinge of disappointment. The disappointment settles deep down inside whenever I experience even minor content down here. I push it deeper into the abyss, as I do with everything these days. None of this is okay. Even the fact that I'm sitting on a comfortable couch, sipping tea and watching a movie. None of this *should* be okay. And I never feel like it is.

Chapter 3.7

"To LIVE IS THE rarest thing in the world.
Most people just exist, that is all."

This quote has been tumbling around in my head more often as of late. It's strange how it stuck in there and now appears out of nowhere, as if I'm having some sort of existential crisis. Maybe I am.

Today marks my third trip outside. I get to breathe fresh air, walk around, and take in the beauty of nature. But at what cost? The cost of my sanity—and the lives of others. I know those people are already captured, and even if I didn't go after them, someone else would. My presence, or absence, won't change their fate. When it comes to the big picture, I am no one. I'm no one even in the small picture. But somehow, that knowledge doesn't ease my guilt.

Unfortunately, I must first be part of the problem to ultimately be the potential solution. I am still impacting and encouraging the organization's appalling actions to some extent. Writing off my actions as a means of survival doesn't give me any level of relief. It doesn't feel like enough justification. These are still my actions, and I am still responsible for every person who gets hurt while I stand around, unable to help them.

To say I have guilt building up throughout every cell of my body would be a comically dry understatement.

Every day, I find it harder and harder to keep moving forward. I find it harder to see the light at the end of the tunnel or any sort of happiness in the future. I wonder if I will ever be able to function as I used to once I get out of here. *If* I get out of here... No, *when* I get out of here. Oh, who cares! I can't stay optimistic. I don't know if I will ever be able to get out of here. Internal battles have become my forte. They're the only thing keeping me sane (relatively).

What even is sanity? I used to think I knew, but now I'm not so sure. If *this* is sanity, maybe I'd be better off letting go, seeing what's on the other side. Perhaps sanity is realizing you wouldn't mind going over the edge but choosing to stay grounded anyway. Or maybe it's just another social construct, a way for society to make us feel inferior. I've started to realize that most things are just that—constructs designed to keep us existing, but never truly living, within someone else's rules.

"Talia, are you ready to go?" Alex calls from below. I asked him to meet me here so that I'm not late this time around. And so that I don't have to go up alone with Luke.

"Physically? Yes. Mentally? Never," I respond as I start descending the ladder.

"Charming. Woke up in a good mood, did you?" Alex asks.

"I woke up in the same mood I've woken up in since I've gotten here. This might come as a surprise to you, but the conditions down here make it really hard for some people to wake up in a good mood," I reply. Kind of rude and snappy, but I am really not in a good mood today. Worse than usual. No further questions.

"Are you doing okay? Do you want some breakfast?" Alex asks, concern lacing his voice.

"No, I'm not hungry. And we're already late."

"You're never hungry," Alex says, still concerned. "Come on, it won't take that long. We can just grab something for the road and go."

"How about we just go," I snap as I start walking down the hallway.

I hear Alex sigh from behind me as he starts to follow. "I'll grab something for the both of us on the way," he mumbles quietly.

Sometimes, I wish he would leave me alone.

Other times, he's not the worst.

I'm conflicted.

"Hey, before we see other people and your mood gets even worse..." Alex trails off as he tries to catch up to me. "I wanted to ask you something—well, not ask... more like... say? Um—okay, so, yeah, I need to tell you something," he says, fidgeting with his hands.

I groan. "What is it, Alex? Spit it out."

"I... well, okay, and please don't get mad about this... I kind of... told... um—"

"For fucks sake, Alex! Just say it!" Irritated and tired, I stop dead in my tracks, causing Alex to bump into me and stumble.

He takes a deep breath and leans away from me but maintains eye contact. "I kind of told Julia about our plan and she wants to join us," he blurts out, all of it sounding like one incomprehensible, jumbled word.

But I hear him loud and clear.

"You *WHAT?!*" I yell, throwing my hands up in the air.

"I told—"

"I fucking heard you!" I cut him off. "What gave you the right to do that? Do you realize you just signed our fucking death sentences? What is wrong with you? How can you be so stupid?!" I start pacing, unable to collect any coherent thought. They're definitely going to punish me for this, maybe even kill me. Shit. Shit. Shit. What am I supposed to do? I guess I can blame it all on Alex and say I have nothing to do with this. Unless he has proof, somehow? Shit!

"She's not going to tell anyone, and she's on board with it. We can trust her. She is my friend, and she won't betray us. She wants to get out of here as badly as we do," Alex says calmly.

POLINA QUINN

I plop down on the ground and put my head between my knees, sighing deeply and trying to regain my breath to somewhat calm down. I'm furious.

"Talia, please, at least trust *me*. I have known Julia since I got here, and she is a good person. She's been here way longer than us and knows more than we do. She can be a great asset to us." I can feel Alex come closer and hover over me as he continues, "Please don't be so upset. This is a good thing."

I raise my head. Unwanted tears start filling my eyes. The tears are more due to anger and anxiety than sadness and betrayal. "Why would you do this without consulting me?" I try to keep my voice calm and steady, but as usual, that doesn't work. "Why would you just *tell her* without asking me first?"

"I need your permission?" He frowns.

"In this case, yes, you do. This is my life. This is all I have right now. This escape is all I have." My voice gives out at the end, and my head settles back down, staring at the dingy, cold floor. The tears are already spilling down and hitting the concrete without a second thought.

You're so weak and pathetic.

I know.

Both of us stay quiet for minutes on end, not knowing what to say or how to feel. I feel Alex's uncertain wavering above me, and I feel my emptiness starting to settle back in.

"I'm sorry," Alex whispers. "Really, I—I know how important this is to you. And I'm sorry I didn't ask before I told Julia. I just thought that—I'm sorry."

I slowly raise my head and internally shake everything off, getting back on my feet and dusting off my pants. "I'm sorry, too. For overreacting right now and for being an asshole always," I say with a tentative smile.

"You are an asshole." Alex nods, but I see a smile breaking through his serious façade.

I laugh. "Sorry," I say again, starting to walk toward the kitchen door. "We're late."

I hear Alex starting to follow me again.

I get to the door and turn around again, coming almost face-to-face with Alex. "But, Alex, seriously, if Julia does anything to mess this up..." I trail off, not knowing how to end the sentence. Should I make him feel bad by saying I will never forgive him? Or should I threaten him, saying I would hurt or even kill both him and her? That seems a bit dramatic and unrealistic. "Make sure she's really up for it and that she will not mess this up," I conclude.

"Promise," Alex responds. "Now let's get going. Luke will not be pleased that we're late together," he states, as he starts walking toward the opposite door.

· · · · ● · ● · · · ·

Time is a strange concept. Technically, time itself isn't all that fascinating. But everything surrounding it? That's a different story. I mean, nothing groundbreaking here—just the usual notions of time flying by or dragging on. When you're not paying attention, time slips away; the moment you do, it slows to a crawl. Figuratively, of course. Time itself doesn't change. But our perception of it depends on our state of mind. Nervous or excited? Time inches forward. Happy or relaxed? It rushes by. Somehow, a year can feel like a few months or like a thousand days. How can that be? It's all in our heads. Time may be one of the only constants in life, yet our brains can trick us into believing it's one of the most uncertain and unreliable variables.

How can the same moment feel like an eternity for one person and a flashing blur for another?

This is what being here feels like to me. Some days, I think about how I've been here for almost three months and wonder where the time has gone. What has happened? And why have I completely lost three months of my life? And then other days, like today—my third trip—feel as if they are taking up the whole span of these three months. It feels eternal. Infinite misery, which I cannot escape.

"We're almost back. Are you tired?" Alex asks as we sit in the van.

"Kind of," I answer, stifling a yawn.

"You can lie down if you want. I'll wake you up before we have to start walking back to the complex."

"Sure." I rest my head against the van window, staring out at the dark sky. It's been raining all day, and though April is near, the days are still short. The moon and stars peek out from behind stormy clouds. Somehow, seeing them calms me. It sounds silly, but in that underground complex, I forget they still exist. I lose all sense of time, of reality, of life. Up here, I'm reminded that the earth is still turning, even if I'm stuck.

"We can play charades when we get back," Alex whispers.

I turn my head slightly against the window to look at him. I frown and question, "What?"

"It's not late. It's only seven-thirty p.m.," Alex states.

"Yes. But charades? What brought that on?" I keep frowning.

"Charades is fun. What do you have against charades?" Alex asks, mock-defensively.

"Absolutely nothing. I'm just confused."

"What is there to be confused about? It is seven-thirty p.m. We will be back at the complex in less than an hour. When we get back, we can play charades. What's tripping you up?" Alex asks, now in a full mocking tone.

I raise an eyebrow and purse my lips. "Don't use that tone with me. I'm not stupid," I reply sassily. "We shall play charades when we get back," I agree before turning back to face the moonlit sky.

I kind of have a smile on my face after talking with Alex, even after our short, weird conversation. It's not that I like him in the slightest romantic sense. I would be honest if I did. It's more that talking with Alex makes me feel like my old self before all of this. It leaves me feeling like my old self for a few minutes before reality comes crashing back in. He doesn't make me feel like a kidnapped victim, a cracked piece of glass, or an unstable person—like most people these days do. He makes me feel like a friend.

Friend.

That word has somehow lost all meaning in our society. People throw it around about whomever, and it doesn't have any effect behind it anymore.

Friend.

There isn't a single definition deep enough for that word. You could google it or check a dictionary, but ultimately, everyone has their own interpretation. To me, a friend is someone I can trust and be myself with. Someone I don't have to hide from. Someone I can have endless conversations with or share a quiet, comfortable silence. Someone who doesn't judge me and sticks around, even when we're apart.

That's a friend to me. And I think Alex might be one. We haven't gone through much together yet, but I feel a surprising level of trust and comfort with him.

It makes no sense, but sometimes you can become friends with a person in a split second. And you trust them. It doesn't make sense because you barely know them, but somehow you do.

I need sleep.

"Deep thoughts?" Alex suddenly interrupts me while I'm in deep thought.

"Will you let me rest?" I snap, keeping my eyes shut.

"I mean, sure. I can let you rest if you want to stay in the van and skip charades. But if you want to get up now because it's time for us to walk, you better get out of those thoughts and that snippy mood. And get your ass out of this van," Alex replies as he gets up from his seat.

"Smartass." I roll my eyes, before scooting over on the seat and getting out of the van.

Everybody is already standing outside, waiting for me. Great. More staring.

"Took your time, Talia," Luke comments. "As per usual."

"Give it a rest," I mutter as I push past him and start walking in the direction of the complex.

"That attitude will get you nowhere!" Luke shouts as I stomp away.

"Sorry!" I yell without looking back, my voice full of sarcasm and disdain.

"You should really be careful with your defiance," Alex says as he jogs up behind me.

"He aggravates me," I respond.

"I understand. I'm just saying you should be careful. He isn't going to roll over on your complicated temper all the time."

"First of all, *'complicated temper'*? Thanks. And secondly, it's worked so far, and he's been less annoying toward me. So I count that as a win."

"His father runs the organization. I'm telling you to be cautious." He eyes me carefully and continues, "But judging by the look you're giving me right now, I'm going to take my own advice and shut up now."

"Thanks. Don't ruin our friendship before we're about to play charades."

"Friendship? Wow, I received an upgrade. Score!" Alex laughs, fist pumping in what I assume to be mock-triumph.

I smile discreetly and keep walking.

I have a friend now. One that says things like "score" and fist pumps.

It feels odd, yet lovely, to have a friend again.

Chapter 4.0

"—TOMORROW," ALEX DECLARES.

"Huh?" I zone back in and turn down the volume on my headphones. I turn my head slightly to look at him and Julia on the other end of the couch. Beth is sitting at the kitchen table.

Somehow— I don't know how, and I didn't ask— Julia and Alex convinced Beth of the escape plan. I won't look a gift horse in the mouth, and I will simply take the win. I am immensely happy about it. Beth isn't happy about it, but at least she's on board.

"We're doing this tomorrow," Alex repeats. "Were you even listening to me?"

"No, I'm listening to 'Happier' by Olivia Rodrigo." I take out my headphones and fully turn to look at them. "Why tomorrow?"

"It's Luke's birthday. He's turning twenty. It's going to be a whole big event. He's out of his teens and all that," Alex rambles.

"Mark said it's going to be huge. Everybody is invited, and it'll be a big party," Julia chimes in.

"Yeah. A party we won't be attending because we're doing something dumb and unnecessary," Beth adds.

"Also, Mark said there will be some kind of surprise, which everyone is super excited about. They're all going to be distracted. There is no better day to escape—well, besides Mark's birthday, but we already missed that opportunity. This is second best. Or else we will have to wait three months till Natasha's birthday," Julia says.

"Do they not celebrate any other birthdays besides the holy family's?" I ask sarcastically.

"They do. Although it's not as big of an occasion, and not everybody shows up to everyone's birthday," Julia answers calmly.

I still don't trust her.

"Look, we can't risk anyone being around when we do this. Everyone has to be drunk and partying for us to pull this off. And nobody is allowed to not attend their birthdays. Last year, a girl didn't come to Luke's birthday, and well... let's just say I haven't seen her around a lot. Ever again," Julia says.

"How wonderful, and what an uplifting story. Thanks, Julia," I say.

"Talia," Alex warns.

I roll my eyes and take a deep breath. "So, tomorrow. Are we ready?"

"What is there to be ready for? We have Beth, which means we have all the keys. We just have to be prepared and ready to go once the party starts to avoid getting caught. I say we grab nothing and go," Alex says.

"I agree. Things will only weigh us down, and I'm sure they can track us if we take any electronics. So we leave everything here and fucking run," I say, nodding.

"We can't take our phones?" Julia asks.

"They're jail-locked anyway, and we can't access anything. And, like I said, I'm sure they can track them. Why would you need it?" I ask, with the right amount of suspicion.

"I just don't feel comfortable without my phone... but okay, I agree," Julia concedes.

I roll my eyes, trying to be inconspicuous so Alex doesn't scold me again.

"Great plan. Can I go now?" Beth asks, sounding simultaneously bored and outraged.

I really don't know how Julia and Alex convinced her to do this.

"Where are you going?" I ask, sounding more concerned than I should be.

"Don't worry, I won't give away your precious plan. I just want to go to the arcade room and have some fun. Something that I won't be having soon enough. Do you mind?" Beth snaps.

"Beth, please—" I start.

"Do. You. Mind?" Beth gives me an icy glare, staying sated but poised to leave.

I stay quiet for a beat. "No," I respond. "Go ahead."

"We'll reconvene later. I have a class," Julia says, jumping up from the couch and following Beth. "Beth, wait up!" She jogs over and disappears through the door into the purple room.

"And then there were two," Alex states.

"Keen observation," I say dryly. "Do you want to watch something?"

"Why not?" Alex shrugs. "*Taylor Swift: Reputation Stadium Tour*?" he questions.

I laugh loudly. "Only if you want to," I respond.

"Always." He scoots over closer and settles down as I search for the film.

· · · ● · ● ● · · · ·

"Today is the daaayy!" Alex sing-songs as he climbs up the ladder into my room.

"What time is it?" I groan sleepily, hiding under my duvet.

"It's time to get ready so that we can discuss our plan of action for today. Because today is the day!" Alex exclaims excitedly, yet quietly enough so that I don't strangle him for yelling in the morning.

"Okay, and what is the actual time in accordance with the sun?" I mutter, still hiding under my duvet.

"Six twenty-five a.m. Now, get up!" Alex says more loudly as he plunks down on my bed.

"Why on earth are we waking up so early? The party isn't till eight p.m.," I groan, finally uncovering my head from under the duvet. "Let me sleep. We have a long night ahead of us."

"I agree that we have a long night, but we'll have adrenaline and all that to keep us going. We have to get up early, as in *now*, to get our plans figured out and make sure everything is set to go," Alex explains. "Hurry up because Julia and Beth are already downstairs waiting." He pauses. "And they made yummy breakfast. So if you don't come down soon, you won't get any."

"I don't eat breakfast," I mutter, blinking at the ceiling. Dark spots and nausea hit me before I even sit up, so I lie still and close my eyes again.

"Up and at 'em!" Alex yells again, now descending the ladder. "We await your presence shortly!"

"You're so weird!" I yell after him as I slowly lift my head off the pillow, followed by the rest of my body, and set my feet on the ground. I try to regain some semblance of stability. Where is gravity when you need it? Lately, I feel like I'm either floating around as if in space or being pushed down into the ground (rather than pulled). It's either one or the other, and neither is pleasant.

I've always been a true believer in science. Specifically, I've found myself captivated by neuroscience—the most vital and fascinating field, in my opinion. Lately, things I once took for granted feel... off, as if reality itself has subtly shifted. In the depths of my cognition, I realize nothing's changed except my surroundings and mental state. The strange perceptions, the distorted sense of time, the overthinking, the loss of appetite, even this newfound fixation on words like *beauty* and *friend*—they're all tricks of the mind. Just defenses my brain has conjured to protect itself from further harm.

I'm no genius who's stumbled onto some groundbreaking insight. I'm more like a lab rat, dropped into an alien environment and forced to adapt however my mind can manage. So maybe I should stop blaming myself for the depression, anxiety, and lack of appetite. It's all just survival instinct. Take a fever, for instance: it's your body fighting off infection, and as awful as it feels, it's a good thing. It's the same here. I'm battling the infection of this place—this cult.

I know that fevers can be fatal, and it's not like I haven't thought about "ending it all." But I'm not at that juncture yet. It's not fatal yet. I can still fight. I can handle this; my mind is coping the best it can. And soon, I'll be out of here. Very soon. Like, *very* soon. So, I better get ready before my mind reaches its breaking point.

"Talia, hurry up, or I'm leaving!" I hear Beth's voice yell down the hallway.

"Leaving to go where?" I mutter to myself. I don't yell it since I don't want her to get upset on a day that is upsetting enough for her. I don't understand her foul attitude, but I'm also not going to actively throw firewood into a burning building.

I'm giving Beth the chance to return to her family, friends, and former life. Or a new life, if that's what she wants. She's an adult. I am giving her a chance and a *choice*—something we don't have the luxury of down here. What is so horrible about that? How am I taking anything away from her besides a miserable life in the underground depths of New Jersey? How did I end up being the bad guy in this scenario? A bad guy to one the only people I ever looked up to and who loved me unconditionally up until a couple of months ago.

"Yeah, I'm coming! Sorry!" I yell instead as I rise out of bed and regain my balance. Fucking dizzy spells. Give me a break.

I dress myself in sweatpants and a sweatshirt. It's feeling chillier than usual down here. I quickly wash my face, brush my teeth and hair, and then drag myself down the dimly lit hallway to the kitchen.

"I've been summoned." I trudge in and sink down into the couch. Everybody else is sitting silently at the kitchen table, munching down some food that is making me more nauseous than when I woke up.

"Good morning, Talia!" Julia chirps.

"Morning, cranky," Alex follows, giving me a big smile.

"Finally," Beth says without sparing me a glance.

"Funny." I make a face at Alex, ignoring the other two. "Anyway, what's so important that we had to wake up at this sinful hour?"

Alex rolls his eyes as he picks up a piece of toast. "We're going over what we're doing and at what time. Everything has to be planned out to the minute for it to go smoothly. I know we discussed it before, but I need us all to be clear. Also, I think it would be a good idea for us to walk around and interact today so that we don't raise any suspicion," he says.

"Nobody would be surprised if Talia stayed here the whole day. She doesn't go anywhere anyway, and she doesn't interact with anyone except for you, Alex," Beth says in her—now standard—bitter and icy tone.

I purse my lips so that I don't snap at her. But right now, in my current mood and state, I kind of want to spontaneously burst her into flames. Alas, that only happens in fantasy books.

"Uh, yes..." Alex gives Beth a weird look. "Anyway, I think that we need to be our normal selves today. Up until the party, that is. Do what you would usually do. Whether it involves staying here, going to the arcade, classes, or whatever it is. Just your typical day—"

"At the end of which, we make a dumb choice to run away from a delightful place and its wonderful people, who have given us a home and any amenity we could ever want," Beth adds resentfully.

How brainwashed is this bitch?

It's your sister you're talking about. Chill out.

P.S. SUPER brainwashed.

"*Anyways,*" Alex continues, obviously uncomfortable. "The party officially starts at eight p.m. sharp. Mark and Luke make it clear that nobody can be late, so people will be gathering and drinking by seven-thirty. Trust me, by eight, everyone will be well on their way to getting drop-down wasted."

"Is that an expression? 'Drop-down wasted'?" I ask, frowning yet also smiling slightly.

"I see that the Turner sisters are not in a chipper mood this morning," Alex comments off-handedly, ignoring my question. "As I was saying, by eight p.m., everybody should be fairly drunk. I say we make our move at seven fifty-five. As we discussed, Beth brings her keys, and nobody brings anything else. We leave all our phones in this room at dinner, just to be sure. Then we make our way down the hallways until we reach the upper-level door, and then... well, I feel like it's self-explanatory." Alex shrugs.

"And why did I have to wake up at six a.m. for this wonderous step-by-step overview?" I ask.

I'm genuinely super pissed off at Alex for waking me up this early. This conversation took all of ten minutes. I haven't been feeling well, and sleeping in would have made it easier to fulfill today's destiny.

"Feel free to take a nap throughout the day. Since you're not a super social person, I'm sure nobody will miss you," Alex says.

"Oh gee, thank you so much. That makes me feel so nice and warm inside. So considerate of you," I reply sarcastically.

"Is this over? Can I go now?" Beth asks, her tone reeking of annoyance.

"And the Turner sisters strike again!" Alex exclaims. "Sure, Beth, go ahead. And Talia," he turns to face me fully before continuing, "I'm sorry for waking you up. I was just so excited for today and wanted get a head start."

I hear Beth's chair screech loudly and her feet stomping toward the door to the purple room.

I roll my eyes and settle deeper into the couch, huddling up in my hoodie. "It's fine. I get it. I'm kind of excited, too. Well, I'm more anxious than excited, but still." I shrug.

"I'm off to get ready for my eight a.m. class. I didn't have much time to study yesterday." Julia smiles and winks at me as she gets up from the table to put her plate in the sink.

I frown and look over at Alex. He doesn't make eye contact. Shit, are they hooking up? I sure hope not because that shit always complicated things, and that is the last thing I need today.

"Have fun," I say quietly as Julia gives us one last look and exits the kitchen.

"Sooooo, you and Julia, huh?" I ask.

Alex is silent for a moment, turning his head away from the door to look at me. "What? Huh? No. No, no, no. Not me and Julia. Nothing," Alex rushes out quicker than a vulture swooping down to attack its prey.

I grin. "Yeah, okay, 'didn't-have-much-time-to-study-yesterday'," I quote Julia. "You're so obvious. And also, we're not in middle school. Grow up and admit you're hooking up. I don't need complications right now," I add.

"There are no complications, Talia. Nothing is going on. We're... hanging out. Yesterday, we watched a movie late at night, and she didn't have time to study. That's all," Alex says defensively.

"I'm not accusing you of a crime here. No need to get so defensive," I try to reason with him. "I'm asking because I would like to—today is important for me, and I want to know that nothing will go wrong. Nothing will stop me from getting out of here tonight."

Alex stays silent and picks at pieces of his toast. Avoiding eye contact.

We stay like this for a while. I turn on the TV and start watching a random episode of *New Girl*. This show always makes me feel better. It's so warm and familiar—a comfort show.

"Fine, we're hooking up." Alex sighs as he gets up and walks over to the couch. He plops down beside me and grabs the remote, pausing the show. "Julia wants to keep it a secret, and she told me not to tell anyone, especially you. I don't know why, so don't ask. I don't understand girls sometimes. But, anyway, I *really super* like her, so please don't say anything. But I promise this will in no way jeopardize today," Alex says.

"How long?" I ask quietly.

"A couple of months. But it only got serious a couple of days ago. We kind of made it official. For ourselves, more than anyone else," Alex answers.

I nod. "I really don't mind, Alex, like I said. I just don't want this getting in the way of anything. And don't worry, I won't say a word—partly because I'd hate to see you fight, and partly because I'm a good friend who knows how to keep secrets." I smile and rest my head on his shoulder. "I hope everything goes smoothly today. Alex, if it doesn't... I'm totally screwed. This is the last ounce of fight I have in me. If today doesn't go as planned, I don't think I'll survive much longer down here." I whisper the last sentence so softly I'm not sure he even hears it.

But it's true. I don't know if I can survive another day down here. Every last shred of strength I have left has been building toward this day—our escape from this horrid place and these wretched people. My sanity is hanging on today's outcome. If it fails, I doubt I'll be able to pull myself back from the edge I've been balancing on for weeks. If we don't leave today, I might finally tip over, plunging into complete and utter... annihilation. Into the abyss. It's beyond rock-bottom; it's a mix of despair, hopelessness, and defeat. Sound fun? Well, that's what's waiting for me if this plan doesn't work.

"I know," Alex whispers. "We will do this today. I promise you, Talia, we will get out of this place. For good."

"Don't give me a promise when you don't know if you can keep it." I sigh.

"I will either keep it or literally die trying because they will kill us if they catch us at any point. So I promise you I will do everything to make this go smoothly because, well, I would like to stay alive."

We stay silent for a long time as Alex turns the show back on.

"Me too," I whisper before closing my eyes and drifting off.

· · · · ● · ● · · · ·

"Isn't this so cute and cozy," I hear a voice break through the haze of my nap.

Can you call it a nap if it happens half an hour after waking up? Or is it simply called going back to sleep? I'm going to go with nap because, technically, I woke up and did my whole morning routine, and then I decided to sleep again. And it didn't last very long, considering I'm still tired and grumpy, so it's a nap.

"Shush, she's sleeping. We have a long day and night ahead of us," I hear Alex whisper gently from somewhere very close to my ear.

"Why is she always so tired?" I hear the voice ask. It's Julia. I recognize her voice now.

"She went to bed late, and I woke her up early. She's not a morning person," Alex says. "How was class?"

"Boring and repetitive. The professor was interesting in the beginning, but I feel like I've learned everything I can from him at this point, and I might start taking..." Julia trails off.

Why did she... oh. Because she will no longer be able to take classes down here after tonight.

"Uh, I mean, I'll take real classes once we're out. Just not in this subject, I guess," she recovers. "Maybe community college. I never finished high school or got a chance to try college. Without a high school diploma, I don't think they'll let me in anywhere. But I'm not going back to high school. I guess I'll have to think about it later." She lets out a slow breath. "Are you staying with her all day, or do you want to go do something? I have another class at noon, but I'm free after that."

I try to tune her out and continue my nap, but it seems like my brain has already switched on. Except the rest of my body refuses to wake up, making the situation more complicated.

"I'm going to stay here for now. But I can meet you in the rec room after your noon class?" Alex asks.

"Yes, I definitely need a rematch on that chess game we played yesterday. I don't appreciate that you cheated," Julia responds teasingly.

Alex faux gasps. "I would never do such a thing."

"Alright, well, I'll see you at one-thirty then?" Julia asks.

Finally, she's leaving. I hope.

"Sounds good," Alex replies.

"Great. See you later!" I hear Julia's hurried steps sprinting away.

There is a moment of awkward silence before I speak. "That was uncomfortable," I say, opening my eyes slightly.

"When did you wake up?" Alex asks as I lift my head from his shoulder.

"Around the time Julia was judging me for taking a nap and judging you for staying with me while I take a nap," I respond groggily.

Alex nods distractedly, looking strangely in thought.

"Anyway, what time is it?" I ask, getting up from the couch and going to make myself some tea.

"It's eleven am. I watched *New Girl* while you were napping."

"Without me?!" I gasp in mock-despair.

"My biggest apologies for the betrayal. It will never happen again," Alex responds sincerely (sarcastically) as he stands up and walks to the kitchen counter.

As I said before, even such a dumb and childish conversation makes me feel like my old self, even if it's for a few minutes. A conversation like this lifts all the negativity that's gathered inside me.

A conversation like this makes me feel a little better in this place for a short while. A conversation like this makes me believe that my old self, although she will never return as she was before, is still somewhere in there. And she might resurface every once in a while. I liked her. She was weird, happy, and excited about life.

I miss her.

Chapter 4.1

"How about you go right, and I go left, and then we can trick them and finally finish this shit," I reason.

"No, that won't work. That's such a basic play, and they will see right through us," Alex counters.

"Okay, we can try like... back to back? Is that an advanced play? A little *Mr. & Mrs. Smith* action?" I ask.

"That's not advanced," Alex deadpans.

"Fine. You come up with something, then. We don't have a lot of time!"

"Shit, okay, let's just go with your *Mr. & Mrs. Smith* idea. Let's go. We can do this. We can beat these motherfuckers!" Alex whisper-yells as we swiftly get out from behind our hiding spots, standing back to back, and start shooting at where we know Julia and Beth are.

"Aaaaand you're dead," Julia says, shooting us both with only one arm on the gun. "That was the dumbest play ever."

"You suck at laser tag," Beth adds.

We decided that before going on our possibly deadly mission of escape, we'd have some last hours of "fun" down here.

"Okay, now we bowl. I know I can beat all of you at that," I say.

"Oh, please. It's dumb luck." Alex rolls his eyes.

"Yeah, dumb luck fourteen times in a row," I reply sassily, giving him the finger.

"I will win one of these times, and then you'll see, and you'll be sorry, and you'll beg and plead for my forgiveness, and I will walk away, and I'll never have to see your face again," Alex defends, a bit over-dramatically for something as mundane as bowling.

"Yeah, because winning once is definitely going to prove you're the better player." I roll my eyes. As my mom would say: "Roll those eyes one more time, and they will stay that way forever". Okay, I'm looking forward to it, Mom.

"How about you two stop bickering and actually play. We can judge for ourselves," Julia says, making her way out of the laser tag room.

We head over to the bowling alley, and of course, I win. No surprise there; I am good at this game. Or maybe it is dumb luck. I guess we'll never truly know.

After bowling, I feel tired again, so I return to the room to take another nap, preparing for the long night ahead.

"Knock, knock," someone says as they climb up the ladder. It's been five minutes. I haven't even drifted off.

Luke.

"You feeling okay?" he asks, climbing up and sitting on the floor, his feet dangling down.

"I wish you would stop asking that," I respond, opening my eyes and raising my head slightly. "I'm fine."

He smiles and stays silent.

"Happy birthday, by the way," I add after a beat.

I guess he was waiting for me to say that because he immediately lights up even more and opens his mouth to speak, "Thank you! It's exciting to be out of the *teen years* but a little scary, too. Surreal. I feel like I was just turning thirteen or fifteen like a couple of months ago. It's kind of crazy how time flies."

"Tell me about it." I nod and lay my head back down on the pillow. "I was kind of trying to take a nap though."

"Oh, sorry. I just wanted to check in and make sure you knew about the party," Luke continues.

"It's all I've been hearing about over the past couple of days," I reply.

"Good, good. Don't worry about a present or anything. Your presence will be enough!" Luke says as he jumps down and lands on the ladder. "I'll see you soon!" I hear his steps slowly descending and then disappearing down the hallway.

Nap time.

I close my eyes, and minutes pass.

For some reason, this nap isn't coming as easily as the previous one. Although I do feel just as tired, if not more.

"Hey, Talia. Are you awake?" I hear someone whisper from below. Beth.

I guess no one is going to let me nap today.

"Yeah," I whisper back.

"Good," she replies and climbs up, perching herself in the same spot Luke was minutes ago. "I wanted to talk to you about tonight..."

I sigh in frustration. "Look, Beth, I know you're not happy about this. But if you're going to back out now, I don't know how to convince you otherwise. You never listen to me. I couldn't even convince you myself the first time around. Julia and Alex had to do it for me. God knows what they said to convince you. But all I'll say is, if we don't do this today, I won't be around for much longer." I whisper the last part, just like I did to Alex. A bit of guilt-tripping mixed with a lot of honesty—maybe it'll work.

"Manipulation at its finest," Beth mutters. "And for your information, the only reason I'm doing this is for you. All Alex and Julia did was lay out the details to me and tell me you would do anything to get out of here. But that you wouldn't do it without me.

So the reason I'm doing this is so that I don't lose you. Although, I still can't understand what is so horrible about his place that you would rather kill yourself than stay here."

"I'm not trying to manipulate you, and I'm not going to explain to you the horridness of this place all over again. You make your own choices, Beth. I just really hope you make the right choice right now. At this point, I *will* leave without you. But I would still like for you to make the right choice," I say.

Maybe giving her an out wasn't the best idea. Perhaps she won't respond to my reasoning. Obviously, I can't leave without Beth. But I have to think about myself, right? It tears me apart to think about leaving tonight without Beth, and I honestly don't think I can go through with it without her by my side. I need to know she will be safe, and the only way to know that for sure is if she is with me.

All I want is for her to understand that I am doing this out of unconditional love, sisterly love. I want to save her—and not in the way this cult "saved her". I want her to be free and do whatever she wants out in the real world. But of course, she is free to make her own decisions even down here. She is her own person, and I would never manipulate my sister or be deceitful to get what I want. I know they have brainwashed her in some way or another, but she is still my sister, and I would never use her vulnerability to my advantage. I need her to come with me, but I can't make her. I can't be selfish, even though I am doing this to save us both.

Silence fills the room like a thick fog, heavy and suffocating. There's no sound, except for Beth's steady breaths and my ragged ones. Silence can be deafening. It can feel like it's tearing you apart from the inside, and all you want is to say something—anything—but you can't. Or won't. I don't know what to say anymore. So, I wait. The silence presses down harder and harder, making it difficult to breathe.

"I will go," Beth finally says after ten agonizing minutes.

I counted.

"I'll go. Tonight. With you. And Alex and Julia," Beth says. She stands up so her feet touch the ladder. "But I want you to know that I am not doing this for myself. I am not doing this because I want to. I am doing this so that you stay alive. Because in your current state, I'm afraid you will actually be selfish and senseless enough to kill yourself if we don't do this today. I would still like to urge you to rethink your stance. But if by tonight you still feel the same... I'll go." With those words, she leaves.

I grit my teeth as I hear her walk down the hallway and slam the door to her room.

Whatever energy is out there in the universe, whoever is out there, please give me enough strength to survive through tonight's endeavors.

· · · · ● · ● · · · ·

I didn't nap. In fact, I didn't even come close to it. After my conversation with Beth, I couldn't settle down, tossing and turning in bed, my thoughts too loud to ignore. Eventually, I gave up on sleep altogether. I guess I'll just be tired forever.

Now, I'm sitting in the kitchen. Alex and Julia are eating dinner while Beth stays locked in her room. Fine. As long as she's ready when it's time to go, I don't care. Of course, I *do* care. I care that she's mad at me. I care that she doesn't want to leave. I care about her all the time. But right now, I can't afford to care. So, I push my feelings down deep into the abyss, as I've done with so many others, and focus on Alex's rant.

"So many people have come up to me today and asked about the party. It's like they don't know it's mandatory, or they think I'm dumb and don't know it's mandatory. I swear, these people have lost brain cells after being down here for so long," Alex rants.

"I feel like I'm losing brain cells right now," I mutter.

"Are you hungry?" Julia asks as she picks up some bread and tears a piece off. "I made way more pasta than I should have, and I also expected Beth to come out and eat. So I can make you a plate?"

"No thanks, I ate earlier. I'm not hungry," I respond, sinking deeper into the couch and nestling into my hoodie.

"Alright. Well, it's on the stove if you get hungry before we leave. I recommend eating something because we have a long, stressful, and physically draining night ahead of us. We have to load up on carbs and protein so that we can make it," Julia says matter-of-factly.

Thanks, Julia. I think I can handle my food intake on my own.

But I don't say anything. Instead, I just give her a tight-lipped smile and turn my head to face the wall.

I zone out, hearing Julia and Alex babble on about nonsense. My mind drifts to tonight, to what could go wrong—which is everything. But what if nothing goes wrong? What if we actually escape? The thought both thrills and terrifies me. If we get out, we'll have to run through the forest, adrenaline pushing us forward, our minds and hearts racing. From our trips, I know the nearest town isn't too far. But can we find it in the dark, when everything feels like a blur? And once we get there, what then? Do we knock on the first door we see? Find a police station? What if the town is full of cult members? That thought hadn't even occurred to me before, but I'm sure I've seen it in a movie.

What if we make it all the way out but then get dragged back because we talked to the wrong person? What if we never make it out of these creepy woods? Will we starve or be eaten by wild creatures? That's a bit dramatic, but it could happen.

I also think about if everything goes right. If we get out, get help, file a report with the police, and return home safely. What happens then? I return to my normal life and go to therapy a few times a week? What about Beth? And what about Alex and Julia? Will I never see them again? I don't even know where they are from or what homes they have to return to. There is so much uncertainty, so I tune back into Alex's and Julia's conversation to prevent myself from any further overthinking. I won't drive off the edge yet.

"It's seven p.m. One more hour till the party. And fifty-nine more minutes until we make our move," Alex says, looking over at me as I turn my head to face them.

"Thrilling," I say, turning on the TV and clicking on the next episode of *Prison Break*.

I know it's a TV show, but it has helped me feel better and a bit calmer about our escape over the past weeks. If a bunch of men can break out of a maximum-security prison, then I suppose we'll be okay. They had it much harder than we have it. I know it's a TV show, and it isn't real, but people have been known to break out of prisons before in the real world. So, I guess that kind of makes me feel less anxious about our escape. Although, I am aware that so many things can still go wrong.

"Alright, I'm kind of involved in a super serious game of *Monopoly* right now. It has been going on for days. I promised to be there at seven p.m. so that we can play before the party. I'll be back as soon as everyone leaves for the party," Julia says, standing up and carrying her dishes to the sink.

A *Monopoly* game? Seriously?

"Sounds good. See you soon." Alex smiles as he stands up as well. He dumps his dishes in the sink and then comes over to sit next to me on the couch. "*Prison Break* again?" he questions.

"Yes. Because it's the best show ever," I respond, not taking my eyes off the screen.

"That's arguable."

"No, it's not. And I will not debate this because you can't convince me otherwise."

"To each their own, I suppose." Alex shrugs and settles down on the couch to watch the show with me.

I hear someone emerge from the hallway and look over to find Beth walking to the stove and grabbing a plate from the cabinet.

"Got hungry," is all she mutters, without even glancing at us.

Alex shrugs again, giving me a sympathetic side-glance, and turns back to the TV. But I continue to stare at the back of Beth's head, trying to figure out what the hell I ever did or what the hell ever happened to her to make her feel so terribly about me.

Chapter 4.2

"It's seven thirty-one p.m." Alex's leg bounces up and down as he sits at the kitchen table, nervously looking at his watch every minute.

"Yeah, and it was seven-thirty one minute ago," I say.

I've changed into my extra-warm pair of leggings and put a long-sleeved shirt on under my sweatshirt. I'm ready to go.

Somehow, I am not as stressed as everybody else seems to be. The adrenaline must be kicking in already because I feel prepared.

"Where the hell is Julia? We agreed to meet here at seven-thirty, and she's still not here!" Alex exclaims.

"Shut up. She'll be here soon. We still have time," I reply calmly.

His constant time-checking is getting on my nerves.

"Alex, you really need to chill out. We are all on edge, but you seem to be losing it," Beth says as she fidgets beside me on the couch. She has yet to acknowledge my presence, but at least she is communicating with Alex.

"Sorry. I'm sorry. I'm just very worried, and this is all getting too real right now. In less than thirty minutes, we are actually doing this. It's too real, too real..." Alex trails off as he looks at his watch again. "It's seven thirty-two."

I sigh deeply and roll my eyes, deciding to abstain from saying anything else to him. Hopefully, he'll settle down once Julia shows up. Where the hell is that girl?

The threatening silence settles in again as we all sit and wait. Alex keeps checking his watch. Beth fidgets and sighs next to me, and I stare at the wall. Not that it's a nice wall or anything; it's actually pretty ugly, like most things around here. But it's something to look at, and it strangely soothes me.

"Seven thirty-three."

"Seven thirty-four."

"Seven thirty-five."

All I can hear is the silence and Alex's murmurs of what time it is every passing minute.

I zone out, staring at the ugly wall. Maybe I shouldn't call it ugly. That sounds mean. It's not the wall's fault that everything that happened down here has damaged my perception of beauty. I guess in any other place, this wall would be neutral. Or even beautiful to some people. I'm overthinking again. It's a wall. And to me, right now, it's ugly. But soothing.

"Seven forty-two. Okay, I am officially worried," I hear Alex's urgent voice sound through my daze of thoughts. "Where the hell is Julia?"

"Stop worrying. She's probably getting dressed or something. We have time," I say in a disinterested tone. We leave with or without her.

"She should have been ready a while ago," Beth chimes in. I start to hear the worry in her voice as well.

Fucking fantastic. Now, I have two people trying to disintegrate my calmness.

"Maybe she got—" I start, trying to calm them down.

"I'm here, I'm here!" Julia bursts into the kitchen, breathless. "So sorry for being late. I got held up with the game, and then everybody left, and I stayed to clean up a bit. And then, I didn't know what to wear, but I decided to dress neutral and warm. It's always better to take off some layers than be freezing, right?" Julia rushes out. She sounds nervous or just out of breath. Probably both. The nerves are getting to everyone.

"Alex was freaking out," Beth says. "He was being super dramatic. Maybe you can calm him down."

"I'm so sorry, babe. I really just lost track of time. But I'm not late, and we're all good, right?" Julia asks as she sits down next to Alex at the table and reaches her hand out to put onto his while her other hand rubs his back.

Ugh, couples.

"Yeah, I'm sorry for freaking out," Alex mutters. "I was just worried about you. It shouldn't have taken so long, but I get it now. You're here, and we're ready to go." He checks his watch. "It's seven forty-four. Everyone, hide your phones and anything else that could be used to track us in the cabinets. We don't want anyone coming in here and seeing a bunch of phones lying around."

We all scramble to our feet and hide our phones in different cabinets.

The anxiety I didn't feel before is now becoming apparent again, and I do my best to push it down into the abyss. I don't have time for this right now. I need to concentrate and be prepared. I need not to feel right now. I can't have anything holding me back. It's us, the adrenaline, and whatever lies before us. Nothing else.

Everybody returns to where they previously sat, and the silence also returns. The nervous fidgeting and early adrenaline in the air make staying seated difficult. But we remain in our seats.

For eleven more minutes.

Silence and invisible electricity coursing through our veins.

"Seven fifty-five," Alex finally announces, barely above a whisper.

"Here we go." Julia stands up from her seat, and we all follow.

Quietly, despite the loud party raging somewhere in the complex, we move out of the kitchen and through the purple room. The door leading to the next hallway has been left open ever since I started going to the arcade. Luke gave his permission.

We walk through the door, and something inside of me spikes. It's hard to explain, but the adrenaline inside keeps increasing with every step. It's like the first time I ever went through that door on the other end of the purple room. The number of times I've gone through it since then is a lot, but right now, it feels like the first time all over again: that rush, yet disappointment, of walking down another dimly lit and dirty hallway and then seeing yet another set of steel doors.

One door leads to the arcade and the living quarters on the other side of the complex. The other door leads to another hallway.

Beth takes out her keys and opens the door that leads us down another hallway. We keep walking, and I see the next steel door. The one that opens into the circular room with a huge, long staircase leading to the outside. My breath catches. This is happening. Now.

I watch, holding my breath, as Beth opens this door too. The power she holds with those keys—and the fact that she hasn't used them until now—surprises me once more. We step into the circular room and stop. The vast staircase stretches before us, the outside so close I can almost taste the fresh air, the moonlit sky, the stars. It's surreal. Beth leads the way, walking toward the staircase. I follow, with Alex and Julia right behind me.

Time freezes as I take that first step up the stairs.

I can physically feel time freeze. I feel like it's taking an eternity for me to set my foot fully down on that first step and then lift my other foot to go on to the next.

I'm in a daze, and it all feels too dreamlike. Too easy. Too strange. Why haven't we been caught? Has it really been this easy this whole time? Why am I questioning this? I should fucking run up these steps.

But time freezes.

Until...

Chapter 4.3

...IT ISN'T FROZEN ANYMORE.

"Talia, stop," Alex says from behind me.

As I turn around, confused, time speeds up. It unfreezes and starts running like it's been waiting for this marathon its whole life.

I turn around fully and stop, staring at what's in front of me.

"What's going on?" Beth yells. She's already turned the corner, so she can't see us. "Are you coming? Hurry up!"

I stand still. Staring. Not saying anything.

"Beth, come down here, please. Slowly," Julia says calmly as she keeps eye contact with me. She is standing a step behind Alex. Completely unmoving and calm.

"What the hell is—" Beth stomps down the steps but then stops in her tracks a couple of steps above me. "What..." she trails off.

Julia takes a deep breath and rolls her eyes slightly. "Look, there's no need to cause a scene or anything. Remain calm and let things happen as they will. I know what you're feeling right now, believe me, but—"

"Alex?" I croak, my voice breaking out in a whisper—it sounds like hurt and betrayal.

I can see Alex close his eyes for a few seconds, but he reopens them and remains standing resolutely calm. So much calmer than a couple of minutes ago. He's standing in front of me, a few feet away.

With a gun in his hands.

Pointed at me.

"Alex. Take it away, I guess," Julia prompts as she folds her arms, looking like a middle school teacher watching over detention.

"Talia, I'm sor—" Alex starts.

"No. No need for dramatics or any of that," Julia interrupts, looking over at him. "Say what you need to say, then do what you have to do. Then we're done."

Alex looks back at me. Gun still in hand. Pointed at what I assume to be my heart, head, or somewhere. I can't tell. I don't even know how a gun works. I didn't realize Alex did. Does he? I've only ever seen it used on TV. I've never had the experience of a gun so close.

Pointed at me.

By a person I thought was my friend.

A person I trusted and relied on.

I feel a sudden surge of newfound hurt flow through me, and I shiver. "Why?" I ask in the same broken voice. I will myself to not sound like that, but it doesn't work. The knot in my throat keeps increasing, and it's difficult to breathe or think about anything else.

"Talia, just listen," Alex begins. "I never wanted to do this. But... I told you about Julia and me the other day, right? How we're together? We've been together for a while now. I'm in love with her. You've been such a good friend, and I couldn't have hoped for a better one in this place. But Julia... she's important to me. She gave my life meaning down here. When I told her about our escape, she didn't panic. She didn't run to warn anyone. But she explained how it was a terrible idea. She warned that we need to stop you. She told me the real reason, the real purpose of the organization. How important it is for us to keep doing what we're doing. We are saving lives. And yes, sometimes we make mistakes." He pauses, his hands still tight around the gun.

"Sometimes, the organization does the wrong thing. But it's for the—the greater good. I won't go into everything Julia told me because it would take too long, but I want you to know that I've thought this through. What she said makes sense. It all makes sense now. I finally see my purpose, a purpose I never knew existed. I didn't know this before, but Julia was saved when she was a baby. Just two years old. She doesn't remember much of her past, but what she does recall sounds awful. She's so grateful to the organization for saving her and giving her the life she has now. Julia is proof of the incredible work the organization does."

Alex pauses, taking a deep breath before continuing, "I know all of this sounds strange, maybe even insane, to you. Julia said you wouldn't believe me if I told you before the escape. She said you'd fight, that you'd try to run, and if you succeeded, you'd ruin everything. So Julia suggested we go along with your plan up until—"

"Alex, honey, wrap it up," Julia interrupts (again) sweetly.

"Anyway, Julia told me this is for the best. And I really do feel bad about doing this. Trust me, believe me, I really do. You're a good friend, and I really never wanted to hurt you, but I have to do this. This is for the greater good and will save so many people's lives," Alex ends his long speech.

Complete and utter shock and betrayal. With each sentence, the hurt kept hitting me over and over. And soon, it turned from hurt into anger, into rage, into hatred.

I don't know what to say. I don't know if I should say anything. "What's for the greater good?" I ask shakily, already anticipating—and knowing—the answer. But I have to ask.

"Talia, dear, don't play dumb. We both know you're not. I can see in your eyes that you won't give up without a fight. You will not let us take you back. And you do not believe in anything Alex just told you. You hate the organization and everything we stand for. You will never trust us, not even after all of this. I see that," Julia says, maintaining chilling eye contact with me.

"You're right," I respond. She is. What can I say? I could lie, of course, but what's the point? Staying trapped down here? Pretending? Cowering under their watchful eyes? I won't do that.

Poor Beth. I hope she doesn't get in the middle of this. I hope Julia truly sees that I made Beth do this—that she's only acting under duress. Maybe they'll forgive her and let her live her life down here. Perhaps she'll get another chance to escape, and she might take it. Or she won't. Maybe someone will expose the organization's crimes and bring it down, giving Beth a second chance at a normal life. Or maybe she'll stay here forever, blissfully ignorant, brainwashed. It's tragic, but at least she'll be alive.

For me, though, that's not an option. I can't wait until some new opening to escape presents itself. I can't wait until the FBI comes bursting down here to rescue us all. And I definitely can't wait out the days until my death down here. Surviving like this. With these people. Being either part of the organization or rotting away in that attic room.

"You're right. I don't believe you," I repeat.

I would rather get this over with.

"Well then, you have made the decision easy for us." Julia steps closer. "Beth, please come with me." Julia extends her hand to Beth.

"What are you going to do to her?" I ask, stepping to the side to shelter Beth.

Julia sighs. "Nothing. Beth is an innocent victim in your game. She never wanted to leave. You manipulated her, and as a loving sister, she was doing this for you. Beth knows about all the good the organization does and believes in us. She believes in herself. She doesn't need all of this drama, and she doesn't need to see what will happen next," Julia states sharply. "Now, come on, Beth, let's go. There's a party waiting for us," Julia says in a calmer, soothing, light voice.

I step to the side and let Beth come down the stairs to take Julia's hand.

"What will happen?" Beth whispers. "Can Talia just come with us? I can watch over her. I can be her guardian if she stays here. I can watch over her all day and night so she doesn't do anything reckless."

"That's really not necessary, Beth. We have much bigger plans for you," Julia says with a dazzling smile. "You will do amazing things. Now, follow along." Julia steps around Alex, pulling Beth behind her.

I watch as my sister hesitates slightly at the steel door, turning back to glance at me one last time with a frown. She looks upset but overall uncomprehending. Beth mouths, "Bye, love you," as Julia gives her a tug and closes the door behind them.

I stand there, staring at the closed door. It feels like time has stopped, but of course it hasn't. I can't tell how long I've been standing like this. Everything seems like it's moving so fast, yet so slow. Time is slipping, but it feels still. My mind is running, yet there are no thoughts— nothing. The usual tornado of thoughts is gone. Instead, there's a strange, empty calm. A rainbow illusion, flickering, but no substance. It still feels like a storm inside, but it's an echo, and there's nothing left. Nothing.

"Talia," Alex speaks, clearing his throat and bringing me out of my haze.

"Alex," I say, looking back into his eyes.

The gun is still pointed at me. Unwavering. I have no way out. Beth had the keys, and she's gone now. Could I beg? It wouldn't change anything—maybe just earn some pity. I wonder how much brainwashing Alex has gone through and for how long. It must be the same thing they did to Beth. I wish I knew the answers.

Alex stares into my eyes, breaking into my broken soul.

I stare into his eyes, trying not to break whatever is left of me.

Go to Sevritulem. You are loved there. You are yourself there.

Flood the abyss. Let go. Let it all out. Finally.

We stare into each other's eyes, and I truly realize there is no hope.

He, Alex, my friend, is in love. He is brainwashed. He is going to do this.

I have no way out anymore. And I don't think I want a way out anymore. I don't see beauty, I don't mind falling off the edge, I simply don't have any fight left.

I don't want to. And I don't need to.

Flood the abyss.

So with every last bit of courage...

Flood the abyss.

with every last bit of confidence...

Flood the abyss.

with every last damn bit of pride...

Flood the abyss.

with every last bit of love from my body, soul, and mind...

Flood. The. Abyss.

and with every last bit of hope...

Without breaking eye contact or faltering for another moment, I say, "Do it."

And he does.

It's done.

Acknowledgments

Writing is a solitary process, but I never truly did this alone. This book wouldn't have come to life without a lot of people who helped make it happen.

First and foremost, to my family—thank you for always believing in me, even when I struggled to do so. Your endless support means everything.

To my editor, Yoanna Stefanova—your keen eye and thoughtful feedback elevated this story in ways I didn't even know it needed. To Krystal Penney, my brilliant cover artist—you brought my vision to life in ways I couldn't have imagined. And to my beta reader and sister, Victoria Quinn—thank you for reading my drafts, giving me honest opinions, and putting up with my writer ramblings. You deserve extra credit for dealing with me outside of book-related matters, too.

And finally, to you—the reader. Whether you picked up this book on purpose or by accident (in which case, I hope you at least found it interesting enough to keep going), thank you for taking a chance on this story. I hope it entertained, surprised, or at the very least, made you feel something.

Now, go forth and recommend it to everyone you know. (Kidding. But also, I wouldn't be mad if you did.)

About the Author

Polina Quinn is a writer whose passion for storytelling began at the age of ten, when she wrote her first short story inspired by Greek mythology. By day, she works in marketing; by night, she plots stories and questions every comma.

Her writing explores themes of identity, societal pressures, self-discovery, and family dynamics. She writes to explore ideas, challenge perspectives, and capture the complexities of human relationships.

Currently residing in Brooklyn, Polina enjoys spending time with loved ones, reading, and traveling. *Missing or Dead* is her debut self-published novel, and she's excited to share her work with the world.

For updates on future books, musings, or simply to say hi, visit polinaquinn.com.

www.ingramcontent.com/pod-product-compliance
Lightning Source LLC
Chambersburg PA
CBHW030426180626
46812CB00005B/2199